# Don't Hang Your Soul on That

Essential Prose Series 190

Canada Council for the Arts
Conseil des Arts du Canada

ONTARIO ARTS COUNCIL
CONSEIL DES ARTS DE L'ONTARIO
an Ontario government agency
un organisme du gouvernement de l'Ontario

Canada

Guernica Editions Inc. acknowledges the support of the Canada Council for the Arts and the Ontario Arts Council. The Ontario Arts Council is an agency of the Government of Ontario.

We acknowledge the financial support of the Government of Canada.

# Don't Hang Your Soul on That

*Robert Hilles*

GUERNICA
EDITIONS
TORONTO • CHICAGO • BUFFALO • LANCASTER (U.K.)
2021

Michael Mirolla, general editor
Gary Clairman, editor
David Moratto, interior and cover designer
Guernica Editions Inc.
287 Templemead Drive, Hamilton, ON L8W 2W4
2250 Military Road, Tonawanda, N.Y. 14150-6000 U.S.A.
www.guernicaeditions.com

Distributors:
Independent Publishers Group (IPG)
600 North Pulaski Road, Chicago IL 60624
University of Toronto Press Distribution (UTP)
5201 Dufferin Street, Toronto (ON), Canada M3H 5T8
Gazelle Book Services, White Cross Mills
High Town, Lancaster LA1 4XS U.K.

First edition.
Printed in Canada.

Legal Deposit—Third Quarter
Library of Congress Catalog Card Number: 2021930893
Library and Archives Canada Cataloguing in Publication
Title: Don't hang your soul on that / Robert Hilles.
Other titles: Do not hang your soul on that
Names: Hilles, Robert, author.
Series: Essential prose series ; 190.
Description: First edition. | Series statement: Essential prose series ; 190
Identifiers: Canadiana (print) 20210110015 | Canadiana (ebook) 20210110023
| ISBN 9781771836081 (softcover) | ISBN 9781771836098 (EPUB)
| ISBN 9781771836104 (Kindle)
Classification: LCC PS8565.I48 D66 2021 | DDC C813/.54—dc23

*Everything is nothing and nothing is everything.*
—Rain Hilles

*If you hang your soul on what is impermanent you will suffer.*
—Buddha

*A commotion in the mind.*
—Katherine Anne Porter

*For Rain Hilles who gave me the title*
*and whose stories anchor this*
*and who has shown me love's clarity.*

*And for Austin, Breanne, Elizabeth, Charlotte,*
*Kyle, Cathi, Robert, Camille and Ben*
*And for the faculty, students, and staff*
*at Vancouver Island University.*
*And for all my friends in Nanaimo,*
*on Salt Spring Island, and in Thailand.*

# Prologue

*WHEN TUUM IS ten, his father and he are in a serious motorcycle accident and Tuum is in a coma for two weeks. After he comes out of it, he can't move his arms and legs and his parents take turns feeding him until he regains the use of his arms a month later. He returns home then from the hospital but it's another two months before he has feeling in his legs.*

*Then every day, his father carries him on his back to the field across the street from the house. There, Tuum walks behind his father but keeps his arms around his father's neck for support. Eventually, Tuum is able to walk on his own and, when he turns twelve, he runs and plays as though the accident never happened.*

# Chapter 1

## *Khon Kaen, Thailand*
## *1970*

By the time she inspects a third papaya, he's already certain that it's no coincidence that she's across the street from him right now. Even from here, he feels an instant connection. This means that they have known each other in a past life. His father has said that: *The full influence of karma is only understood through dedicated, daily meditation.*

He ignores those words and watches as she hands the papaya to the vendor who wraps it in newspaper and hands it back to her. She lowers it into a wicker basket and then turns slightly away from Tuum to pay. With her back to him, he notices that her skirt nearly touches the ground. She wears flat sandals and her hair is gathered in a single knot at the back.

She lifts the basket with one hand and with the other raises her skirt above her ankles and walks briskly north and doesn't stop at any of the other vendors.

He pays for his meal and hurries after her, uncertain what he will say when he catches up with her but will come up with something. He works as a teacher so is used to thinking on his feet.

She is too far ahead for him to catch up, so he stops and watches her upright posture and quick steps and wonders if she's a dancer. She alertly pivots her head from side to side—likely to take in each vendor's wares. When she reaches the main gate of the market, she vanishes in the crowd.

It's a Wednesday in mid-June and for the next month he eats lunch in the market every day but doesn't see her. He wonders if her long absence means that she lives in one of the neighbouring villages.

He twice dreams of her. In the first dream, she hurries past riding an elephant. Any dream with an elephant means good luck. In the other dream, he's departing the very bus she's waiting to board. When he wakes from that dream, he tries to remember what bus he was on but can't.

Then one afternoon he emerges from school after a day of many difficult pupils and pauses halfway down the front steps just as she passes, riding in the back of a *samlortiip,* or pedicab. She turns and looks in his direction. Her glance is brief but long enough to indicate interest. He hails another pedicab and follows hers and, when his is a few lengths behind hers, he asks his peddler to slow down.

Her pedicab stops in front of a large white cement two-story house with red ceramic roof tiles. An eight-foot-high brick and cement wall surrounds the house and hides the first story. The house is significantly larger than any of the others on the street, most of those constructed from wood. The backyard contains four towering eucalyptuses and one massive yang na tree, and behind those and along the back of the property is a tight row of taller palms.

He recognizes the house and has heard much gossip about it and its owners—a high ranking local official and his wife. He'd ridden past it on his bicycle only three months earlier for a salacious peek. He didn't see her then and knows that the couple has no children so she must work there.

She pays her driver and gets out of her pedicab and comes over to his. She wais—a customary greeting and sign of respect consisting of a slight bow with hands together in front of the chin—and he does the same.

"You know where I live, but I can't be seen talking to you," she says.

He watches her hurry across the street and through the front metal gates past the guard station. She continues through a second gate and down the short driveway to the main door. She doesn't enter there but goes to a smaller side door farther down.

He pays his driver and gets out and walks home because on his teacher's salary he can't afford a pedicab both ways.

The next day is Sunday, which he has off, so he rides his bicycle to her street but stops a block south and on the opposite side of the road. He knows enough about the house that he can't simply knock on the main door and ask to see her. Nor would the local official take kindly to him loitering out front. So he walks as close to the house as he dares and sits in the shade of a tamarind tree.

In the late afternoon, she comes out of the main gate and walks down his side of the street and joins him. She carries a small basket and retrieves two plastic bags from it. One of them contains pork *laarb*—a popular ground pork dish, and the other, hot sticky rice. She takes out two sets of forks and spoons from the basket and hands him a set.

She says that she noticed him from the second story window of the prayer room and brought leftovers from her mistress's afternoon meal. He asks if she works as a cook there and she says she doesn't but that her mistress likes some of her traditional dishes and insists that she prepare those whenever the mayor and his wife visit.

He learns that her name is Roong, which means rainbow. She is from a village near Chum Phae, west of Khon Kaen. Her village is only two away from his father's village, so he assumes that his father has been there before, but Tuum hasn't.

"My mother died when I was fifteen and my father died last year," she says. "It's his debt that I am working off."

He tells her that his father is still alive, but his mother died when he was fifteen.

When they finish eating, she repacks her basket and says she must get back before her mistress notices that she is gone.

"I work from sunrise to sunset seven days a week. She gives me one day off a month and it's usually a Wednesday or a Sunday. All other days, I'm only allowed out on errands."

It's another month before they spend a Sunday together. In the afternoon, they take a pedicab to Kaennakhon Lake in the middle of the city and sit on a bench near the water and eat chopped mango and papaya and a fist-sized ball of rice. Later they rent a rowboat and he rows them to the middle of the lake and they talk under the shade of the flowered umbrella she's brought with her. This is a traditional courtship although neither of them speaks about it that way nor have immediate family to please beyond his father. But Buddha specifies that lovers must maintain propriety.

The afternoon heat bears down on them despite the protection of her umbrella, so he rows them to shore. The whole way back, she deftly adjusts the umbrella, so it always keeps the sun off them. By the time they reach shore, he's fallen in love with her.

The heat doesn't wane when Roong and he are back on land. They escape it as best they can by sticking to the shaded side of each street as they walk back to her mistress's house. They talk comfortably and laugh often.

Less than ten blocks from the house, the street is less crowded, the buildings bigger, many with gates and walls so high it is impossible to see over them. On a corner a woman sells *Kai Pahlo* from a cart—a dish of boiled eggs and cinnamon, cilantro, and soy sauce—but Roong says that she gets a bad feeling from her, so they don't stop to buy any. Farther along, the street is lined with more vendors selling either hot food or *Kha Nom Thai*—various popular Thai desserts. They stop at one and he buys them each a bowl of coconut milk and chopped mango.

They sit on a low cement wall to eat, and after they finish, she says that she's ashamed to be working at her mistress's and then tells him how she's ended up there.

"One afternoon, I came home early from harvesting with my father. I wasn't there long before she knocked. When I opened the door, the first thing she said was: 'Aren't you lovely.' Those were also the kindest words she's ever said to me. She then stepped back and asked where my father was. I told her that he was in the final rice paddies north of the house. She thanked me and walked in that direction. I watched her go and was struck by how straight and proper she walked despite wearing high heel shoes—better suited for sidewalks than our gravel road and the uneven footing of the rice paddies. That day, I'd thought she was a good and kind person.

"When my father finished work that evening, he told me that she'd seen me riding my bicycle through the village a week earlier and had asked after me. She told him that she knew people in high society and that she could give me a better life. She would pay for me to go to school and study to be a nurse and make sure I married someone well off. I told my father I wasn't interested in leaving him or our village. He said he would think about it."

Roong tells him how her mistress returned the following week. "This time my father introduced her formally to me. She spoke forcefully in Thai and not Isaan. She was very insistent that a wonderful life waited for me if I was willing to choose it. I remember thinking that her insistence made her seem less kind. After she left, my father said that she told him that she'd make sure I was well married and any debt he incurred would be a minor investment in my happiness. Those words should have been a dire warning to us. He told me then that what mattered most to him was that I was happy and had a good life."

Not long after her mistress's second visit, government agents appeared at their farm asking to do a full inventory of her father's crop, something that hadn't occurred in many years because her father kept meticulous records. He'd answered all their questions astutely from memory never once needing to consult his ledger, as most farmers would have done. The agents complimented him on this and said they could find no fault with his accounting. Her father had beamed for hours afterwards. Neither of them guessed that he only had a month to live.

The day her father died she hadn't gone to work with him as she usually did. Instead they'd both agreed the night before that she should stay behind to clean the house. They'd been working so intently on the harvest that the house hadn't been cleaned in several weeks. She scrubbed the windows starting with the two in her father's bedroom and then cleaned every room and finished with plenty of time to prepare dinner.

Her father didn't come home for the evening meal, and she waited a full hour thinking that he was working to finish the harvest that day.

"When it got completely dark, I went in search of him. I hurried toward that final paddy and I shouted his name as I went but he didn't answer. That wasn't like him and dread quickly knotted in my belly. There was a full moon that night so I broke into a run and called his name as loudly as I could while running. When I reached where the harvesting stopped, I circled the area and shouted until I heard him cough and then moan.

"I spun in that direction, but it took me a few seconds to locate him in the dark. When I reached him, he was lying on his stomach with his head turned toward me. He raised his head as much he could and I bent down and put my ear near his lips. He said: 'Thank you.' I told him everything would be okay. He nodded. I'll never forget how vague his eyes were and how long they took to focus on me."

Roong stops now and Tuum sets down his empty dessert dish beside him on the cement wall.

She sets hers next to his and then closes her eyes and keeps them closed for several minutes. When she opens them, they are welling with tears.

He wishes he could reach over and take her hand but that wouldn't be proper. Instead he reaches in his pants pocket and retrieves a napkin he always carries with him and offers it to her.

She takes it and daubs below each eye and then straightens her back and squares her shoulders. She rests her hands on either side of her. After another long pause, she says that, when she found her father, she fully believed she could save him and that everything would be fine. Her father was the strongest person she knew, and she couldn't imagine anything harming him. She says that she wishes now that she'd simply stayed and talked with him at least they'd have had that time together.

Instead she encouraged him to sit up, which he did after much wheezing and coughing. She offered to help him stand but that proved impossible, so she suggested that he crawl the short distance to a mango tree. She then helped him to sit up and lean against it for support.

She told him that she wouldn't be long and ran back to the house tripping several times in her haste. Each time she fell, she got right back up and kept running, not even taking time to catch her breath. At the house, she quickly located the wheelbarrow. It was full of rice harvested the day before. She dumped that on the ground and pushed the empty wheelbarrow ahead of her. It bounced erratically over the uneven ground and flew out of her hands twice and turned over on its side. Each time, she grabbed the handles and righted it and pushed it even faster.

When she reached him, his head had lowered to his chest and his breathing was very shallow. She raised his head gently and he opened his eyes and fixed them on her. Even in the moonlight she recognized terror in them. She'd never seen her father afraid before that day. His forehead was covered in sweat. She wiped that away with an edge of her skirt.

"He said: 'There's just one more day of harvesting left.' I told him to save his energy and after a short rest I got him to crawl to the wheelbarrow and then I helped him lean in headfirst and I picked up his legs and rolled him the rest of the way inside. He had to pull his knees to his chest to fit in it and even then his feet stuck out the front of the wheelbarrow."

Her father shook violently, and she rubbed his forehead and told him again that everything would be okay. He smiled briefly but that quickly faded. Then he smiled a second time and said: "I haven't always strived to be good, but you are my true goodness." She thanked him but didn't encourage him to say more, wanting him to rest, but wishes now that she'd let him talk. Then, she'd been solely focused on saving him.

She gripped the handles of the wheelbarrow and lifted it and pushed but the wheelbarrow wouldn't move. Although her father was short and thin, he weighed more than she could manage in the wheelbarrow and she wondered how she'd ever get him back to the farmhouse. She lifted the handles a little higher and pushed again and this time she felt a surge of power enter her body and the wheelbarrow moved. At first the soil was so soft she made little progress even with that surge of strength. But she persisted and eventually she reached firmer ground and the wheelbarrow moved freely. She was running then and pushing the wheelbarrow as though it were empty.

At the house he shook even more violently, and she felt the back of his neck and it was icy. She lifted each of his legs out of the wheelbarrow and then helped him sit up and asked him to put his arms around her neck and lean on her. This way she was able to lift him out of the wheelbarrow and set him on the ground. He then crawled to the house and up the two steps and inside.

He stopped just inside the door and leaned against the living room wall for support. He wheezed so noisily she wasn't sure if he had the energy to make it to his bed. She got him a glass of water from the kitchen and he took several shallow sips and then handed the glass back to her and crawled on his own energy to his bedroom. He managed to lay his head and shoulders onto the bed and she raised his legs and rolled him the rest of the way.

"I then helped him onto his back, and he put his arms at his sides and gasped loudly. I asked if he wanted anything to eat and he said no. I said I'd get help and he said that sounded like a good idea. He closed his eyes then and I thought he was sleeping. But he opened them again and said: 'Don't wait up.' I said alright and left him there."

She rode her bicycle to the nearest neighbour with a phone, which was a kilometre closer to the village. From there she called the local doctor who said she'd ride her bike over right away. Roong rode home and hurried to her father's room. She remembered opening the door and sensing immediately how quiet the room was. She froze and couldn't advance. She listened for his breathing but heard nothing. Eventually she sat on the bed and the mattress didn't give much under her weight as though a heavy stone had already been set upon it. His forehead was warm when she touched it and she yelped and pulled her hand away. She sat there in that impossible quiet for a few minutes and then told him that she was sorry.

"I remember weeping until there was a loud knock on the door. I ignored the knock at first no longer in my right mind. The doctor knocked twice more and then called my name and I hurried to let her in. She must have seen the truth on my face for she lowered her head and said she got there as fast as she could.

"She went in to check on him and listened at his chest with her stethoscope and then came out into the kitchen and said there was nothing I could have done. She asked if I wanted her to call someone. I said my uncle and aunt were still alive and she could call them. I told her that beyond them, I was all he had."

All the time that Roong has been telling him this, they've remained sitting on the same wall. He feels such sadness from her story that he doesn't know what to say. Instead he asks if she would like to chant for her father and she says that she would.

When they finish chanting, they slip off the wall and continue slowly toward her mistress's house. They speak little these final blocks but walk close enough that their arms brush against each other from time to time.

Eventually they stop at the main steps of a school and sit again. He's amazed that they both stop at the same time without verbally agreeing to it and he's uncertain which of them instigates it. The street is busier this close to her mistress's house and many people hurry in both directions.

They sit very close to each other and he notices that she smells of the lake. Her story has chilled him and he can't begin to imagine the horror and pain of such a night. He also realizes from her story that she is fiercer and more determined and courageous than he is.

When it is fully dark, they continue on their way so that she doesn't get back too late. They walk faster now and when they reach her mistress's house, it's lit up and party noises spill out into the street.

They stop in front of a clothing shop across the street. In the darkened windows he sees several mannequins but their clothes are mere shadows covering their nakedness. He turns back to Roong and her eyes are fixed on him. They don't waver.

"More people come by in the evenings," she says. "The house can be very noisy then. That's when I am expected to serve drinks or dishes of food. Whatever she decides is needed. That is not at all what she promised after my father died. She came to the farm two days after he died. She said that she'd lent my father a considerable sum of money recently to see him through to the end of the harvest and that he had yet to pay any back. She also said that his death didn't wipe out that debt so now it was mine. She said that she had an easy way for me to pay it off and that I would see in time that she is a kind person and that I would be thankful for her kindness. I was a fool to believe her. When she told me how much he owed, I knew she was lying because the amount was too large and very unlike my father. It seemed like a made-up number. But before I even had time to think it through, she produced a contract and insisted I had to sign right then or I could be arrested."

He stays facing her the whole time she tells him this.

Buddha says that kindness is the greatest power. His father has stressed that to him often and yet he hasn't always seen kindness in the deeds of others or even in his father. He wishes right now he could free Roong from her debt, but his meagre schoolteacher's salary is no match for the size of debt her mistress claims she owes. He also knows from his father that such debts are often greatly exaggerated and meant to take a lifetime of forced labour to pay off.

She is shivering but not from cold and he senses her reluctance to go in. He tells her that he loves her but hears immediately how empty that sounds after her story.

She holds him and says she loves him too and says that today gives her hope.

They don't kiss because it's too soon to kiss.

She hurries across the street and inside the main gate and past the guard station. When she eventually opens the side door, the sounds of many voices rush out, along with the loud, quick notes of a saxophone and piano playing American jazz. The instant glare from inside highlights briefly the contours of the main wall. She looks smaller in that abrupt light and doesn't linger but goes straight in without looking his way. After the door closes, he hears a burst of laughter followed by muffled conversations. He can't make out any of it. Then there's a squeal of delight followed by more laughter. A drum and trumpet join the saxophone and piano. They play slower and a woman sings so sweetly he recognizes the hurt feelings being conveyed even without making out any of the words. When the song finishes, there's no applause only a jumble of more voices.

He turns toward home, and as he walks, he thinks about his father and can't imagine lifting him into a wheelbarrow and pushing him to safety. His father would be light enough that Tuum could manage it, but his father would refuse to climb into the wheelbarrow and would insist that doing so could break his karma.

Despite Roong's slight stature she'd wheeled her father home and allowed him the dignity of dying in his own bed. She doesn't yet see the goodness in that but he does and believes in time she will. There is a karmic completeness to it too that appeals to him and likely would to his father as well.

Thinking of his father triggers dangerous feelings. It is true that his father had been instrumental in helping him to walk again after the motorcycle accident, but without his mother to guide Tuum, he's come to blame his father for the accident. It hasn't helped that he has little memory of it, and that his father has never discussed it with him.

He and his father haven't exchanged even a single letter in the past three years.

*The memories will return in time.* His father had promised after the accident. That hasn't happened and so those words sting now and remind him of the continuing rift between his father and him.

Lately he's come to accept that that rift runs deeper than the accident and is likely attributed more to events in their past lives than this one.

He can't remember the last time he's touched his father in the past decade even during those final molten years that they shared the same house. They came and went most days without seeing each other.

When he first told his father that he wanted to teach mathematics in high school, his father had said he shouldn't get too attached to numbers because what they count isn't really there. But by then Tuum had already discovered numerical patterns in many places and he'd argued with his father that numbers replicate what Buddha teaches. Those patterns aren't there by coincidence but are manifestations of what Buddha discovered buried within everything. Numbers are but one way to explain the *core.*

Thoughts of his father cause him to hunch forward as he walks, and his footsteps sound noisy and aimless in the street even though he's headed straight home. Near his apartment, his footsteps lighten because he remembers the thrill of hugging Roong and their declarations of love. She may have told him the saddest story he's ever heard—a mournful story—but he doesn't feel sad or mournful.

Three nights later, he dreams that Roong is running alongside his bicycle and the faster he pedals the faster she runs. He expects her to drop back but she keeps pace with him and eventually passes him and runs so far ahead that she stops in the distance and waits for him. He pedals faster and faster but never catches up to her. He gets winded and quits pedalling and his bicycle coasts to a stop. He plants his feet on either side of the bicycle and gasps for air. He gasps deeper and deeper until he's suddenly awake and realizes that someone is knocking on the door of his apartment.

Roong is there when he opens it. He doesn't remember telling her where her lives, but there she stands. He blinks twice and wonders if he hasn't yet woken from his dream but quickly realizes that it's raining too heavily to be a dream and she's dripping wet. He steps out of the way and she hurries inside.

"Let me get you a towel," he says, and goes to his small bathroom and returns with a folded amber cotton towel. She takes the towel from him and sits at his dining table and dries her left arm and then her right and then slips off her sandals and dries her feet and ankles and any other exposed skin. She passes the towel to him and asks him to dry the back of her neck. She tilts her head forward and lifts her long, wet hair out of the way. He daubs the towel along the neckline of her top first and then lightly daubs up and down her exposed neck careful to dry everywhere. She keeps her head lowered and doesn't move.

He hands her the towel back and she excuses herself and goes to the bathroom and returns a few minutes later with her hair wrapped in a green towel.

They sit across from each other at the table and don't speak right away although he has so many questions beginning with how she has managed to be here at this late hour. Despite those urges he knows it's best not to bombard her with questions, so waits for her to tell him whatever she wishes to tell.

He hears the rain die down outside his open window and several loud voices carry up from the street. A man and woman are having a noisy argument that ends with the loud revs of a motorcycle before it accelerates away. He gets up and closes the window and feels a rush of humidity as he shuts it. The floor around the window is damp but he leaves that to dry on its own and returns to the table. He's giddy that she's here but that's tempered by his knowledge of all she's risked. He realizes even more how brave she is.

"I shouldn't have come?" she asks, perhaps having sensed something unintended in his expression.

He says that he is delighted she is here and asks her how she's managed it, even though he's promised himself he wouldn't.

"I waited until everyone was asleep and slipped out my bedroom window. It's on the ground floor so I could have done that months ago but I didn't have anywhere to go to until now. When I got to the main gate, the guard was asleep. He woke as I passed but he simply nodded. Either he thought I was a guest leaving late or decided that he and I didn't have any karma in common so wasn't about to interfere and create one now. I know it's foolish to come here but I've missed you so much and needed to see you tonight. I'll have to be back before anyone wakes up and notices I'm gone." She tightens the towel around her head and says that her long hair dries very slowly.

He likes the ease with which she adjusts the towel and that hastens thoughts that he must push aside because intimacy between them isn't possible yet and her being here doesn't change that. He shifts his gaze to his hands as he slides them along the surface of the table to distract himself.

She says the overhead bulb is rather bright so he turns on the bathroom light and leaves the door open and turns off the main light. The bathroom light spills across the table. The rest of the room is dark except where fresh moonlight illuminates a thin swath from the main window to the middle of the room.

This close, she smells of rain but also jasmine and roses. The faint hint of her breath across the table is a pleasant blend of honey and lavender.

He slides his hand and takes hers and squeezes it. She squeezes back. This connection pleases him but he draws his hand away so that all remains proper between them. At first, their conversation is halting with many awkward pauses. This is so different from the day at the lake and is due to the suddenness of her being here. In time, though, the words flow more easily between them.

They talk until the first rays of daylight enter the window.

He says he'll give her a ride back on his bicycle. In the street, he collects it from the rack outside the main doors of his apartment building and mounts first and balances the bicycle with his left foot so that she can sit on the top bar in front of him. She lightly grips his left arm with both her hands to steady herself.

The streets are deserted except for two other men on bicycles that pass going the other way. Near her street, a motorcycle comes up quickly behind them and then speeds past and the woman passenger briefly looks back at them. The streets are wet and slippery from last night's rain so he slows his pedalling and twice swerves to avoid large puddles.

He stops a block from her mistress's house and leans his bicycle against an electric pole and walks with her the rest of the way.

Three houses before her mistress's, they slip into the shadows and hold hands. They kiss once but very briefly. Her breath is warmer than he expects and when they move apart her eyes flicker, reflecting a stray streetlight.

Neither speaks. She takes his hand and draws him to her again and they kiss longer. A slight breeze blows the morning heat away from them and in that cooling moment, time slows and his aching abates. He senses the urgency of the hour and breaks from the kiss but holds her. She holds him too and the moment extends.

"I must go," she says finally, and drops her arms. He does the same. She says that she will try to get away that night but can't promise. "If I don't make it don't worry, I will return when I can." She grips his hand and then slowly lets go of it and hurries in the direction of her mistress's house. At the main gate she stops and opens it only wide enough to slip through. She hurries past the guard station.

The guard steps out from the shadows and stands there for a moment and then steps back again out of sight. By then she's vanished from view.

He leaves the door to his apartment unlocked that night and every night for the next week, but she doesn't return. The following

Saturday, he wakes during the night and she is sitting on the edge of his bed.

"When did you get here?"

"About an hour ago. I let you sleep. You moaned once and turned from one side to the other as though having a bad dream. I've come for good."

It takes a moment for that last part to register but when it does, he smiles and goes to her and holds her and feels his reckless heart race.

They sit together on the edge of the bed and she says she wishes to chant and he joins her.

Later they lie fully clothed on the bed. This is the first time they've lain together and this close she smells different: partly of lemongrass, and partly of lime and mango mixed with rain and damp towel, because it has rained again tonight, and of lavender too like before. The rain has washed off any smells of whisky, cigar smoke, teak, or bamboo.

They fall asleep hugging each other as an easterly breeze blows in through the open window and runs cool along his bare arms.

Later he wakes to sharp morning glare and Roong is still asleep beside him. Cheery birdsongs alternate with a branch rubbing against the now closed window. She must have gotten up at some point. He realizes that a dark reckoning is brewing. From what he knows of her mistress and her husband they will insist the debt be paid and they will not stop until it is. They are rich and powerful enough and will act swift and mightily. But at this early hour his mind drifts from that peril to the pure joy of her being here with him. He foolishly wishes that a love as strong as he feels can defy everything, and even prosper—despite all threatening evil.

He inches up onto his elbows so as not to wake her and then eases into a lotus position and meditates deeply. He is soon gripped by strong sensations of foreboding, but he lacks his father's ability to focus and connect to the forces swirling around him. His father is able to experience the past and future as fluidly as most people experience the present.

When he comes out of his meditation, he knows that Roong's being here is his mother's doing and he thanks her. For weeks now, every time he's chanted or meditated, he's asked for her help.

He wakes an hour later from a dreamless sleep and the first thing he senses is Roong's warmth beside him. She's awake and kisses him as soon as he opens his eyes.

He tells her how he's asked his mother for help and she says that she's asked her father.

She kisses him again and, when they break apart, her eyes stay fixed on his. He recognizes doubt in them. But he sees gratitude too and love. She's right to doubt him and worry about the precarious position they are in now.

She's safe in his apartment for the moment, because her mistress won't know yet where she's gone. But she has spies everywhere and will soon find out.

"We should leave as soon as possible," he says

"And go where?"

"South or north. You choose."

"What about your job? Your students?"

"The school will find someone to fill in. They'll make do."

"What about references? How will find you find work elsewhere?"

She's thought more carefully and thoroughly about their predicament than he has. He's simply believed that their love will be enough to provide for them but realizes now what she already has, that it may not. There are significant practical hurdles to overcome.

*It is the day-to-day details that matter*, his father warned him before he left for university in Khon Kaen. *Don't get swept up by romantic feelings. The young have a tendency to do that. They think love conquers everything but it doesn't. Love can be very dangerous and is often our undoing. Love might feel permanent but nothing is. Not even love. Nothing lasts. Love is an illusion.*

He didn't believe his father then nor does he now. His father has always lived as though love were very important to him.

"I'll speak to my father," he says, and saying that aloud commits him to seeking his estranged father's help, something he's promised himself he'd never do. That way is fraught with danger but it's a knowable danger. He doesn't tell her any of this.

They make love then for the first time and are awkward with each other and leave their clothes on until it is absolutely necessary and then remove them with haste and toss them off the bed with little care for where they land. When they make love a second time, they are slower and the feelings are more intense for him. At the moment he climaxes he experiences a magnetic pull from her eyes. She then shows him ways to please her too. Afterward they settle into each other's arms and the day's busyness is muted to street noises at the window.

They sleep again and he doesn't wake until late into the day. She is already up and sitting at the table.

"I've chanted and it is clear that our best chance is to go east to Cambodia."

This is a different plan and he considers Cambodia foreign, hostile and dangerous and is now regularly being bombed by America. Still if that is where she wishes to go, he will go there with her.

They decide to leave in the morning.

He wakes first and packs a leather duffle bag with the few items of clothing she brought with her in a paper bag. He then goes to his closet and picks the first items his eyes light on, feeling no particular attachment this morning to anything there. He then prepares a breakfast of boiled rice and chopped pork. The smell of boiling rice wakes her.

He remembers then a dream he had last night. In it he climbed a steep set of stairs. When he reached the top, there was another set of stairs and at the top of that another set of stairs, each set steeper than the one before. He'd felt so tired in the dream he just wanted the stairs to end. He didn't care where they led. After the fourth set he woke and felt relief that it was only a dream and didn't care that he never learned where they led.

They eat slowly and partway through eating she takes his hand and squeezes it.

She tells him that she is glad to be away from her mistress's daily cruelty. "I didn't know until I went to work for her that anyone could be so cruel. She seems kind and caring in public and when she visited my father, but in private, she is brutal and hits us often with a belt if we don't work fast enough."

She tells him of how the woman used her belt on someone different every day. She rotated her beatings and they seemed to fire her up and her eyes glowed pure evil. Sometimes she beat Roong for the smallest complaint. Each time she did so, she flashed a gleeful smile when she finished. Not a wince as one might expect of someone after inflicting pain on another, but a joyful smile so broad that it exposed a full set of straight, white teeth.

"She looks ugly when she smiles, her mouth is too large—too stretched out, too exaggerated. She smiles past a smile so it becomes a grimace. I had to look away because the darkness of her soul surfaced then and was visible in the dark centres of her eyes." She stops talking and collects her dishes and walks them to the sink.

He does the same and says he'll clean up. When he's finished, he puts the dishes away uncertain if he will ever use them again. He's paid the rent for two more months and hasn't planned past that. Someone will likely claim whatever he leaves behind. *So be it.*

Later they sit at the table and she tells him that on the first day he saw her in the market, her mistress had sent her to find the best papaya. She had very important guests coming for dinner. The papaya Roong bought that day was the ripest she could find, and when she tasted it later at home, it had been superb. But after the guests left, her mistress yelled at her and said that the papaya was sour and hopeless and it had ruined the meal and caused her to lose face. She beat her with her belt until Roong's arms and backside were bruised and bleeding.

Roong had to sleep on her stomach for a week afterward. She'd cried into her pillow the first night sleeping little because of the pain.

He reaches his hand across the table and takes hers and feels it tremble. He squeezes lightly not wanting to hurt her. She squeezes back firmly and her trembling stops.

She tells him of a dream she had last night. In it they were on a bus going to Cambodia, and in the dream, she'd said to him: *Look, we're wearing our silken finery.* Later in the dream the bus arrived in Phnom Penh and they got off and hurried along a crowded chaotic street and it started to rain and they ducked into the nearest café. A woman greeted them at the door and said that today was an auspicious day although when Roong looked around the café, it was deserted. The woman said she was happy to see that they were wearing silk as that meant that they could come inside and sit at any table. After they'd sat down at a table near the back, she handed them each a menu and said: "You'll be safe here." That was when Roong woke.

"The dream means we must wear silk when we leave. That will bring us good luck and ensure our safety," she says. "As poets have written. Lovers should wear silk whenever they travel."

She tells him that when she woke from the dream she realized that today was the 14th day of the month, which is an auspicious date for travelling to a different country. She must go out and buy herself a silk blouse. It is important that she buy it with her own money. She has managed to save a little and wishes to use that. To cross such a powerful dream would doom them.

He hears the decidedness in her voice and trusts her instincts. *To resist karma is to seek peril.* That warning from his father registers with him now.

He walks with her to the street and she says she won't be long and hurries in the direction of the morning market. He watches her run in the quiet street. She goes a full block west before turning south. When she disappears from view, he returns upstairs and sweeps the floor and then checks through his closet again but hasn't left behind anything he'll miss. He hopes that she buys more clothing for herself. He knows that whatever she comes back with will be lovely.

She does not return in an hour. He waits. After two hours, he knows she isn't coming back.

# CHAPTER 2

## Chum Phae, Thailand
## Present Day

HE DOESN'T NOTICE the change in weather until dark clouds balloon overhead. It's too late to take cover so he drops his scythe and arches his back to the warm downpour. When the rain shifts sideways, Ed straightens and widens his stance to keep from losing his balance. His robe soaks through and droops heavily but the rain is a welcome reprieve from the steady throttle of afternoon heat.

The rain stops as abruptly as it starts, and beyond the rectangles of golden rice, he sees layers of green clear to the humps of mountains in the grey distance to the north. The lighter green of the *bo* trees (or sacred fig) gives way to the darker greens of the *pradu, doc jan, yang na,* and coconut trees. The more distant tamarind and mango trees add an in-between, serious green similar to the firs and cedars he's familiar with on the west coast of Canada.

Song works a short distance north of Ed and swings his scythe in steady, graceful arcs. Although he is over eighty, he works in his rice paddies every day. He is thin and sinewy and his arms and legs tightly muscular. There's no visible fat on him, and he walks with more energy and determination than Ed, despite being forty years older.

Ed notices another man working farther north from them. This is the first day that anyone else has been helping, so likely Song and he have fallen more behind with the harvest than Ed has realized.

Ed goes back to work but within a half hour the heat presses in again, and he stops to catch his breath. He notices that a second man has joined the first. They aren't working but face each other, and the second man is gesturing wildly with both hands.

Song drops his scythe and runs in their direction, and Ed does the same. He has worked alongside Song long enough to know if Song is running, he should be too.

Before Ed gets very far, the second man raises an arm to shoulder height and points a pistol at the other man. Ed shouts: "No!" But his words don't carry, so he shouts it more loudly. In that very instant the first man is thrust up and back and drops to the ground. The crack of the shot echoes in the mountains, and the shooter lowers his gun and turns and walks east.

Ed has never witnessed anything so terrifying and all he can think to do is keep running. He's soon in the thick of nearly waist high crop and this slows him as he pushes stalks out of his way. When he reaches Song's trampled path, he takes that and runs faster.

A silver half-ton truck appears from behind a row of trees and stops for the shooter who immediately gets in and the truck speeds north, trailing a cloud of dust behind.

A second or so later, Ed reaches Song kneeling next to the fallen man. Song's breathing is loud and wheezy, as he lowers his head to the man's chest.

Ed crawls to the other side of the fallen man and pushes ripe plants out of the way so he can get closer. *Stay calm,* he reminds himself but feels a painful throb at each temple. He watches Song attend to him. *Today now contains this.*

Song raises his head and looks briefly at Ed and then back to the man on the ground and rests a hand on his shoulder, and the man's arm twitches and then goes slack.

Ed checks for a pulse without knowing that is what he is doing until he does it. The pulse is very faint.

The man's eyes are closed, and his shirt has a growing bloodstain at heart level. Ed lowers his head to the man's chest and listens. He hears a single raspy intake of air followed by a long moan that fades to nothing. The significance of that doesn't register at first and he waits for the next inhale, but there isn't one.

The startle of that causes him to lift his head and take out his cell phone from the waterproof pouch dangling from his neck. He dials the emergency number and hands it to Song.

While Song talks in Thai on the phone, Ed pumps firmly on the victim's chest several times, but when this doesn't work, he nests his fingers together and pounds the chest twice and listens. Nothing. He tilts the man's head back and forces apart his jaw and places his lips on the man's and blows in forcefully and waits for the exhale and then blows in again. He does this fifteen times, but there's still no heartbeat.

Song has finished on the cell phone and hands it back to Ed and looks at the body on the ground and says: "*Mai Dee. Mai Dee.*" (This is bad. This is bad).

He turns to Ed and fixes his gaze briefly on him and then glances away.

Ed is used to this limited eye contact between them. He isn't certain what he should do next so lightly grips Song's upper arm and then lets go. The older man nods but doesn't come any closer. This is the first time he's touched Song and this proximity feels awkward, so he steps back to a more comfortable distance between them.

A fly buzzes near his ear, but he doesn't shoo it away, as he once might have, but ignores it because any encounter, even a brief one like this, can have serious karmic consequences. The fly and they could have been enemies in a past life, or lovers, or father and daughter.

The fly is soon gone and Ed senses dampness on his cheek and touches a finger there. When he draws it back, there's blood, and he brushes the spot several times with the fingers of his left hand until his cheek feels dry. He then wipes off his fingers on flattened rice stalks.

Song watches him do this.

Ed isn't certain if this means it's okay or if this too has karmic implications he'll regret later.

He glances again at the man on the ground and except for the bloodstain on his shirt, he could be sleeping. Ed notices that the victim's feet are bare, and he quickly locates the man's sandals a metre or so away in the cleared part of the field. He retrieves them and puts them on the man's feet.

He hears a siren but it's another five minutes before the ambulance locates them. It stops near where the murderer got in the truck.

Song and Ed make room for the paramedics. They kneel next to the body and a female paramedic places her stethoscope at heart level and listens while the male paramedic readies an oxygen mask. She shakes her head and her partner puts the mask back into the equipment bag beside him and the two of them return to the ambulance and carry back a metal stretcher and set it on the ground next to the body.

The male paramedic lifts the man's head and shoulders and the female paramedic grips his feet and they position him onto the stretcher, covering him with a brown blanket. They carry the stretcher to the ambulance, which is a half-ton truck with a canopy over the back—a common form of ambulance. They load the stretcher inside and the woman closes the door.

A police officer arrives on a motorcycle, and after a brief exchange with the paramedics, he opens the back of the ambulance and climbs inside. He lifts aside the blanket and takes pictures with a cell phone and then lowers the blanket and comes outside. He talks to Song for a long time and writes frequently in a notepad he retrieves from a shirt pocket. When he finishes with Song, Ed asks if he needs his statement, and the officer says in English if that is necessary, he can give it later at the police station in Chum Phae. There will be someone there to translate it into Thai.

After the ambulance and police leave, Song tells Ed in his limited English that the dead man is his cousin's youngest grandson, Sutum. "A good and kind man. Bright."

He stands for a while beside Ed and then chants aloud. Ed closes his eyes and listens but doesn't know any of the Pali.

When Song finishes, he says: "*Pope gun mai,*" (See you later) and walks south toward the hut where Ed is staying. He stops at his motorcycle, which is less than halfway there, and gets on it and with a tap of a sandalled heel releases the kickstand, and then with his other, he kick-starts the bike. He rides very slowly to the highway and maintains that same speed after he turns onto it.

The rice paddy is eerily quiet now and Ed feels the skin on his bare arms prickle. He stands amongst untrampled rice and can't take his eyes off where Sutum was only minutes ago. A larger area of rice has been trampled down there. He has the urge to rip out those flattened stalks and toss them into a pile but instead walks back to his hut. It takes him longer than usual, and at the hut, he opens the door to let out caught heat but doesn't go inside. Instead he sits on floor of the shaded porch.

He glances back the way he's come, and his gaze falls immediately on the scene of the murder. From now on he'll always know exactly where it happened.

Everyone involved today, including him and the paramedics and police officer, now have a karmic connection to Sutum and his killer. He takes in the significance of that but doesn't yet fully understand the implications. For him, karma is still a vague notion, but for Song and Ed's wife Nan, it has deep intricacies and each day contains a myriad of risky, karmic criss-crosses. There are no accidents, which means Sutum's murder was always going to happen today and everyone in attendance, including him, are caught in that karmic chain of events. He knows that his life has changed because of this murder but doesn't know yet how it's changed.

Nan has told him that when someone dies their soul remains in close proximity to their body but when their body is taken away the soul may stay behind. Those nearby at the time of death risk being drawn into past and present karmic complications. He chants to inoculate himself against such consequences but knows it's already too late to block them all.

A flock of chestnut-tailed starlings drops one by one onto the short grass in front of him. Once on the ground, they appear singular in their actions and peck individually in the grass as though no longer part of the flock. Hunger and other urges drive them, and he envies the clockwork of that and how they appear to live free of moral choices.

A starling breaks away from the others and stops on the patch of exposed earth next to the gravel driveway in front of him. It pecks at the ground several times and draws out a long worm and dangles it in equal halves from its beak and then tilts its head back and swallows the worm.

Birds have poor memories and live mostly in the present, guided by instinct more than thought, or so he's believed until recently. He's assumed that they don't have the capacity for thought. But now he's not so certain. He knows they have quick, active brains but he hasn't a clue about the workings of those brains. Through his daily Buddhist practices, he's come to accept that birds have souls like all other living creatures. He knows too that the fact he's focused on these starlings right now could mean that he was a starling in a past life.

He should see a progression to here from all that's happened today but sees only that a man has killed another man, and a bird has killed a worm. Beyond that, he can't make sense of the intersections.

Five more starlings join this one and peck the ground nearby. One of them draws out an even longer worm and bites it in half and lets each half fall to the ground. The starling then picks up one half of the worm and swallows it and then picks up the other half and swallows it.

Maybe the worm's soul will be reborn as a starling or tiger or human.

He turns back to the rest of the flock, and they are busy pecking and for a few seconds their activities calm him, and he forgets that this too is a karmic drama playing out.

A fox charges from his right and the starlings instantly scatter into full flight. They converge and form a black flurry that expands and contracts as they fly east and then abruptly turn north and angle up and then down, and then go sideways again, and then up once more, moving always as an amorphous dark presence, that fluidly changes size and shape many times. Their threat avoidance mesmerizes him, but he recognizes fury in it too. Their high-pitched noises fade as the flock levels off and flies in an elongated column northward.

He returns his gaze to the ground in front of him and watches the fox press its snout down and shake its head from side to side. Feathers fly up and float on still air. The fox chomps and then lifts the dead bird in the grip of its jaws and hurries into the nearby trees.

Ed finds the flock again now already at the distant Tamarind trees in the north. He watches the dark shape break apart, as one after another, the starlings drop into the cover of uncut rice. Everything is still again except for the slight sway of the trees around him.

By killing the starling, the fox has freed its soul so it can jump into its next body as Sutum's soul may have already.

He thinks about all that and how each day is like this and yet not like this. Run, the master monk that he's met through Nan, has said: *Being is a mirror and is not a mirror.*

He gets up and goes inside. The hut has cooled enough that he shuts the door. He sits at the table and chants. His hands and legs shake, and when he closes his eyes and focuses on his chanting, he sees an image of Sutum lying on the ground. He opens his eyes and reaches for the small bell that Song gave him and that he keeps on the table. He rings it three times as Song has shown him and closes his eyes again and his arms and legs stop shaking.

He stays like that and soon his body calms. He waits. Nothing. The moment settles and then another. He presses his fingertips to the tabletop and says: "*Satu, Satu, Satu.*" (Amen.)

Ed has lived in Thailand for five years with his wife Nan, and for the past three weeks, he's been staying alone in this bamboo hut north of Chum Phae and eighty kilometres west of Khon Kaen. He's here to work on his Buddhist practices and to help Nan's great-uncle Song harvest his rice crop.

Nan has said that Ed and she were lovers in a past life, but it mustn't have gone well because their souls have sought another chance. According to Run, Ed lived in Thailand two hundred years ago and again in the last century. In this life he was born in Victoria, Canada, grew up there, met and married his first wife Teresa there, and divorced her a decade ago.

He's eager for glimpses of his past lives in Thailand but that requires a higher level of meditation than he's mastered so far. That prospect hasn't deterred him and every day he meditates hoping for a breakthrough.

It is soon dark, but he can't stop thinking about Sutum's murder. Those thoughts cause such restlessness in him that he goes outside and paces in the front yard and shouts profanities into the night. When he's all shouted out, he sits in a wicker chair on the front porch. A full moon rises in a dark corner of the night sky and, here and there, small puddles formed by today's rain reflect a shimmering, misshapen moon. Frogs and crickets sing so uniformly that it seems intentional.

He closes his eyes and chants but no matter how much he focuses he can't block unwanted images. First there's the close up of the blood on Sutum's blue shirt. That image reappears no matter how many times he wills it away. Later he sees a detailed zoom of Sutum's face—stopped by death. His face is boyish—a mere twenty-five, Song has told him. Other details come like a small round scar on Sutum's right cheek and several days' growth of whiskers, and above his upper lip a thin moustache. Were those actually there?

He opens his eyes to stop the images. The frogs and crickets have gone silent and he goes inside but leaves the door open.

He calls Nan to tell her about Sutum, and she is quiet at first and then tells him that she's had a bad feeling all day. Twice she broke a glass at the kitchen sink in their apartment. She rarely breaks dishes.

He asks her why Buddha would allow people to kill each other and she says that Buddha doesn't determine what people do. What exists in the world is what exists. His teachings point the way to enlightenment. It is up to each soul to reach it. Before hanging up she says that she'll ride to Run's later and chant for Sutum and says he must do the same.

He goes to the table and sits but doesn't light a candle. When his eyes adjust, he can make out the vague shapes of the furnishings he knows acutely in daylight. He scans from left to right and stops first at the vague hump of the double wide bamboo cot in front of him and to the right of that he can make out the top of the wooden chair he's lined up with the door. He sits in that chair whenever it's too hot at the table. The furnishings are scant, with only the most necessary items arranged for utility. This makes the hut feel more spacious than its four-metre by five-metre size. It was built more than eighty years ago to provide temporary lodging for couples who came from the deep south or far north to help with the harvests. It has withstood the years remarkably well despite minimal repairs.

He slides a hand along the rough wooden surface of the table. It's more of a picnic table than a proper dining table but the wood's roughness comforts him. All of this is temporary, he reminds himself, especially his sitting here and yet here he is. He stops his hand when he snags a sliver and pulls it out. He then pushes his chair back and stands and goes to the door and shuts it and returns to his chair. He closes his eyes and chants: "*Pra Nip Paan Knaw,*" (Nirvana)—until his mind quiets and he enters a deep calm.

He wishes he could cross time like Run. When Run meditates, time buckles, bends, splinters so he sees many strands at once. *Soul memory* is how Ed thinks of it as Run is able to connect to the memories of past lives locked in souls, both those in bodies and those not in bodies, and by perusing those memories he can travel forward and backward in time. Nan has explained that those locked memories reveal the karmic timetable that regulates all that has occurred or will occur.

More random images of Sutum come to him. He slows his breathing until he is only taking a few breaths a minute. His thoughts slow then too and the images fade.

More than an hour later there's a light knock on the door. By then, Ed has lit a candle and is at the table reading his daily teachings.

When he opens the door, Song nods, and Ed steps to the side so he can come in. At the table, he hands Ed three warm plastic bags. One is full of white rice fried with chopped onion and garlic and lime squeezed over it. Another contains chunks of chicken seasoned with coconut sauce. The third bag is full of balls of tofu fried with ginger and cilantro.

Ed gets two bowls from the cupboard above the sink and spoons out a larger portion for Song than himself and puts the leftovers in the small propane fridge.

Song eats his portion without saying anything. Ed is used to this preference for not talking while eating. Nan and he rarely speak during meals to avoid choking or other mishaps.

When Song finishes, he folds his hands and closes his eyes and Ed does the same. Song chants aloud and Ed repeats the Pali as best as he can, but Song chants faster than Nan does so several times Ed has to guess at the pronunciations. Song doesn't correct him as Nan might.

They end with "*Satu, Satu, Satu.*" (Amen)—and Song stays quiet for another half hour and doesn't move in all that time.

Ed is unable to sit still for that long. Twice, he catches himself adjusting his robe and later he absentmindedly moves a foot up and down.

Eventually Song gets up from his chair and carries his and Ed's dishes to the sink and picks up a drying cloth. Ed washes them and hands each to Song who dries them and then places them in the cupboard. He doesn't have to ask Ed where any of them go.

Later at the door they stand side by side and Song says: "Chai." (Yes.)

"Sutum?" Ed asks.

Song nods but doesn't speak. After a long pause he say: "He was a good boy, but foolish in love." And then: "It's okay."

Ed is heartened by those last words and is thankful to Song for them but also senses that this is the most they'll ever speak about what's happened.

When they go outside, the moon is hidden behind the hut, and in the more limited light, Song's face looks vague and timeless. He falters slightly on the first step and Ed reaches out a hand and catches his shoulder and steadies him and then lets go. Song grips the handrail and continues down and doesn't look back.

Away from the hut he is half lit by the moon as he walks to his motorcycle. He straddles it and kick starts it twice before the engine catches. He revs it for a few seconds and then lets it idle. He turns on the headlight, and the bulb is so dim Ed wonders how he can see his way.

Ed stays on the landing to take in the night sky overhead. Tonight, there are fewer stars and those he sees are far apart, except directly overhead where they appear bunched together, even though they are millions of miles apart.

The total number of stars is so large they can't be counted, only approximated. Normally that fact comforts him but tonight he longs for what is knowable and finite. He shifts his gaze to a section of the empty night sky and that dark makes the sky appear flat and two-dimensional.

He knows from his daily readings that the magnitude of stars isn't what's important and to look at the sky is to look inward. He stands for a while longer and considers how every star is moving away from him at an ever-increasing speed. But from here they appear stopped. Where exactly are they going? Physicists have proposed theories about that and those notions of the cosmos dwarf our daily lives. His practices are helping him to see that existing in the midst of all this movement means he's travelling too. Tonight, though, the sight of the stars adds to all he doesn't know and likely never will.

Earlier, when he and Song were chanting for Sutum's soul, he fully concentrated on his chanting even though he still doesn't have proper sense of what the soul is, or its size, shape, or location.

Nan has said that the soul is elusive and that there isn't any point locating it. "Just assume it's there," she's said, and so he has accepted that his soul lurks somewhere inside him.

But seeing these stars, so nebulous and far away, he wishes he could feel around his body and locate his soul, and that it would always be in exactly the same place, like his heart. Nan says the soul shifts locations and doesn't take root and can't be boxed in. It isn't tangible like an organ or bone. At times it's an energy source, and at other times it's nearly dormant. The soul is ever accumulating like the night sky.

He returns inside the hut and blows out the candle and in the dark goes to the bamboo cot and sits on the edge of it and keeps his back straight. This is not an easy posture for him to maintain for long and it has taken him weeks of practice to do it as easily as he can tonight. He focuses on the bamboo cot and senses each layer of it from the floor to the criss-crossed bamboo strips and woven grass that forms the top layer he sits on now.

*I shouldn't be here,* he thinks but then immediately counters that with: *But I am here and can't be anywhere but where I am right now.*

He feels time pull him along and senses its pace hasten for the first time. Before tonight, time has been steady and insistent—an expanding bubble that absorbs everything it encounters. There is no existing outside of it. He used to think of time as a culprit and thief but tonight sees it as his travelling companion. It's part residue and part vapour trail, a rolling forward. Its urgency may be vague but it's still an urgency. He can't yet imagine the complexities of Run's time travel but accepts that it occurs.

*We mostly stand still and time swirls,* Run has said to him.

He hears now in his head what Nan said to him earlier this evening on the phone: *Don't look for reasons. Don't search. Don't seek. Be a chamber. By standing perfectly still you will sense the movement of all things. That movement is constant and is what holds you here. What happened today was always going to happen. You are merely one of the participants.*

He lies down on the cot and sees today's tragedy differently than he would have before he'd married Nan. The arc that includes a given event may span many lifetimes. What may seem mysterious or impulsive in this life may be the culmination of many misdeeds, betrayals, or wrongdoings in previous lives. Tragedies repeat because all involved are unaware of previous tragedies they participated in. It takes someone like Run to unravel all the interconnections, and even then, the way ahead is never certain.

A rat wakes him as it claws along the thatched roof. He stays on the cot and listens to its noisy progress and worries that it will find a way inside and climb down a wall. But he reminds himself that he's here to let go of worries. According to Run, worry is an impediment to a clear mind.

The wind picks up and shakes the roof and the rat works louder and moves quickly along the southern slope of the roof. Near the eaves, it makes a jubilant high-pitched chirp and goes quiet.

He considers getting up and grabbing the straw broom to shoo it away if it's come inside, but he stays where he is and repeats: *Let go. Don't listen. There's no rat here just as there is no wind. There is only this cot and my noisy heart.*

The wind dies down again, and the rat noises return but it's busier and noisier than before and moves quickly from the eaves back to the peak of the roof and then down the far side. *This is proof that I exist and that I can't escape myself.*

The rat could be the reincarnated soul of a farmer who once lived in this hut. Lives shimmer and blend in ways he hasn't known until now. Being anywhere is not a certainty. To master more filaments of his life, he must first accept that the divide between the living and dead is not absolute. What he sees isn't all that there is. These ideas are new to him but enthralling and liberating.

He closes his eyes and slows his breathing until there is no rat.

A fork or spoon scrapes across a plate. At first, he thinks the noises are lingering sensations from a dream, but as he listens, the noises don't fade but move toward the fridge. He doesn't lock the door at night, so anyone could have come in and gone to the fridge for something to eat. He sits up in the cot for a better view but can't see anything in the dark. The noises stop not long after he sits up. He gets out of the cot and goes to the table, but it's exactly as he left it earlier. Nan has warned him that there could be unexpected disturbances during the night. She'd said if he hears anything out of ordinary or has the urge to burp or fart or his nose is runny, he must chant: "*Phen Dukkang Aniccang Anatta*" (It is suffering. It is impermanent. It is uncontrollable)—to ward off any bad spirits. He returns to the cot and closes his eyes and repeats that chant three times.

According to Nan, some souls don't realize that their bodies have died. They continue with their daily routines thinking they are still alive until they discover that no one can see or hear them. Once they discover that, they flee to some place they had a connection to in their most recent life or a past one.

He returns to the cot but isn't able to fall back to sleep and listens for any unusual sounds but there aren't any. Nor are there the usual wind and animal noises. The night is so perfectly quiet that he shakes even though the hut is hot and muggy. The trembling doesn't let up until it's getting light and he finally falls back to sleep.

For the next week, no one comes to the rice paddies to harvest so Ed stays inside with door and window open to let in any available breeze.

During the day he focuses on his Buddhist practices and each night his sleep is interrupted by ever-stranger disturbances. The second night loud noises at the table and sink again wake him. The next night, his own sneezing and burping wakes him. He sits up in the cot and chants until they stop. The night after that, his violent coughing wakes him, and he has to get up and puts his head between his legs to get the coughing to stop.

He's so tired during the day that each afternoon he naps for several hours. When he wakes from these naps, he always calls Nan to report the latest disturbances. She urges him to chant often and stay dedicated to his practices and to be *Sati.* (Being fully present and attending to every movement.)

By the third day of this, she tells him that the disturbances mean he is making progress. *He's made a breakthrough.* She doesn't say that specifically, but he infers it and understands that a shift has occurred. She tells him that Run says that such activities mean he's a conduit and that the spirit world is more exposed at the hut allowing for powerful connections.

She then tells him how her grandmother's ghost rode the bus from Chum Phae to Khon Kaen every week for five years until Run helped her soul move on. Recently, Run woke in the morning to the distinct scent of cherry incense except none had been lit. That meant that another world was nearby and that someone there was burning cherry incense. Run lit cinnamon incense and chanted and meditated until he only smelled cinnamon. By that time, many images had come to him and much had been changed in this world and that one.

Ed asks Nan how long these disturbances will continue, and she says until they stop and then she adds that he can no more control them than he can move the moon a centimetre.

The next night, a very noisy rat wakes him so abruptly that his heart pounds loudly in his ears and he feels lightheaded and thinks he is still dreaming. In time, he's fully awake but all the details of his dream have vanished except for the sensation of being locked in a small room. He can't shake off that feeling and gets up and goes to the window seeking the comfort of the view. The slight shimmer of morning light exposes details on the mountains to the north and he watches that fade as the sun gets higher and the mountains become a vague backdrop. When the last stages of morning end, he returns to the cot and is soon asleep.

A week after the murder his loud burps wake him. He gets up and paces until the burping stops. It is fully light by then, so he goes to the window and stays there for a half hour chanting with his eyes open. He ends with "*Satu, Satu, Satu,*" but doesn't step away. He slides his fingers along the rough wooden surface of the windowsill to remind himself where he is.

He's about to step away when a red Toyota half-ton appears from behind the hut and stops where the gravel ends. Three young men get out and walk below his window but don't look in his direction. They disappear around the front of the hut and a few seconds later he hears a soft knock. He isn't expecting anyone at this hour so doesn't answer right away hoping they'll leave.

There is a long pause and then two more knocks closer together but as light as the first. He says: "*Pra Nip Paan Knaw*" three times and the opens the door. One of the three men stands there, the other two have stayed at the bottom of the steps. All three wai him.

"Come," the man says, and then tells Ed in Thai that his name is Ta and that Song has sent him. His hair is cut close to his scalp but not as short as a monk's.

Ed slips on his sandals and steps outside. Ta has joined the other two and turns first and leads the way to the truck. Ed follows Ta and the other two walk behind him. Ta points to the passenger side and Ed opens the door and gets in. The two men climb into the bed of the truck and Ta gets in the driver's side.

At the four-lane highway, Ta turns south and doesn't speak as he drives but stares straight ahead and keeps both hands on the steering wheel. They come alongside a truck so overloaded with cabbages that it teeters dangerously into their lane, but Ta expertly speeds past it. After three more kilometres, he turns onto Song's gravel road.

From there, Ed has a direct view of Song's two-story cement and wood farmhouse. This far back, it looks like a house in the country in Canada, but as they get closer there are large Thai symbols at the front peak of the house. When he came here three weeks earlier with Nan, she'd told him that it's a Pali chant to ward off bad spirits. The first floor of the house is constructed of cement and four cement pillars support a large overhang to the right of the house under which a table and chairs have been arranged out of the sun and rain. The second story of the house has teak siding. Blue ceramic tiles cover the peaked roof.

In a fenced area to the west of the house, brown chickens run, hop, and flap their wings in a panic because of the noise of the truck. Ta backs up onto the grass next to the parking pad and Song's new white Toyota Yaris. Today other new white Hondas and Toyotas are parked next to Song's Yaris.

The chickens continue running about now wildly dodging each other.

When Ed visited here before with Nan, Song and his wife, Aom, had prepared them a meal of *Phad Mee* (stir fried rice noodles), sticky rice, and papaya salad. Later Song showed them pictures of his two sons and one daughter and five grandchildren who all live in Khon Kaen. He also pointed to a picture on the wall of his sister, Nan's grandmother, who had died a year after Nan and Ed were married.

Ta steps out of the truck first and waits on his side until Ed gets out. The other two jump out of the truck bed and join Ta. The three of them go up the main steps ahead of Ed and remove their sandals at the front door and carry them as they go barefoot inside without knocking. Ed does the same and then follows them.

The living room is empty and he listens for voices, but the house is quiet. They continue out the back door and a small crowd stands silently around a plywood coffin. Two sets of black handles have been screwed to each side of the coffin.

Everyone turns at the same time and wais the newcomers. They give Ed a slightly higher wai than the other three and he wais them back one at a time. Most of the mourners are close to Song's age.

Song steps forward and nods to the four of them and says: "*Kop Khun Krup*." (Thank you.)

Ed and the three men wai Song in unison and Ta says: "*Mai Pen Rai.*" (No problem.)

The crowd steps away from the coffin and Ta and the two men put their sandals back on and each take one of the handles and wait while Ed also puts his sandals on.

He then grips the fourth handle and they all lift the coffin. It feels surprisingly light to Ed as though there's no body inside. It occurs to him then that the others are lifting more than their share, needing him only to balance a corner.

They go around the side of the house and toward the front. They walk very slowly taking two steps and then stopping for a full minute before taking two more steps and stopping again. Song walks behind them and Aom behind him and then everyone else behind her. Some ring chimes while others hum or chant or moan. When they eventually reach the front of the house, a teenage boy runs ahead and lowers the tailgate of the truck.

Ta and the other man rest the front of the coffin on the tailgate and they come around back, and Song joins them and they slowly push the coffin forward until it bumps against the back of the cab. They then slide it out again so there's a small gap. The coffin extends out of the back of the truck, so the tailgate has to be left down.

The two men climb into the back of the truck and sit cross-legged on opposite sides of the coffin and far enough away that they're not touching it.

Ed gets into the passenger side and Ta gets in his side and drives away from the house before all the other vehicles. Song and Aom follow next in their car. The rest of the cars and a few motorcycles fall in behind them. Ed watches the procession in the side mirror. Song stays so close behind that any sudden braking by Ta would send Song's car smashing into the tailgate and the coffin. But Ta drives so slowly there's little risk of that. It takes them more than twenty minutes to travel the two kilometres to the centre of the village.

Ta continues through the village and past two temples before turning south and stopping at an open field adjacent to the largest temple in the village. The size of the temple indicates its importance and Song's status.

Ed has been to this temple once before with Song. He'd brought Ed here after his third day of harvesting. Song left an offering to help ensure a bumper crop and then they'd chanted in front of the main altar and its fifteen-foot, golden Buddha. Next to it, there's a Buddha bone in a glass container. A video camera is focused on the Buddha bone and a magnified image is streamed to two flat screen TVs, one on either side of the altar.

Nan has explained that the Buddha bone intensifies the abbot's powers so that he connects directly with the forces of the sun and moon. He uses the moon when someone is too hot and the sun when someone is too cold.

The abbot, who looks about Song's age, is waiting out front of the temple. His hands are folded at his waist. Ta stops just past the abbot and the others park behind him. Song gets out first and approaches the abbot. Everyone else stays in their vehicles. Ta turns off the engine and Ed cranks down his window to let in any breeze.

Song wais the abbot and they speak for more than ten minutes and then a dozen novice monks emerge from the temple and line up in three short rows behind the abbot. The novices wear white robes and their heads have recently been shaved. More villagers arrive, some walking and others in cars or on motorcycles. They form a large half circle behind the novices.

Song returns to his car and opens the passenger door for Aom. The two men in back of the truck hop down on opposite sides and stand where they land. Ta gets out next and then Ed, and when they reach the back of the truck they each grip a handle and slide the coffin out until the other end balances on the tailgate. The other two men each hold a front handle. Ta and Ed step back, and this time he feels his share of the weight. They turn in the direction of the temple and then stop. Song and Aom stand at the front of the coffin and are joined by a couple only a little older than Ed. These must be Sutum's parents. The rest of the mourners line up behind them.

Sutum's father sets a prayer wreath on top of the coffin and several mourners do the same. Song and Aom go to the abbot and Sutum's parents join them and then they walk ahead of the coffin.

The novices and the rest of the mourners line up behind, and the procession advances alongside the temple. As they walk, they follow a similar halting rhythm to the one at the house.

When they pass the last temple building, a side door opens and loud Thai rock blasts out. This loud intrusion causes the procession to stop. Ed expects a novice to hurry inside and turn off the music or at least close the door. Instead the music is allowed to continue. When the song ends, everyone walks until the next song plays and they stop again until that song ends and then they advance again but stop when the next song plays. This third song is louder than the other two and has a much faster tempo. Ed recognizes the distinct rhythm of *Mor-Lam* (Isaan style of music and dance) that he's heard in the streets of Khon Kaen. No one sways or dances to the hypnotic rhythm. The tempo speeds up and the procession starts again but maintains a slow pace, despite the driving music.

When they reach the end of that building, they turn and cross the street to a large field. At the north end of it, a two-story pyre has been constructed from lumber and straw.

It takes them twenty minutes to reach the pyre. Up close it smells of coconut oil and gasoline. Ta raises his corner of the coffin and Ed does the same and so do the other two. Ed knows to keep the head and feet of the corpse at the same level as they lift the coffin to four novices waiting above in the pyre.

The novices grab the coffin and swing it around and set it into place. They then climb down, and other novices circle the pyre lighting incense sticks and candles.

The abbot stands in front and raises both arms. The distant music is finally turned off mid-song. Everyone forms a half circle facing the abbot, who chants: "*Metta Knaw*," (Kindness) and "*Pra Nip Paan Knaw*," repeatedly. The crowd repeats each phrase in unison after the abbot. This lasts for nearly a half hour and then the abbot changes to a longer chant also in Pali. Again, the crowd repeats each line after him and the rise and fall of those voices sweep Ed along and he joins in too even though he has to guess at the pronunciation of most words.

The abbot stops chanting and he waits for the crowd to finish and then turns ninety degrees and walks slowly to the far side of the pyre, and as he walks, he keeps his hands folded in front of him.

A boy of about seven runs from the back of the crowd and when he reaches the front, a novice hands him a lighter. The boy walks it to the pyre and then flicks it twice before it lights. He cups his hand around the small flame and presses the lighter into the thick of the straw and holds it there until the straw catches fire.

The straw burns quickly and the flames rise to the layers of kindling and from there to the wooden frame. The abbot circles the pyre chanting, and everyone forms a paired line behind him starting with Ed and Ta and behind them the novice monks. No one repeats the abbot's chant.

A man and woman stand in the back of a pickup nearby and the woman releases two birds from small bamboo cages and then the man releases four balloons from a large bundle he is holding. The man and woman then continue to alternate between releases. The birds scatter immediately to the cover of nearby trees. The balloons float straight up for a long time, and when they reach an upper current, it carries them quickly northward even as they continue to climb. Ed watches the first set of balloons until they disappear from view.

When he returns his gaze to the pyre, it's fully engulfed and the flames have burned their way inside the coffin revealing the contents. The other mourners move forward for a better view of Sutum, but Ed stays back.

He's never watched a pyre burn before and is surprised when Sutum's corpse is exposed and his head rises as heat constricts muscles in his neck and shoulders. He continues to rise until he's nearly sitting upright in the partially burned-away coffin.

Ed turns away then and hurries in the direction of the main temple.

Across the street, he stops and sits under a tall mango tree facing the pyre but he's still too close and hears many pops and hisses. The smells of lavender and coconut oil have been replaced by the stench of burning flesh.

He stands and walks alongside the main wall of temple until he reaches a massive tamarind tree. The wind shifts and he's far enough away that the smells and noises don't reach him.

He sits facing the pyre and watches a thick cloud of black smoke stall over the fire. The cloud swells to three times its original size and then starts to slowly move eastward. The sounds of chanting occasionally reach him but fade in and out so often that he can't make out any specific words. He drags his fingers along the dry grass and presses his back against the rough bark of the tree. Those tactile sensations keep him alert despite the afternoon heat.

He sits watching for another hour before any of the mourners begin to leave. They break away in small groups of three and four and most are talking and laughing as they pass him. Not a single person is crying. Earlier there had been times when the tone seemed sombre, but no one cried.

The abbot, Song, Aom, Ta, and Sutum's parents stand so close to the pyre that they must feel the intense heat, but they don't move away until the pyre is reduced to smouldering ashes.

Ta approaches Ed then and waves for him to follow. At the truck the same two men get in the back and he joins Ta in the cab. They don't speak the entire trip back to the hut. Ta smells of smoke and coconut oil.

At the hut, Ta and the other two walk behind Ed to the front steps. He turns to face them and they wai him in unison, a higher wai than they gave him earlier, but not as high as they gave Song or the abbot. None of them says a word to him. Ta turns and walks back to the truck, the other two follow him.

He watches the two men get in the back again and Ta in the cab. Ta doesn't start the engine right away and Ed realizes that he's chanting. The two other men sit with their backs to the cab of the truck, but don't appear to be chanting nor are they talking. They face Ed and from this far away he can't tell if they are actually looking at him or at something in the distance.

He waits until Ta starts the engine before he turns and continues up the steps and into the hut. He goes immediately to the window and watches the truck disappear behind the hut.

He looks across the empty rice field to where Sutum died. From the heated confines of the hut he could be looking at any field anywhere but he's looking at a murder scene. He decides he'll give it a wide berth from now on.

That evening he calls Nan and she tells him that Run has seen Sutum's ghost in the cabin and Ed needs to chant very diligently so that Sutum doesn't get trapped there.

For dinner he eats a palm size ball of rice and two pieces of tofu and has no appetite for anything more. When he finishes, he cleans up and returns to the table to read and practice.

Nan calls back and she is now at Run's and they have been chanting for Sutum. Run says that there is much black magic at the hut that Ed is now caught up in it. She says there is much danger there but Run will keep him safe.

After a pause she says: "We are always living the strands of our past lives too, in this one." She explains how the actions, betrayals, loves, and accidents from past lives ripple into this one. Maybe the man who killed Sutum used to be his enemy in a past life or his father or aunt. Maybe he killed Sutum because in a past life Sutum killed him or betrayed him in some devastating way. Or maybe they were lovers and Sutum jilted him.

The compounding of these possibilities astounds Ed and he wonders if it is possible to get free of them or do those interferences simply accumulate? Do all the intersections between this life and earlier ones become so tightly wound that in time everyone is trapped?

He asks her about this.

She says he's still thinking like a *forang* (foreigner), and adds: "Don't hang your soul on that. Run will help sort all that needs to be sorted out. It's what he does."

She calls back a half hour later, and he puts the phone on speaker and listens as Run chants for him. In the slow rising and falling of the Pali, Ed feels nudged along and in time drifts deeply inward and senses his self flatten and become dimensionless. When Run's chanting stops, Ed surfaces and thus gains an emotional footing.

Sutum's ghost wakes him again during night, and the hut is engulfed by the powerful competing scents of cinnamon and garlic, although he hasn't cooked with either in several weeks. He hears no unusual noises, nor does he burp or sneeze. He repeats: "*Pra Nip Paan Knaw,*" to himself but the odours linger. He continues to chant "*Pra Nip Paan Knaw,*" until he falls asleep.

He wakes later than usual the next day and is ashamed to have slept in. When he opens the door, Song is not working in the field. Three more days pass before Song returns to work. That morning Ed sleeps in too and, when he wakes and goes to the door, Song is working alone and has already cleared all the rice from around where Sutum was shot and has progressed a good distance beyond that.

Ed eats quickly and joins him.

# Chapter 3

## *Khon Kaen*
## *1970*

When a second hour passes and Roong hasn't returned, Tuum rides to her mistress's house and leans his bicycle against the outside wall right next to the main gate. It's open at this hour and he walks past the guard without stopping. The guard stands and wais him but then quickly sits again and doesn't attempt to interfere with him. At the front door, Tuum knocks twice, and when no one answers, he knocks longer and louder.

Almost immediately, a woman, about Roong's age, opens the door. Her hair is pulled behind her head in a ponytail and she wais him and then smiles.

He asks if Roong is there and she says that she ran away two days ago. This admission surprises him so he presses her for more details and asks if she's heard from her. She suggests he try the police station and quickly closes the door.

Back at his bicycle, he remembers Roong's words from just days before: "I've died young in every previous life and I worry that I will again in this one."

He'd assured her that she would live a long life this time and that he intended to see to that. She said he was lovely but then added that she wasn't sure such a karmic pattern could be broken.

He then foolishly blamed her past short lives on Buddha.

She'd said that she wished he hadn't done that as his words could trigger something dangerous. Then after a short pause, she'd fixed her eyes on his and said: "This doesn't concern Buddha. He isn't the adjudicator."

*Buddha is the place we lay down and go to sleep,* she'd said later.

"What does that mean?" he'd asked.

"We are all Buddha in Buddha. All animals and beings are Buddha. You are Buddha, I am Buddha."

"Even your mistress?"

"Yes, even her."

*Before Buddha there was another Buddha and before that Buddha another Buddha and so on. In the year 5000 this Buddha will end. For a while there will be no religion and then in time the next Buddha will appear.* This is how his father has explained that chronology to him but he likes Roong's notion better and wishes to believe that all beings are Buddha. He realizes now that time is Buddha. His father has alluded to that this way: *Nothing is standing still and nothing is moving.*

The street is already busy with afternoon shoppers. He mounts his bicycle and rides to the main Khon Kaen police station five blocks back toward his apartment. The station is on a wide street busy with bicycles, motorcycles, *tuk tuk* (three wheeled taxi), pedicabs, and a few cars.

The main room of the station is crowded, and someone occupies every wooden chair against the wall on his left. He scans for where he should go and sees the receiving counter at the very back of the room.

To his right three police officers are gathered around a single desk. They are filling out forms and, at another desk to the left of that, an officer is interviewing two people. A man with his hands cuffed behind his back sits in a chair off to side of them and appears to be connected to the two people being interviewed. The man's head is lowered and Tuum thinks he is sleeping, until he passes near him and hears his quiet chanting.

One officer sits behind the receiving counter and is talking to a woman standing very close to the counter. One of her legs is shaking and when Tuum gets close enough he hears her stutter several times. She stops abruptly as Tuum approaches the counter. The officer points to his right and tells her to try in there. She disappears through double doors and they snap shut again loudly enough behind her that the room noticeably quietens for a second or two and then everything resumes.

Tuum steps as close to the counter as possible and the officer wais him but doesn't ask why Tuum is here. Instead he sorts through the stack of papers directly in front of him and picks up a sheet and skims it and then sets it in the larger stack to his left. He then selects another piece of paper and examines it even longer and sets it on the smaller stack on his right.

He looks up then at Tuum and wais him a second time as if he's forgotten that he's already done that. He asks if Tuum is here to report a crime or turn himself in.

Tuum says that he wishes to visit Roong who he believes is being held here. The man picks up a thick ledger to the right of the tall stack of papers and cracks it open pushing the splayed ledger flat against the counter. He asks for Roong's full name and then runs his finger down the page and then flips to the next page and does the same until he reaches a blank page.

He says her name is not on the list so she can't be here.

Tuum asks him to look again as he says that he believes that she has been falsely arrested and charged. This causes the officer to go back to the page he opened and scan very carefully down each page, running his finger very slowly down the left margin. When he reaches the first blank page again, he closes the ledger and looks up at Tuum and says she's not here. He asks what crime she's been falsely charged with and arrested.

Tuum says he doesn't know.

The officer then asks how he knows then that she has been falsely arrested and charged.

He says because she couldn't have possibly committed a crime. He then says that she left for the market yesterday and didn't return.

"Maybe she decided to not come back."

"That's not possible."

A couple in their fifties approaches the counter and waits quietly behind Tuum.

The police officer likely seeing that his work was getting backed up suggests that Tuum try the Khon Kaen Remand Prison, she may have been taken directly there. If her crime is serious, officers will not bring her here but take her directly there. "To await trial," he says.

He gives Tuum directions and then asks the couple behind him why they are there. Tuum doesn't wait to hear their answer but hurries to the street and rides immediately to the Remand Prison. It's three blocks east of his apartment.

He realizes that he's past this building many times without knowing that it's a prison. On the outside, it is plain and utilitarian and blends in with all the other government buildings on this street except it doesn't have a large plaque displaying the department name. Nor is there a spirit house next to the main doors.

He doesn't go directly inside but sits on the cement bench outside the front doors and meditates. When he reaches mindfulness, he doesn't hear passing footsteps or traffic noises in the street. Later, as he resurfaces, he asks his mother for a good outcome. Before opening his eyes, he focuses on being *Sati*.

Just inside there is a security booth and the guard there smiles and wais him and then asks his business. He returns the wai and says he's here to visit someone. The guard tells him to check at the main counter through the mahogany doors just down the hallway.

The doors are thick and heavy, but he pushes forcefully on them and goes easily through. The bright glare from massive windows on the other side disorientates him and he stops to get his bearings. People blur past.

When his eyes adjust, the open area is larger than two combined classrooms at his school. The floor is polished, white-marble tile. Teak-framed windows circle the room and each reaches nearly to the high ceiling. The only furniture is a mahogany counter against the back wall. On either side of it are wider and taller teak-framed windows.

He approaches the counter and the guard behind it smiles before he does and they both wai at the same time. He asks the guard if Roong is here and is told that he has arrived during visiting hours.

The guard's nametag says Ven, and Tuum asks him again if Roong is here. Ven says that is difficult to know. Tuum asks why that is but already senses the Buddhist trick. They're discussing the impermanence of *here* without discussing it. There is no here, no clock, and no continued rush of time. Everything including this building is perfectly still and not moving nor is anyone inside it moving, including the guard and him. Everyone is exactly where they should be. No one is out of place.

He asks a third time if Roong is here and points to a list attached to a clipboard on the desk. Ven picks up the clipboard and runs a finger down one page and then another and another. He goes all the way through and then returns to the first page and starts over. This time he pauses on the third page and shows Tuum a name written there. It's Roong's.

"Someone will bring her," Ven says and points to another set of mahogany doors to the right of the counter. The room on the other side is small and cramped. Six narrow metal tables have been arranged in two rows. Each table has four straight-back, wooden chairs—two to a side. All of the chairs are occupied except for two in the very back corner. A guard motions for him to sit at one of those. A man and a woman occupy the other two chairs. The man wears blue prison garb and a woman sits across from him and they hold hands and the woman talks rapidly. The man listens.

When Tuum sits beside them the woman lowers her voice and the man leans forward across the narrow table until her lips are close to his ear on the other side, away from Tuum.

He folds his hands on the table and waits. It's fifteen minutes before Roong is led into the room by a female guard. They both come directly to his table and the guard leaves before Roong sits across from him. She is wearing the same blue garb and her face is blotchy. She's been crying recently.

She slides her hands across the table to his. Her hands are icy and dry, and she has bruises on her wrists and the backs of her hands.

He asks about them and she leans forward and says: "Not now. Not here."

He hands her a bag of hot *Phad Mee* he bought in the street for her. The guard who escorted Roong comes over and inspects the bag and nods and gives it to Roong.

"My mistress has charged me with stealing her gold worth a million baht. The guards say my best chance is to confess. I will get a lighter sentence then, but I haven't done anything wrong. They aren't interested in the truth only in a confession. If I don't confess, they will arrest my aunt and uncle and hold them in prison until I tell them where the gold is. If I don't produce the gold, it won't go well for me here or in court. But I can't produce gold out of thin air. I don't think she ever had the gold that she claims is missing. That makes it easier for the gold to disappear. I'm being charge for stealing gold that doesn't exist. The only gold I ever saw her wear was a ring and bracelet and neither of those were worth more than a few thousand baht. If there's gold in that house it is well hidden and if it is gone then most likely she made it disappear."

She then tells him she'd been in the middle of picking out a silk blouse in the market, when a policeman approached and arrested her. "I was foolish to go, and I realize now that I incorrectly interpreted that dream. I see the warnings I'd missed. The silk was meant to warn me not to go to the market and woman in the café had really been the fruit vendor in the market that recognized me and reported me to a policeman on duty in the market. A bad spirit caused me to miss those warnings."

She says that guards have also shown her the amount of debt her mistress claims that she owes and that her mistress has greatly exaggerated the sum, well beyond their original contract. Her mistress has already taken possession of her father's farm and sold it but none of those proceeds have been included in the documents shown to her.

She stops and fiddles with the bag of food and then says it is best if she eats it here because if she saves it for later it will be confiscated. Her hands shake as she eats the whole bag of thin noodles, fried eggs, green onions, and pork. Some of the other prisoners and their visitors look briefly in their direction as she eats and then go back to their conversations. He says he will bring her more food when he visits again and says that he'll get help.

"I might be beyond help. It is my word against hers and she has the money to pay the right people. A million baht is an impossible sum for me, for you, for us." She says it would take a lifetime to save that much.

Soon after, the guard sitting at a desk in the far corner rings a bell. Two minutes later he rings the bell a second time, and the other prisoners stand and Roong does too.

Tuum remains seated with the other visitors. The male prisoners line up on one side of the room and the female prisoners on the other. No one talks. A guard leads the men out first and then the guard who brought Roong in leads out the women. Roong is the very last one in line. None of the prisoners turn around for a final glance at their visitors. He watches as Roong keeps her head up and her shoulders pushed back and walks very straight and purposeful unlike many of the prisoners who slouch and keep their heads down. She lifts each knee high as she walks, and he takes that as evidence of her defiance. As soon as she exits, the doors snap closed.

The visitors stand then at random but one at time. He waits until everyone is standing before he gets out of his chair. The visitors don't line up nor or parade out but disperse quickly from the building into the street.

*If you don't fight you can't be a winner*—THAI SAYING

*During war with Burma a Thai general told his men on the morning they were about to cross into Burma that they should eat a big breakfast. He then told them to break all of the dishes and throw out all remaining food. He said no matter what happens that day they wouldn't need the dishes anymore, and if they lost the battle, they shouldn't leave anything for the Burmese if they crossed into Thailand. 'They must have no rice or chicken to give them strength. If we are victorious then we will be eating in Burma tonight.' They won that battle and stayed in Burma for ten years.*

He sleeps very little that night. At first light, he's out of bed and at his prayer corner and chants. He asks Buddha for guidance. For a few seconds he sees a half moon in his inner darkness, but it fades. Then he sees shifting tones of blue and thinks the word *blue* and then *why.* But that is all he gets except for a steady hum coming from somewhere outside his head. He tries not to listen but it persists.

He stays kneeling and keeps his eyes closed, but nothing comes, and he finally gives in and leaves his prayer corner. By then, morning heat has thickened the air in his apartment. If his father were here, he'd scold him for his neglect of his practices. By now he should have better access to time and be able to see months and years behind and ahead for *all time exists. There is no true past, present, or future but a weaving and bending.* He needs to only find the key to enter it all.

When Tuum left home for university, his father's powers were so well known that people came from all over Thailand to consult with him. They sought advice on the best day to marry, where and when to plant crops, whether to lend money or borrow money. Over the years his father has assisted many powerful people and collected many favours. His father says that power is an illusion. *Buddha says there is more power in a grain of sand than in the most powerful human who has ever lived.*

He skips breakfast and arrives at the prison even before morning visiting hours begin so all the tables are empty. He selects the one nearest to the door that Roong came through and left by yesterday. The other tables fill up one at a time with visitors. A half hour later the male prisoners are brought in and once they are all seated the woman prisoners are escorted in. Roong is not amongst them. He asks the woman guard who paraded the women in and she tells him to go back to his table and wait.

It's another half hour before she's led into the room by two women guards, one on either side of her. She sits across from him and he sets a bag of *Kai Pahlo* (boiled eggs and cinnamon, cilantro, and soy sauce) on the table and Roong doesn't touch it until the woman guard comes over and pokes in the brown liquid with a knife and then hands the bag to Roong.

She eats using the spoon and fork he's brought. When she finishes, she tells him that her aunt—her father's only living sister—and her husband were arrested yesterday and are being held here too. Guards brought them to her cell this morning as proof that they're here.

"They're very old and frail and both were trembling as they stood in my cell."

She felt each of their foreheads and they were feverish which meant that bad spirits had attached to them as well. They asked her why they had been arrested because no one told them why they'd been brought here and locked up. A car had come for them at first light.

Her interrogators now accuse her of selling the gold and hiding the money. They demand that she tell them where she has hidden the money, or she will spend a long time in prison and her aunt and uncle will die in prison. She has told the interrogators that she didn't steal any gold and has no money hidden anywhere. They have said that claiming innocence is not an option. Her mistress knows judges and prosecutors and her words have much more legal weight than anything that Roong might say.

"I told them that I've recently learned that she sells young girls to Hong Kong and China. She goes into the villages in the far north near the Burma border and tells the families that her husband is a high-ranking official. She says that she will take their daughters to Krung Thep (Bangkok) and educate them so they can become nurses and marry policemen. But once the young women reach Krung Thep she has them sent to Khon Kaen and she puts them to work and if they refuse to work for her or one of her husband's powerful friends or refuse to go to China then she accuses them of stealing her gold and they go to jail for a very long time. I have seen them pass through the house.

"Her husband profits as much from her activities as she does. How can laws stop such corruption if those who enforce them are corrupt? Only the Karmic wheel can correct all of these wrong doings, but it spins too slowly for me. Maybe two lifetimes from now it will put right but that won't help us today.

"One of my interrogators then said that the guilty always make outrages claims. *They squawk but say nothing,* he said."

*If you are a good person time will take*
*a bad person out of your life.*
*If you are a bad person time will take*
*a good person out of your life*—Thai saying

Immediately after his visit with Roong, he catches a bus to his father's village just north and west of Chum Phae. The house his father lives in now is much smaller than the one Tuum grew up in. His father's new one is in the very centre of the village, and all the streets fan out from it like spokes of a wheel so that many have a view of it. It had once been the mayor's residence, but the mayor now lives in a large house on the edge of the village. For many people, his father is more important than the mayor.

Nong, his father's current wife, opens the door when Tuum knocks. She nods and he wais her. She is only a few years older than Tuum and wears red shoes and smiles often.

"You father will be so glad to see you," she says and doesn't at all seem surprised that he's here after more than three years, and without a word of warning that he's coming.

His father doesn't leave his office to investigate the commotion. Tuum remembers his father being in his office most days when he was growing up, except for the two miraculous years when he helped Tuum to walk again. When his father worked as a lawyer, he had an office near the courthouse, but worked most evenings at home. Later when he left law and became a devout monk, he used his office as a place for meditation. Since becoming a village elder, he's conducted his interviews in the house, but his influence is now considerably more powerful and far reaching than it was then.

Nong opens the door of his father's office without knocking and goes straight in, something Tuum's mother never did. She always knocked first and, if his father didn't answer, she'd find some chore to attend to and return later.

Tuum enters behind Nong, but his father doesn't turn around to greet them. He continues to flip through a binder bent open at his desk. There's a row of other binders that line the back of the desk and still more in the bookcase on the wall to the right of his desk. His father stops to write something with a fountain pen.

Tuum stands beside Nong and waits for his father to turn around and acknowledge him. He goes on scribbling into his binder until Nong says: "Jan."

His father turns around then and nods to both of them and they wai him.

Tuum is shocked by how much older his father has become. He's 72 now but looks closer to 80. His handsome features remain but his face is frailer, his arms are stick thin and there are many darks spots on his cheeks and the top of his bald head. His eyes are bloodshot, and his cheeks are sunken.

His father turns back to his desk and closes the binder and puts it back with the others. The binders contain a detailed ledger of his father's powerful influences. Before Tuum left for university, his father had shown him the contents.

There are rows of names on each page and beside each name are several columns with symbols written in red ink that only his father knows the meaning of. As far as Tuum knows, his father has rarely collected on these debts but continues to list them perhaps as a necessary accounting of what he's accomplished. This is some instinct pushed forward from a past life, his father has told him. The reasoning is not clear, only that he must do it. Still from time to time these have allowed his father to wield great power.

He slides a stack of papers to one side and then piles others on top of those so that there's a bare spot directly in front of him. He then turns back and says: "You've come," as though he's summoned him.

Nong slowly steps back out of the room but leaves the door open.

"Sit," his father says and points at the wicker chair beside him.

It's firmer than Tuum expects. This is the chair visitors sit in whenever they seek his advice. Tuum doesn't look around the office except to notice that it is considerably more cluttered than he remembers it.

"I suppose you are here about Roong?" his father says.

"Yes," he says. He had a planned to work up why he was here, filling in his father on his last three years, starting with his teaching post and then later, after they'd settled in, telling him about Roong. But his father clearly already knows why he is here. It doesn't surprise him to learn that his father has kept tabs on him. People bring him news and gossip from far and wide every day and certainly anything involving his son he likely would be eager to hear.

He's also certain that his father already has decided whether he will help Roong or not and what form the help will take and what that help will cost Tuum. For his father will insist on that because Karma and the Law of Action will require Tuum to assume karmic responsibility for what his father does on his behalf. There undoubtedly will be many karmic hurdles to manage. He will expect Tuum to abide by his duty.

"The help you seek is difficult," his father says. "But it can be done." He rings a bell and turns back to his desk and slides another paper in front of him.

Tuum stays in his chair and watches his father scribble on the paper and then set it on the pile to his right. His back is hunched and rises and falls with the slow regularity of his breathing.

Tuum had come prepared with arguments and now that he doesn't need them he realizes the karmic requirements his father will demand will be significant. But, if it means Roong will be free, he will do what is asked.

Nong opens the office door and comes inside and puts her hand on his father's shoulder but doesn't say anything. He raises his hand and taps hers with an affection that his father hasn't displayed since Tuum was a boy.

Tuum slides his chair back and rises and steps out into the hallway. Nong stands awhile longer next to his father and then joins him.

She goes ahead of him to the front door and opens it. He wais her and then steps out into immediate heat. He's been in the house less than an hour, but it has become considerably hotter outside. It strikes him now that his father's house had been very cool. How is that possible without a single noisy fan? He realizes that the coolness is partly because of the thickness of the walls and the tall tamarind trees that shade the house all day.

Nong doesn't shut the door right away but stays to watch him go. At the bottom of the steps he turns back one more time but doesn't wai her. He wishes at that moment that his father had joined her at the front door, but she remains alone.

He walks to the bus station and buys a ticket for the next bus back to Khon Kaen. Once on the bus, he takes a window seat and watches the passing rice paddies. Although it is now getting dark, many of the fields are full of people harvesting rice. He sees a water buffalo pulling a wagon heaping with bundles of fresh cut rice. A small man, or boy, rides up front. The bus slows for traffic and the buffalo and wagon continue alongside for a while. He can see now it is a boy at the reins and they are headed toward a large fenced area. Inside that, men and women are shaking rice bundles onto a large pile of rice. He counts more than a dozen people before the bus moves past them.

He looks back briefly and thinks one of those could have been Roong's father less than a year ago working in oppressive heat to finish his harvest. He thinks of his father huddled at his desk in his cool house. Despite living several villages away, Roong's father may have known his father but never sought his help. His father likely knew her father's fate and perhaps knew of his financial woes and what happened to Roong after his death. This latter part troubles him and makes him wonder how well he knows his father.

Nong comes from a family of rice farmers too and she may have known Roong's father. All these possibilities occur to him, but they confuse him more than settle him. The bus increases speed and the highway is smoother and he lets go of that line of thought.

A large dog runs alongside the bus for a short distance and he sees that farther back a boy chases after it. The dog cuts hard to its left and bolts away from the highway into an open rice paddy. The boy stops and faces away from the highway, likely keeping track of the dog's progress in the diminishing light. Tuum shifts his gaze to where he last saw the dog and it takes him a few seconds to locate it again. It is much farther away from the boy and is chasing a sizable dark shape. At first, Tuum thinks it's water buffalo but it moves too fast to the left and then right to be a buffalo.

The dog could be chasing a bear or tiger and Tuum worries for the boy and dog's safety. He looks back for the boy, but the bus enters a long curve to the right and the boy vanishes from view. He nearly gets up from his seat and asks the bus driver to stop but hopes the dog is merely rounding up a stray horse or bull.

He pushes back in his seat and chants for any dark spirits to let go of the boy and dog. He opens his eyes a while later and the bus is passing lit houses as they near the edge of the city. Soon after the first lights of the city come into view in the front windshield of the bus and eventually that light spreads wider and wider out from the centre, filling up the whole windshield. He can't stop thinking about the boy and the dog. He has no idea what will happen to them, but senses that what he's just witnessed may mean the undoing of all he's accomplished today.

The next morning he's at the Remand Prison as soon as visiting hours commence, and this time, Roong is the first prisoner brought out and the guard doesn't escort her all the way to the table but stays near the door and allows Roong to go the final distance on her own.

After she sits down, she tells Tuum that her aunt and uncle were released at sunrise.

"They've already left for their village. A guard brought me a large breakfast of boiled rice and chopped chicken, and about an hour ago a guard told me that they have requested that my mistress report to the main police station for questioning. He said they are worried she will flee so have insisted that she not delay."

They talk longer than all the other prisoners and, even after everyone has left, no guard hurries her out. He feels most joyous at these turns of good fortune.

That afternoon a messenger comes with a note from Roong telling him she is about to be released and for him to hurry there. When he reaches the prison, she is sitting on the cement bench out front.

"They released me a few minutes ago. By some miracle, my mistress has been arrested. They wish to locate her gardener who vanished four years ago. Others have come forward and said that the gardener has intimate knowledge of her various deceptions."

This is his father's doing but the speed of it impresses Tuum and indicates that the reach of his father's influence is much greater than anything Tuum has imagined. As connected as her mistress and her husband are, his father's connections have proven to be much higher.

They embrace briefly and then sit side by side to chant. As he finishes his chant, he knows that the speed of his father's action also means that his father will demand much of him in return. He's certain in a day or two when Roong is exonerated, her accuser facing the charges she should have faced years ago, his father will summon him. He doesn't tell Roong this.

# Chapter 4

## *Chum Phae*
## *Present day*

*With back to sky and face to earth.*—Thai farmer saying

After that first day back at work since Sutum's death, Ed calls Nan and she says that Run told her today that two hundred years ago Ed had been a soldier in the Thai army and Nan had been married to a doctor. She had five children and they only met once. She was hanging up clothes to dry and he was on a horse. They spoke briefly and then he went on his way. They fell in love during that brief encounter. That's all it takes sometimes. Shortly afterwards, Ed, the soldier, was killed in battle.

"That is just one of our lives. Run says there are others. Don't look for a purpose in our lives," she says. "That is your western thinking. Such thinking will make you very tired. Focus instead on kindness. But kindness is tricky. It doesn't mean being weak or a push over or easy on people. Nor does it mean giving people whatever they asked for. Kindness means being strong, resolute—knowing exactly what form of kindness is required.

"Run says that Sutum's ghost is at the hut but Run has also detected other disturbances likely stirred up by Sutum's presence. This hut may be the meeting place of alternate paths and we may have links to that hut too. Past lives zigzag, swirl, become, and then slip away, and become by some turn this life. Run says that whatever you are feeling involves us and doesn't involve us. The link between it all is not yet clear.

"You must attend to these sensations you are having though. They are real. Run says that in time all will be revealed."

He thinks of an evening a month ago when he was still in Khon Kaen and he and Nan went to Run's at six pm as they did many evenings and sat on plastic chairs in a circle with others and faced Run. Ed had asked Run if he'd been a good man in his past lives.

"I don't know. But such distinctions don't matter."

Ed then asked him how much good is there in the world?

"As much as there needs to be."

"Are there more good people than bad?"

"Only Buddha can determine that. But what would it prove?"

It is dark now but he doesn't light a candle. Instead, he sits at the table and places a hand on each of his legs to take in his body's heat. He thinks about what Nan has told him about seeing by not seeing.

He rises from the table and pushes on his sandals and goes out into the rice field, letting sparse moonlight guide him. Several times his feet sink ankle deep in warm water, but he doesn't turn back. When he reaches near where Sutum died he stops. He's never intended to come here again but feels drawn by an unexplainable urge. Even with all the rice cleared away he knows the exact spot.

He sits, and in the semi-dark hears a blend of animal noises: frog, crickets, mosquitos, flies and now and then the distant bark or howl of a dog, coming from the direction of another rice farm. When Nan was a girl, she used to bring lunch out here every day for her grandfather. After he died, his ghost sat in his favourite chair on the porch at home. Her grandfather's ghost was there to look after Nan's grandmother and did so for many years.

In daylight, the hut is the only building visible from here. Maybe that's why Sutum has ended up there. Ed focuses on the short distance back to the hut. He chants and then meditates but feels nothing. *It was a mistake coming out here.*

He returns to the hut and the moon is now behind a cloud so he pauses at the top of the steps and opens the door but doesn't go in. Without candlelight inside, the hut seems to have no interior and night reduces it to a vague wooden structure. He smells hay and aging bamboo. The frogs and crickets sound louder here but their locations are more difficult to pinpoint, and he's accepted that they are simply out there somewhere in all that dark. He sheds his sandals at the door and goes barefoot inside.

A different noise wakes him hours later. He lies on the cot only half awake and hears the metal bucket slide along the wood floor. He wonders if the rat has finally found a way inside and is after any water still in the bucket. He turns from his back to his right side facing the noises and they stop.

He closes his eyes and chants aloud: "*Pra Nip Paan Knaw,*"—and the noises start again. He slows his breathing and feels his perceiving mind slip away. He senses the edges of his self expand and then drop away. In this altered state he seeks to connect with Sutum but there's only a vast inner dark. He has no idea how long that lasts as all sense of time passing fades. He has no sensation of being anywhere, no sensation even of himself. He has vanished. Then as though a switch has been flipped, he is back in his head again, the hut quiet.

In the afterglow of what has just happened, he senses briefly how heavy and burdensome his ego is. But, as his self comes rushing back, he does a mental inventory and feels that nothing is missing. He gets up and moves toward the sink and immediately senses a rush of air so cold he shivers. He stops and can't take another step. *This is new.*

In time, the air warms again and he feels the warped ridges of the uneven floorboards beneath his bare feet. They remain icy as though he were standing on an un-insulated cabin floor in Canada in the middle of January.

It rains abruptly then and so heavily that the glass in the window rattles but doesn't crack or shatter. The south side of the roof lifts but holds.

There are two flashes of lightning close together. In the first flash he sees a shadow to the right of the sink and away from the bucket, but in the second flash, the shadow is gone.

He goes to the small bamboo shelf next to the window where he keeps a flashlight and extra candles for emergencies. He grabs the flashlight and aims its beam toward the sink and the bucket on the floor and then scans the area around that. But everything is as he left it. With the flashlight, he inspects the rest of the hut and again all is as it should be. He then goes to the bucket and shines the flashlight inside it. It's completely dry. He swings the flashlight beam from the floor to the roof looking for any signs of a rat. There are none.

He returns to the cot and sits but doesn't lie down. He has a powerful urge to call Nan and ask her to come here. But it's the middle of the night so will wait until morning.

He shuts off the flashlight and keeps it in the cot with him. He lies down and listens to the rain. When the storm fades to the west, the hut is quiet, and the mysterious noises don't return. He lies on the cot and discovers that there are layers to the quiet he hasn't noticed before. He keeps his eyes closed so he can better focus on those layers and in time can map them. He again does a mental inventory: Nan, him, this hut, this cot, the table, the window, Sutum, Song, and Run. He expands that outward and feels his mind lift and then his thoughts float out the window, float past the rice field, past the highway and soon soar above it all. *And here,* he thinks. *And here.*

When he wakes three hours later, morning light streams into the hut and it smells fresh and earthy from the rain. The light reveals the unevenness of the floorboards and highlights the natural grooves in the wood and he easily makes out where he stood last night and how ridged and rippled the floor is in places.

He gets up and dresses and then discovers a dead gecko in the corner of the hut near the sink. A parade of tiny ants has already laid claim to it and they are in the process of dismantling it. They form a busy line from the corpse to the outside corner of the hut. The line is so thick in places that it's visible even from the table.

He stands over them and studies their progress but doesn't interfere because he's learned from Nan that ants mean good luck, and the more ants he sees, the more good fortune he will have. To kill even one is to risk losing that.

Last month when ants invaded their apartment in Khon Kaen, she'd scooped out a handful of rice from their lunch and shaped it into a ball and set it near the balcony door. The ants swarmed it.

"Better to feed them than kill them," she'd said. "See, they aren't scary." By the next morning the mound of rice and the ants were gone.

He spoons out rice from the bag that Song brought yesterday and forms it into a ball and sets in on the floor a foot away from the dead gecko. The line of ants forks immediately so that one prong leads now to the rice and the other continues to the gecko. He pulls up a chair and studies them. This is a valuable lesson.

The ants remain singular in their task and don't stop to wonder, or contemplate, or fabricate. They work together against all obstacles.

He realizes, as he watches, that he's witnessing all that is wrong with his life. He takes his notebook from on top of the fridge and writes a note to himself about how purposeful they are, and how fiercely they obey bodily imperatives. These are creatures tightly bound to time-held duties.

By the time he leaves to harvest rice, the flesh from the upper part of the torso of the gecko has been stripped, exposing a tiny skeleton beneath. The rice ball is half its size too. The ants are relentless.

When he returns from work in the late afternoon, only the skeleton of the gecko remains in the shaded, muggy hut. The ball of rice is gone and so are the ants.

He doesn't know what to do with the skeleton so leaves it there. If he could ask Buddha what lesson he is meant to learn from this he suspects Buddha would say: *This is life. This is how ants and geckoes are. And you are.* There are no rules to learn, no longing—all of it a wheel turning. Each being is stitched into time and unable to work free of it. Ants and geckoes are obedient agents and act as they have always acted—lively participants in what each day offers. To live is to engage, to be. To know that intricacy is to know all that there is. Each life is but one link in a long chain of lives. The souls of ants and geckoes hurry and scramble and eventually succumb and then begin again—hurry and scramble. That is a worthy lesson.

Nan has explained how that chain of lives works by saying: "When I'm angry it isn't me that's angry but someone from long ago angry about something that happened long ago, not now. When you're angry it isn't you that's angry. This is our journey to enlightenment."

When he'd asked her if she'd ever experienced enlightenment, she'd said just once and very briefly.

"What was it like?" he'd asked

"Like looking over a ridge and being blinded by the sun."

The next afternoon Nan rides her Honda Click from Khon Kaen. When Ed finishes work, she's waiting for him on the front porch. He changes from his robe to his jeans and a shirt because he isn't permitted to wear a robe if they sleep together.

During the evening meal, Ed asks about Sutum and she raises her finger to her lips to indicate he isn't to speak of that yet. After they finish eating, she reaches across the table and takes his hand and says they need to chant.

They finish by saying: "*Satu, Satu, Satu,*" together and then sit quietly with their eyes closed. His breathing slows and soon he can't feel his hands and his feet. That numbness continues even after he finishes meditating. He is unable to move at first and she comes around and rubs his arms and he then rubs his legs and can stand. This hasn't happened before so her being here has helped him to reach deeper inside.

She walks to the sink and he joins her. They do the dishes together. He washes and she dries and puts them in the cupboards.

"It is not a good idea to leave any dishes out," she says. "That's an invitation."

"The chairs too?"

"Chairs we have to leave. Furniture is furniture but—"

She goes outside and leaves the door open and he follows her, and they stand together in the dark.

"Show me where—" she says after a while.

He leads her by the hand to where Sutum was shot.

She sits in a lotus position and he sits next to her but keeps his legs out at his side because of the numbness earlier. She takes out her cell phone and calls Run. They talk in Isaan at first and then she puts her phone on speaker and Run chants.

Ed closes his eyes and listens. Run chants longer than usual but asks *Bowel Mai Krup* at the end as he always does. He is asking them if they feel better. Ed answers with *Bowel Krup* meaning that he does. Nan says, *Bowel Ka* to indicate that she does too.

After she hangs up, she says: "Good"—and then stands and walks back to the hut but doesn't go inside. From the doorway she asks him if he's heard noises anywhere else besides at the table and the sink.

"No just there."

She rubs her hand on his back in a steady circular motion.

"It may not be Sutum that you are connecting with but traces of other lives, earlier or future, yours and others, the swirl and tangle of it all. Maybe even you were here before and all this is to let you know that."

"How will we know which it is?"

"Run will know in time. We'll call him from inside. He can see all the energies around us."

"Even over the phone?"

"Yes. All he has to hear is our voice to make a connection."

When they do call Run, he tells Nan that he senses Sutum sitting in the corner of the hut near the sink and near where the gecko died. He is facing the two of them. There have been others here too, he says, but they are gone now. Some helped to harvest rice, and some didn't. *Each circle is inside another circle,* Run says before hanging up.

In the middle of the night Nan wakes him and whispers in his ear: "Hear that?"

He thinks she means Sutum, but the hut is perfectly quiet. Within seconds it starts to rain lightly at first and then a noisy downpour.

"It's so romantic," she says.

"How'd you know it would rain?"

"The quiet. Even the frogs had stopped singing."

She slides a hand over him and their lovemaking is feverish and frantic, intensified by the tempest outside.

Later they lie in a cool aftermath holding each other and by then the rain has slowed to a light drizzle.

He's never made love during a rainstorm before and all that lightning and thunder had stirred up a fury in him that lingers still and leaves his skin tingling.

The next day Nan works alongside him and Song, and after work, she and Ed sit out front of the hut. He looks to the bare patch where the starlings last were. They still haven't returned. He's come to accept that they might never come back. Likely they've found a less dangerous place to feed. Even if birds seem habitual, they live in flux as he does, as all living creatures do. The only difference is that they aren't impacted by property lines or deeds, or trauma or morality, but rather by the proximity of predators.

Nan leaves her chair and walks in the direction of the rice field. He follows her but she waves him to stay back. He returns to his chair and watches as she continues to the scene of the murder and stops in the exact right place even though it had been dark when they went there last night. She turns to face the setting sun and then kneels and lowers her head until it touches the ground. She maintains that position for a long time and he knows that she is chanting for Sutum.

He closes his eyes and chants until he hears her footsteps.

They lie on the cot that evening and chant. Afterwards they talk but only in whispers. He asks if she's whispering so Sutum's ghost can't hear.

"Ghosts don't hear us," she says. "It doesn't work like that." She's whispering because she has a headache from kneeling in the field. Something attached to her there. She can't say exactly what but says she feels different. Her throat is constricted, and she burps loudly several times.

He retrieves his cell phone, and she calls Run, and he chants for them and when he ends the call, she says that her headache is gone and so are her feelings of unease.

"Does making love bother ghosts?" he asks thinking of last night.

"No. Sometimes they make love more fiercely than we do. The more we make love the more they do."

"With whom?" he asks.

"With past lovers."

"They are here too?"

"No, but they have powerful memories of them, and for ghosts those memories are real."

He wakes hours later from a dream and the hut is unusually dark. One moment he is in a dream where he and Nan are attempting to load bundles of rice into an already full wagon and the next, he is wide-awake in an unfathomable dark.

He slips from the cot careful not to wake her and goes to the table. The moon comes out from behind a cloud and the room brightens just enough he can make out Nan lying on her side on the cot facing him. Her stillness mesmerizes him, and he takes that as further proof of the intense shimmer in each moment. Awake or asleep their bodies churn and possess. The moonlight fades again and she turns away from him. With her back to him now, she is less visible in the dark and he has to really focus to see her. He moves to the window and looks out into night. The harvested field is a vague flatness lit here and there by moonlight, as it comes out from behind another cloud. The moon looks jaundiced and all alone in a night sky surrounded by many fingers of white clouds.

*Ghosts are funny creatures*, he thinks just then, and he wonders why that occurs to him.

"Ghosts aren't like they are depicted in movies," Nan has told him. "They don't go about scaring people. They are often members of a family stuck somewhere they really don't want to be stuck except they are ghosts and that is what happens to ghosts until enough chants help them move on to where they need to be next."

The moon fully vanishes this time behind a thick, dark cloud, and he senses that, like the moon, ghosts can be here and not here at the same time.

"You are too hard on yourself," Nan has told him and then stressed how lightness of being is more helpful, more advantageous. He does take himself too seriously, he admits now, and yet also knows that his self is paper thin and more like puffs of mist in the air, adrift and of no more consequence. He needs to strive to not be and by doing that he will be more completely here. In Canada he thought of ghosts as imaginary creatures but understands now that, if all it takes is for a soul to become adrift and get attached to someone or someplace familiar, then ghosts do exist.

He goes to the sink and rinses his hands under the tap. He is careful to keep the flow of water weak so he doesn't wake Nan. He likes the feel of cool water flowing over his skin. It holds him in the moment. He attends to every sensation and feels solidified and attached in ways he hasn't before.

He listens for Sutum but there isn't a single foreign sound anywhere here. He'd like to know more about Sutum and the man who killed him, but Nan has warned him that it isn't a good idea to pursue his curiosity about the killer. That is his western mind intruding and wanting an explanation. The true forces of this world run deeper than he has ever imagined and often there are many dangerous ones at work. He should avoid connecting with those. To think in terms of motivation is to oversimplify what is transpiring. He's used to settling for what he wishes to be true, but the roots of truth run very deep and branch every which way.

The more he fixates on Sutum's killer the more he risks having that evil enter him and if he is not careful it could entice him to kill. If such a dark power were to attach to Ed even Run couldn't break the spell. Then, there would be no knowing what horrible consequences would result. Even worse, he could be unwittingly drawn into an ancient feud between Sutum and his killer. The less he knows about the killer, the safer he and Nan will be.

"Maybe in a past life you and the killer got in a quarrel and perhaps you hurt him so you had to witness him killing Sutum as a warning." She'd said last night shortly before he fell asleep.

"Oh no," he'd said.

"Yes. Oh no," she'd said.

Earlier he'd asked Nan what becomes of murderers when they die, and she'd said they'd go straight to hell and stay there for five hundred lives.

He'd then asked her why anyone would commit murder given such dire consequences.

"Murder is murder. Some of those who commit murder have no more lives to jump to. It is easier to kill someone when there is nothing to lose."

After drying his hands, he goes outside into damp, stagnant heat. He sits in a wicker chair and closes his eyes and focuses. In a short while he hears noises in the kitchen. Maybe it's Sutum or maybe Nan is getting a drink of water. He doesn't go in to investigate. Instead he focuses on not listening, and for a short while, every noise is amplified but that gives way to a pure, inner quiet. It is then, empty of all thought, that he glimpses Nan hurry past and then a figure that could be Sutum chasing her. They pass just the once and very briefly. He hears noises in the grass below him that could be them or the wind. But he resists that and keeps his eyes closed and his dark head soon quiets again. When he opens his eyes later, the sun has risen and is high enough to indicate that several hours have passed.

He goes inside, and Nan is at the table setting out dishes for breakfast. She spoons out a small lump of rice on each plate and then spins the rest of the rice in the plastic bag and squeezes the bag until there is no extra air in it. Finally, she twists her hands several times and secures the bag with an elastic band wrapped around the top. She does this with such fast hand movements that she could be doing a magic trick.

She then serves two chunks of fried tofu onto each of their plates, setting them on top of a small mound of sticky rice. She finely chops cabbage and broccoli and adds those next to the rice on each plate.

Certain foods are off limits for her like beef and crab. Today, she warns him about eating duck and says that if anyone offers him duck, they're wishing to curse him and bring him harm.

"My uncle and his neighbour argued over the property line between their respective rice fields. They stood on either side of the fence that had been put up many years earlier by different owners and each insisted that the fence encroached on his land. They stood across from each other for hours and didn't budge even to pee or drink water. The heat bore down on them and still neither gave any ground. My uncle buckled first. He picked up his scythe and walked home.

"A few days later his neighbour's wife brought him a plate of chopped barbequed duck and claimed it was a peace offering. His wife had been dead a few years by then, so he welcomed a prepared meal. He ate the duck but saved half for his dead wife as he did for every meal after she died. If he hadn't the curse would have worked faster.

"The next day, his water buffalo died, and then, the day after that, the engine in his car seized up. This forced him to drive his Honda motorcycle to and from the rice paddy. He had no more problems for a week and then riding home one evening a Toyota pickup swerved to avoid a dog and hit my uncle head on. He lived for a week in pain but never left the hospital. After he died, his neighbour had the fence torn down and built another a metre in his favour. All of that because my uncle had eaten duck."

After telling him this she slides her chair away from the table and carries her dishes to the sink.

That evening they sit out front of the hut and meditate until the mosquitoes get to him and he goes inside. She follows him soon after and pushes him to the cot and they make love. Later when she holds him, he thinks: *This is new.*

He wakes in the middle of the night again. In the dark he focuses on various events in his life and realizes that the memories of his life in Canada are fading but his memories of his past five years in Thailand are intensifying and becoming more vivid.

He hears a glass clink at the table and then a bamboo chair creaks.

Nan must hear that too because she rises up and looks down at him and presses a finger to her lips.

The noises shift from the table to the corner where the dead gecko's skeleton was. He hears a muffled hum, which then shifts to a moan that isn't really any moan he's ever heard before. It quickly fades.

He rolls to his side to better get off the cot, but Nan stops him and again raises her index finger to her lips. Like Run, she hears sounds that Ed can't.

She takes his hand and slides a finger up and down his palm in a seductive manner and then grips the hand firmly and squeezes. She gets out of the cot and takes a step toward the table and he does the same. She turns instead and goes to the window and sniffs around the sill. Then she goes to table and sniffs there too. He follows her but doesn't interrupt.

She sits at the table and moves a second chair next to her and taps it for him to sit.

"He won't be active anymore tonight," she says. "I can't smell even a hint of him."

"And you could before?"

"Yes, very strongly?"

"What did he smell like?"

"Like lavender and honey."

"Lavender and honey, really?"

"Yes most certainly."

"I would never have guessed that," he says.

The next morning, Nan is sitting cross-legged in the cot watching him when he wakes. He asks her if she has been awake long and she says that she never went back to sleep.

"How long have you been watching me?"

"Not long. I sat outside and watched the sun rise. I liked the feel of cool morning air on the skin of my arms. I spent a lot of time thinking about Sutum and what might have brought him here. Perhaps he looked in this direction just before the gunshot and saw you in the distance and remembered a scene from a past life where someone else was standing where you were. It is most important what a person thinks just before they die. If they have happy thoughts, even eager thoughts, then they are more likely to go to heaven. If they have a lot of worry, they could end up anywhere. Maybe even as a rock or piece of paper on the floor.

"Or perhaps something good happened at this hut in another life or even in this one and when he died he wanted to return to a place of happiness. It is up to us and Run to assist him.

"If we leave now the next occupants may not care or will ignore him or worse will not even be aware that Sutum is trapped here. Many ghosts remain trapped for many years until someone like Run comes along and can see them and assists them in their transformation to the next life."

He sits up and slides his hand down her arm.

"We must chant," she says.

Later the next night, he wakes yet again in full dark and listens. He is now used to these nightly interruptions. After an hour Nan wakes too and shifts on the cot and runs a hand softly down his arm. He turns to face her. She puts a finger to her lips and points toward the table, but he doesn't hear anything.

They lie side by side for another hour and by then the hut is fully engulfed in morning light. Nan rises and goes to the sink and makes them coffee.

He joins her and slides his arms around her waist. She stops her work and turns around and smiles. Her heat is soft and different from the heat in the room and draws him closer. Her breath is hot and minty when they kiss. In those uncountable seconds of the kiss he settles even more deeply into the moment. In the past he would have travelled away and then hurried back, but not now.

They move apart and he reaches around her and takes the two cups of coffee she's poured and walks them to the table. She joins him and they sit facing each other and sip before speaking.

"We are fortunate that Sutum is not a hungry ghost," she says.

"What is that?"

"Hungry ghosts have huge bellies and very small mouths and throats, so they can't eat fast enough to fill their bellies. They consume everything in their path. They are at the level just above hell and did something very terrible and ruinous in a past life to end up there.

"To get entangled with a hungry ghost risks getting sucked by them into hell. These are the five realms: The heaven realm, the human realm, the animal realm, the hungry ghost realm, and hell. A soul that becomes a hungry ghost is confined there for five hundred lifetimes just like in hell. The only way for them to get out is if a living soul guides them out through chants, but first a living soul must detect them. It often takes many lifetimes for them to be discovered."

Nan goes to the propane fridge and takes out the pitcher of water and pours some into a glass and sips it. She asks if he wants any water and he says no.

She returns to the table and rests her head in her hands, which means she is meditating. It's twenty minutes before she speaks again.

"Sutum is here now."

"What's he doing?"

"He's waiting for someone. He doesn't know that we are here. I can sense him but he can't sense us. He can't harm us or hurt us. He's just here. Others have been here too but they are gone now."

"Sutum is waiting?"

"Yes," she says. "But with Run's help we can free him. He doesn't know he is trapped or that we can free him. He is simply here.

"He could be waiting for a lover that died a long time ago, but his soul doesn't know it yet. Ghosts don't know time nor experience it passing the way we do. Ghosts are weak when it comes to love just as the living are. Now that we've fully connected with him, he's our responsibility."

Ed stands and slides his chair against the table. She smiles up at him and he's drawn to the crooked part in her hair and how she's pulled the rest tightly behind her in a ponytail. Sometimes when they make love she unties her hair and lets it fall on her shoulders, but it is how she has it now that he prefers.

"Good," she says, and nods as though she's read something different in his gaze.

That evening after work, he arranges the covers on the cot. Once they are smoothed over top the bamboo, he lies down but still feels the uneven bamboo strips underneath.

"Move over," she says, having followed him.

At first, he thinks that she wants him to give her more room, but she pulls him closer to her.

He is sweating now from the heat and especially on his forehead and wrists.

"That's a funny place to sweat," she says, pointing at his wrists. "It's something you brought with you from a past life."

The thought of that comforts him because until now he's always wondered why he's sweated there. He has no sense of this continuity she speaks of but believes it. He understands that a soul is an accumulation of all its past lives whether that soul remembers them or not.

They lie in each other's arms and don't speak. He fights to keep his eyes open but can't. He hears water dripping in the sink and a few other kitchen noises that could be nothing at all, a rat even, or Sutum.

Later, he hears light feet hurrying across the counter and realizes he has been asleep for hours. How did that happen? He last remembers talking with Nan and is now abruptly awake. The heat in the room is lighter and in fact he feels a bit chilly. He rolls over to check the time on his cell phone and it's too early to get up.

He remembers then that he's just dreamt about Sutum and tries to recall the details of the dream, but can't beyond that he'd dreamed of Sutum and that the man in his dream had not been the man who'd died in the rice field but a taller and younger man. His face was completely different too and not at all familiar and yet he knew with complete certainty in the dream that it was Sutum.

In any case, the dream means something, he thinks, and listens to the comforting sound of Nan's breathing as she sleeps.

# Chapter 5

## *Khon Kaen*
## *1970*

TWO DAYS AFTER Roong is freed from the Remand Prison, a man knocks on the door to Tuum's apartment and hands him an envelope. He doesn't wait for a reply but quickly disappears down the stairs.

Tuum opens the envelope and the note inside reads: *Come home.* This is but the first salvo in what's to come. But at least Roong is free. He can ignore this note, but they will keep coming and each note will be more insistent than the one before it and in time his father will take to reminding him of his duty and that ignoring his father's request will put him in serious karmic jeopardy.

The smell of gasoline reaches him from the street below, and that odour causes him to step back into his apartment and close the door. The smell triggers a memory from the accident. It's the first he's recalled in many years. He inexplicably can feel the vibration of the bike on his legs and then there's an abrupt impact and he's lying on the ground looking up at his father. His father kneels next to him and his face is very close, and he says: *It's okay. You'll be alright.*

Thinking of that reminds him of something his father said years later: *Higher powers also have higher powers to answers to. But above them all is Buddha. Do not be reckless with your time.*

He returns to bed and shows Roong his father's note. By now he has prepared her and let her know it will be coming.

"Perhaps if we chant, Buddha will show us another way."

"We can try," he says.

They chant for an hour side by side in bed not touching. Nothing comes to him in that time and she says that nothing has come to her too.

He holds her and she closes her eyes, and she breathes as shallowly as he does. Then she runs a warm hand along his arm.

"How long will he want you there?" she asks.

"A month at least. He will think this is for my benefit more than his."

"Is it?"

"Around him I am never certain."

She doesn't respond then and he senses that this weighs on her and that she sees it as being because of her. But she's done nothing wrong and can't be faulted. He attempts to convince her of that, but he feels her pulling back, suspects this isn't what she wants to hear but, in this moment, can't anticipate what she really needs. All he is certain of is her goodness.

"I want to believe that we have crossed to some place better. So I will. This will take as long as it takes and in time—" She stops there, and he senses why.

Her heat beside him weakens him and he lets go of all but the two of them here in this moment and all its glory.

*Don't fight the wind,* his father would warn him whenever, as a boy, he'd come against an immoveable force. *The wind is but one fury.* His father also said it when Tuum was a bit older. At the time, Tuum couldn't have named other furies, although he'd been certain his father could recite a long list of them. Now Tuum's list includes bloodline, time, karma, and greed.

His father also warned him that those in love will face many furies and as they defeat one, another will take its place. True love will be constantly tested. If it is true it will flourish, otherwise it will falter. He is certain that this love he feels for Roong is as true a love as is possible and together they can defeat whatever furies come their way.

When he was a boy, his father told him many stories. Most of them featured a monk and a little boy. Sometimes they were on a long journey to a faraway land. The reason for the long journey was always to escape a betrayal or treason of some sort. He sees those stories now as his father preparing him for this moment.

"I can delay a day or two," he says.

No one is home when he arrives at his father's house and he assumes that Nong and his father are still at the temple for afternoon chants. He could walk there but decides to wait in the shade on the front steps. It's the hottest part of the day so there are few people in the street. He watches a mother and two boys pass. A mangy dog walks beside the younger boy and stops when the boy stops. He can tell that this is a loved dog by how often the boy stops to pet him.

As he waits now, he chants to quiet his mind and images of Roong speed past so fast that he can't make sense of what she is doing, only that it is her. He slows his breathing until the images stop. Later, when he emerges from meditation, he has the acute feeling that he's made a mistake coming here. What possible karmic danger would compel his father to require him to be here? As bumpy as these recent years have been between them, he is certain his father loves him.

When the sun is a little farther west and his father and Nong have still not returned, he rises from the front steps and moves into the small rectangle of shade at the front door. He isn't there long before he sees them approach from the direction of the temple.

"You could have gone inside," his father says, when he reaches Tuum.

Nong opens the door and enters the house but his father waits for Tuum to go in first and then follows him.

Although Tuum had never thought to try the door, he would not have gone inside anyway because of the potential danger from all the charms and spiritual pieces his father has likely arranged around the house.

His father doesn't go to his office but stops in the living room. There are so many framed pictures on the walls that Tuum feels unsettled by the clutter. He is thankful he doesn't live here. On his last visit he'd simply passed through here to get to his father's office. Many of the pictures are of famous monks, but others contain lotuses or roses and have sayings written on them. The closest one to him says: *A cluttered mind is not a free mind.* The one next to it says: *Shifting weight off one's shoulder makes each step lighter.*

His father and mother left the walls of their house mostly unadorned except for a few family photographs. Those are likely hanging in some other part of the house. He recognizes the influence of Nong in these pictures, but others tell him that his father has grown sentimental.

Nong sits in the chair closest to the kitchen and apart from the two of them. His father gestures to Tuum to sit in the bamboo chair opposite his teak chair, which has no padding on the seat. His father waits until Tuum sits before he does.

His father closes his eyes and chants loud enough for Tuum to chant along with him, but he chants a different chant quietly to himself and keeps his eyes open.

Nong doesn't close her eyes either, but she has drawn her legs up into in the lotus position on her chair like his father. Tuum keeps his feet on the floor so he can then get up at any time and leave.

There's a blue hatch in the drawing directly across from him and the writing next to it says: *Blue hatches lead nowhere.* He has no idea what the purpose of a blue hatch might be then.

His father chants for a long time after Tuum has finished. Eventually his father says: "*Satu, Satu, Satu,*" and rises from his chair and moves as slow as a monk as he walks in the direction of his office. Tuum follows him and it takes them nearly a minute to reach his office. At the door his father stops and he turns to Tuum.

"Before we begin, are you sure you want this?"

Tuum hasn't expected his father to ask him that, although he realizes that his father really isn't asking nor is Tuum permitted to say no. He is not really offering his son a way out and nor is he inviting Tuum to say what he really thinks. Rather this is merely his father's way of forcing Tuum to say aloud that he agrees to be here.

Tuum is certain that, if he were to say *no* now and hurry back to Roong, within hours all the agreements his father has put into place would unravel and Roong would be back in prison and her mistress free again. Such is the accordion nature of power.

Tuum says what he must say. That he is certain.

"Good," his father says, "Then we'll begin."

Once they are inside the office, his father pokes his head back out the doorway and looks in both directions and then closes the door. Tuum wonders why his father would do that and assumes that it's a recent habit.

Tuum remembers his father's lessons about this. *We may develop habits or mannerisms we can't explain and that means they come from a past life. Only through deep and stern practice and meditation can we discover their source and what they mean and why they persist. Knowing that can help us to make progress and to even allow us to stop those behaviours. Most often though, such habits serve no purpose in our present lives but are simply residues of a past life. Knowing their source and purpose will not change what we do in this life, and if we don't make them stop, they will become a necessary part of this life too. And so does much strangeness spread from life to life.*

His father goes to his desk and slides out his chair. He sits and then swivels it to face Tuum, and suggests to Tuum that he pick a chair, as he swivels back to his desk.

Tuum glances around the office and notices that it is more of a jumble of books and papers than it was only a few days ago. New stacks of books are scattered about the room and more piles of papers cover his father's desk and the tables on either side of the desk. He wonders if his father has been preparing in a rush for his return.

He settles on a teak chair with a cushioned seat wedged into the corner next to a tall bookcase spilling over with books. He knows his father has read every one of them. He grips the wooden arms of the chair and lifts it high enough to clear two stacks of books on the floor. He sets the chair down to the left of his father and leaves a large space between them to act as a buffer.

This close to his father he notices right away familiar odours of coffee and jasmine incense, but there is something new too—a staleness comingled with dust that suggests aging.

When Tuum was a boy, he rarely set foot in his father's office. The door remained closed most of the time and that meant that his father was not to be disturbed. His father didn't venture out of his office during the day except to rush off somewhere without warning. As a result, Tuum turned to his mother for guidance.

Tuum never learned the nature of those urgent interruptions that called his father away, and whenever he'd asked his mother, she'd claim ignorance.

He once resorted to blocking his father's way when he'd returned from going out and asked him where he'd been. His father eyes narrowed perhaps surprised at being confronted in this way and leaned to one side as though nursing an injury. After a few seconds, he smiled at his son and rubbed the top of his head and then stepped around him without answering. He slouched slightly as he walked to the kitchen to wash his hands at the sink. He returned from there and dried his hands on the towel that Tuum's mother brought him. He then kissed her cheek and returned to his office. He didn't emerge until dinner and by then acted as though Tuum hadn't asked him anything.

All that changed after the accident. His father rarely went into his office all the time Tuum was healing. Most days were taken up with Tuum's exercises. When he was able to walk again, they would sit in the front porch in the afternoons after his exercise and watch various villagers pass in the street. His father told him stories about some of those who passed. Now as Tuum reflects on those, he realizes that they were in fact most likely made up to make some point. Then he'd taken his father on his word and had been impressed with his vast knowledge of village life.

Most of that time on the porch was taken up with his father teaching him various Buddhist lessons or telling him more adult versions of the Monk and the boy stories. By then Tuum saw through the simple morals in his father's stories but in time they became more nuanced and only later would Tuum recognize the deeper threads running through them. All of that and this would be very different if his mother had lived.

His father turns to him and his gaze isn't the formidable, unbreakable fatherly gaze he'd known as a boy, but simply a man like himself caught in the karmic webbing of daily life.

His father's eyes are darker and less hardened than they were after Tuum's mother died. Tuum understood later that that had been grief manifesting in his father's eyes.

Tuum had been angry then and once spit at his father after something he'd said about Tuum's mother. He doesn't remember now what his father had said. He only remembers spitting and then running from the room and out into the street. He kept running and stayed away for hours and only returned home when it was getting dark. His father was sitting on the front steps waiting for him. He didn't say anything to his son as he passed him on the steps. Instead he stood up and a followed him inside.

His father said then that he understood his anger and that had made Tuum even angrier, but he found a way to contain it. He'd gone to his room and didn't come out until the next morning. He and his father had then acted as if nothing had happened.

Now his father's eyes are so dark the irises appear to be all pupils. They flit back and forth and don't stay on him for long. This too is new. His father's eyes have always been steady and unwavering. Now he blinks frequently and between blinks Tuum catches winces of pain. He wishes he could ask about that but can't yet. The lower rim of each eyelid is a half-circle of redness and the whites of his eyes are crisscrossed with spidery red veins.

His father turns back to his desk and slides his hands noiselessly along the smooth wood surface. Tuum has witnessed him doing this many times and eventually his father told him that it's his way of slowing his mind in preparation for chanting.

There's not a single sound and that quiet amplifies the noises in Tuum's head. His father's hand movements don't slow Tuum's mind but speed it up even more, so that when he closes his eyes, images flash by without fully registering. The more he concentrates on them the faster they appear and disappear. He gives in and allows them to flit past without grasping any of it. In time they stop on their own and he floats above the room and is looking down at his father and himself.

It is then that more memories from the accident return. Not full memories but partial ones, no more than quick glimpses. His heart races in his chest and its pounding speeds up. He glimpses his father holding his motorcycle helmet in one hand. Then he is looking down at Tuum. Then three people appear beside his father and he drops his helmet and kneels. Tuum's perspective changes and he is looking up at his father and his father's eyes are at first porous and then become bright mirrors. He hears a scrape of leather on pavement and he isn't looking at his father anymore but someone else. A face he doesn't recognize. A complete stranger. He thinks then that forgetting is such a heavy science, and then: *Move. Turn your head. Get up.*

He sees below him that his father's hands on the desk have stopped. Tuum eyes open and he is instantly back in his chair beside his father who folds his hands together and rests them in front of him and closes his eyes as though to chant but opens them again after less than a minute. He slides open the top drawer of his desk and reaches in and retrieves several sheets of papers held together by a folded left corner.

The top page is written in his father's distinctive hand.

"This is my list of certainties," he says. "Some of these you know already, but others will be new. I started this list for you after the accident in case—" He stops then and looks at the papers in his hands.

Tuum can see that the papers are shaking, not just a bit but noticeably even from where he is sitting. After a few seconds, the shaking stops.

"I've saved the list in this drawer for this day. I've added to it from time to time. But most of what I've written I wrote the day you came home from the hospital."

His father raises the papers from the desk and reads the front page to himself and then flips through the remaining pages stopping now and then to consider something he's written there but doesn't study any page for very long. Then he flips back to the first page and sets the papers down in front of him on his desk and turns the chair so he faces Tuum and then turns back to his desk.

"You are expected at the temple after dinner so we only have time for one item on this list today. We'll go through the others in the days ahead," he says, and smoothes his broad hands along the creased list and then rests them on either side of the paper and turns yet again to Tuum. "I'll walk you to the temple."

He pushes his chair back a little so he is farther way from Tuum. He inhales very slowly and then says: "Despite what you might think, I loved your mother very deeply and still carry that love with me today. Such a love only gets stronger after the beloved dies. You'll learn that in time. Nong understands that and knows that my love for her is different from my love for your mother. Both can exist at the same time. Love doesn't end just because someone dies. It continues from lifetime to lifetime. I know your mother has been reborn already and is somewhere in Thailand. I don't know where, but I know for certain that she has not left the country. We won't meet again in this life nor the next one but the one after that.

"My love for your mother has a different span and origin than my love for Nong. She has known more than one great love too. Our souls carry many loves. That is one of the complications we must live with. What might feel like the most powerful of loves often isn't. That is the mistake those new to love make. Love transcends any given birth and death and what feels powerful and whole in the present may in fact be no more than a momentary infatuation. It takes years and much meditation to determine which loves are momentary and which ones transcend beyond one life. In time you will discover which those are for you. But now is not the time for me to lecture you on love."

As Tuum listens, he realizes that he is no longer pressed against the back of the chair but has inched forward and his feet are firmly planted now on the floor. He straightens his back and takes a long silent inhale and holds the air in until he feels his lungs burn and has the most powerful urge to exhale but he still waits. He grips the hard arms of his chair and continues to hold his breath. He doesn't reply to his father. Instead he pretends not to have heard him.

He'd normally get up and flee after such comments, but his father has a strong hold on him this time. He closes eyes and says: "*Satu, Satu, Satu.*" He then opens them and realizes that his father has been staring at him this whole time, his head tilted in the peculiar way he's used to seeing him do when he knows something more that he is not saying and is waiting to see how someone reacts.

Contrary to what his father might believe, Tuum has often meditated about the karmic consequences of his love for Roong. Because of that he's learned through his dead mother that what his father just said is wrong. He's certain now that his feelings for Roong run much deeper than this life and will continue into future lives too. His father's words make him all the more certain of that now.

He lets go of his grip on the arms of the chair and at last expels a long silent exhale and as he does so he feels the burning dissipate from his lungs and throat and feels a release drawn up through his core. He waits to a count of twenty before he inhales again and quietly thanks his father and defiantly waits for him to go on.

"Today we'll skip ahead to the most powerful item on my list," his father says and flips through and stops on the fifth page and reads:

> ***5. The cycle of birth and death.***
> *Neither birth nor death is certain but what happens between them is, and those events repeat often. You have already learned the karmic necessity of lives repeating. Your soul might be my ancient great aunt's soul or someone I don't know at all, just as my soul this time might be in a human body for the first time in five hundred years. You must focus on the cycle. We are here now because we are here now. We are father and son because we are father and son. We are not to derive extra meaning from that. It is simply where we are at this moment and nothing more.*

His father stands and steps away from his desk but picks up the list. What his father has just said to him is not new and he wonders if his father is toying with him or testing his seriousness at being here.

His father motions for him to join him at a small table in the back opposite corner of the office from where he got his chair and away from the large windows with heavy curtains closed over them now to keep out afternoon heat.

Tuum hadn't noticed this extra work area. There are several stacks of paper on the either end of the table too but the middle is bare. His father goes to a nearby bookshelf and takes down a photo album and flips through a few pages without stopping. Tuum can't make out who is in the photos, only that they are in black and white.

"This is your family on my side. I know you have seen these when you were a boy but likely haven't recently. You need to study them. Buddha has said that *to mistake one life as the summation of all lives is to mistake the present sunshine as the only sunshine, the present happiness as the only happiness.*

"These people made it possible for your soul to be where it is now. Most of these people have already died and been reborn. When you look at me, I don't want you to see your father but to see your son and your son's son. We have a very long way to go."

Tuum prefers when his father speaks of his love for Nong or Tuum's mother because that fixes them to this life, in this room and not a confusion of many possible lives and many possible rooms. He could equally argue that his father is not his origins but merely another soul he shares this time with. Still he is at this moment his father's son and will remain so and by doing his duty he is able to be with Roong, and they can flourish with their love. What were the origins of his father teaching him to walk for a second time? He almost asks that question, but his father speaks first.

"Study these now. Commit them to memory. Then it will be time to go to the temple.

His father walks behind him all the way to the temple and every time Tuum slows his pace his father slows his too so he remains two steps back. Tuum thinks of those countless afternoons in the open field when he walked behind his father clinging to his neck. Now his father walks behind him. This too is a test, but he isn't sure yet what it is being tested.

The temple is a kilometre from his father's house so it is nearly dark by the time they arrive there. Once they are through the main gate and at the front steps, his father tells Tuum to wait and goes up the steps ahead of him. At the top, he sits on the cement bench to the side of the main doors and takes off his shoes and leans back against the building.

This is Tuum's cue to join him. When he does, the tiled floor is still warm from the day's heat. They sit together in silence for ten minutes before the gold-plated doors of the temple swing open and four monks step out, one behind the other. They are led by a thin monk, older than his father and perhaps in his late eighties. The others are much younger but likely at least a decade older than Tuum.

The oldest monk high wais his father to show respect and gives a lower wai to Tuum. The other three monks wai Jan in unison and then wai Tuum. The oldest monk tells Tuum that his name is Kay and he is the abbot. He then addresses Tuum's father as Khun Jan. He says what an honour it is to have him and his son here. He assures Khun Jan that everything has been arranged for Tuum.

"Will you join us for the evening chant?" he asks Jan.

His father says he will.

Two dogs and a cat pass. They appear well fed and energetic but their mottled furs hint at an iffy lineage and difficult lives before coming to the temple. The monks accept all strays and feed them because any animal may contain the soul of an ancestor, a parent or grandparent even. One of the dogs stops and tilts its head back and howls a long howl that triggers the other dogs at the temple. The night air is immediately filled with the howls of dozens of dogs and it makes Tuum think it is a dog's version of a chiming bell—listen and pay attention, they say.

His father closes his eyes and the other four monks do the same and Tuum does too. Within a minute, all the dogs go quiet.

"Thank you," Kay says to Jan, "We love them, but they can be so noisy after dark."

Kay opens the door and enters the temple and everyone follows him. Tuum goes in last. The temple feels smaller than he remembers. Before his mother died, he came here a few times with her and looked forward to the walk here and back and to the time they sat in lotus positions, neither of them uttering a sound for a full hour. She'd always compliment him on the way home for his attentiveness.

After his mother died, he didn't wish to come here but his father reminded him that his mother would have wanted him to. His father never once said it was what he wanted. Tuum wished he'd had. In time

Tuum understood that coming here was what his father needed more than what his mother would want. Whenever they left the temple, they would walk home in complete silence.

The other three monks appear ubiquitous in their yellow novice robes, but as he studies them now, he notices that one is shorter and slower than the other two and walks with a limp. Another looks back often and is closer to his age than he first realized and handsome in the way that means he likely has an easy life outside the temple. The third monk walks behind the other two and is Tuum's height but much closer to his father's age. He stays just ahead of Jan and Kay who walk side by side in front of Tuum.

The shortest monk is named Win and the handsome monk is named A and the older monk is named Pon. They stop in front of the five-metre tall golden Buddha, which is flanked on either side by spirit houses overflowing with pink and white flowers. Each spirit house has a smaller Buddha in the middle and a wooden horse the size of child's doll and white cloth draped over it and a dozen sticks of incense, none of them lit. Each has three round, fist-sized unlit candles. Behind them and in middle between them is a wooden arc placed on a golden pedestal. He learned from his visits here with his father that that this is where a Buddha bone is encased in glass.

Win kneels first on the far left of the golden Buddha and he is quickly joined by A and Pon. His father and then Kay sit to their right and Tuum kneels to the right of them and is the most distant from the Buddha bone. His father is directly in front of it.

Two piles of orange monk robes wrapped in plastic are set in front of each of them. Normally people would be asked to pay for the robes before they are blessed. But his father's blessings are so sought after that he is not asked to pay.

His father selects two robes and rests them in his lap and chants. Kay does the same and then each of the other three monks select one robe and also chant. Tuum waits a few minutes, as required, and then selects a robe and places it on his lap.

Tuum chants but his thoughts drift. He hears himself chanting but above those words he is thinking about Roong. He sees her again with her hair wrapped in a towel and then later she stands in the hot sun just before he boards the bus here.

He returns to the present and realizes he has reached the end of his chant, so he starts again. Soon he is thinking about the other three novice monks and assumes he will be sharing the days with them. He has already guessed from the way Pon speaks that he is from Krung Thep. Of the two others he isn't as certain although he senses that Win is from the deep south, perhaps Hat Yai.

His father stops chanting and Tuum stops too. He opens his eyes and watches his father set both robes in front of him to the floor to his right and take two more from the first pile and start again. When he completes one stack a novice will bring others. There will be a note attached to each, which he'll read first. The note will indicate for whom he is chanting and what they need.

Kay stops chanting and sets his two robes to his right too and selects two more. The other three monks stop but hold onto their single robes as does Tuum.

His father and Kay will bless many more robes today but he and the other three will only bless the ones they are holding and later tonight, they will each return to their room and put on their new robes. In the morning, another novice monk will collect his street clothes and they will be washed and ironed and returned to his room and left in full view on the shelf next to his narrow cot. He must wear a robe while he is here.

He's reached the end of his chant so stands and positions the folded robe under his arm and walks back the way he came. Once outside the temple doors, he sits in the lotus position on the same cement bench he and his father shared earlier.

In time, he closes his eyes but doesn't chant. Instead he listens to the slap of sandals against tile and then the noises of metal plates hitting together and water splashing, as someone washes dishes. He doesn't open his eyes to find the source of these sounds. Instead he continues to listen, separating each in his mind. He also hears a motorcycle in the street and a distant car horn. A door opens and closes not too far to his right. There are more footsteps and then another motorcycle powers away.

He opens his eyes and estimates without looking at any clock that he has been sitting here for nearly an hour. He unfolds his arms and legs slowly to minimize the rush of blood back into them.

Shortly after, Win joins him and overhead the clear night sky is bright with stars. Pon comes out next followed closely by A. Pon joins Win and Tuum on the bench while A sits on the bench on the other side of the main doors. He doesn't sit there long but stands and slips back in the direction of the sleeping quarters.

Jan and Kay remain inside for another hour. Kay comes out first and then finally his father. Tuum knows that by then his father has likely blessed more than two-dozen robes and Kay nearly as many. Someone will come later and collect all of them, and by morning they will be dispensed throughout the temple.

The moon is out now and a wide swath of greyish light illuminates the walls of the temple.

"I will leave you now," his father says and puts on his sandals and walks very slowly down the steps and toward the main gate.

"He's a great man," Kay says.

Tuum does not answer but his gaze stays on his father until he vanishes in the dark beyond the main gate.

Kay walks with Tuum to the door of his room and pauses there without speaking. When Tuum opens the door, Kay nods and then says good night and turns around and hurries off much faster than earlier.

In his room, Tuum gets down on his knees and feels the rough floor with his hands, noting where grit has bunched and feels all the dirt the novice monk who cleaned this room has missed. He pushes it along with a hand and slides it into the palm of his other hand and carries it to the wastebasket in his room. He does the same in another part of the room until he has cleaned the whole floor to his satisfaction.

He then goes to the toilet down the hall and washes his hands and watches dirt and grime stream off them and down the drain. The coolness of the water on his hands soothes away all the strangeness of the day, and he lets the water run over them. As it does, he adjusts a little more to being here.

There have been times in his life when he has felt hollow and even the sight dirt washing off his hands has troubled him, but today it grounds him, and he senses exactly where he is and what he is doing and why. He smiles and believes whatever his father intends or will attempt won't stop him from returning to Roong.

He thinks of his father blessing the robes and doing what is required of him, and in thinking that, he feels some love for him for the first time in a long while, but that love will not alter his plans.

He returns to his room and the floor feels clean now under his bare feet. He sits cross-legged on the cot and chants for another hour, then turns out his light and is soon asleep.

Later that night a persistent mosquito buzzes noisily around his ears and lands several times on his bare arm. This wakes him and he gets up and turns on the main light and sits on the cot until the mosquito flies close enough that he traps it with the quickness of a hand and carries it to the door of his room and sets it free outside careful not to let in any others.

"*A death is a death.* You might be bringing a creature closer to enlightenment by killing it. But you could just as easily be forcing its soul to jump too early to another life. Each death causes a karmic ripple and it is best to make as few ripples as possible." That had been the second of his father's certainties. He'd called that certainty: *The death after death.*

Perhaps he has forgotten that he'd told Tuum this in those months they laboured together on that field as he helped Tuum to walk again. He didn't call it a certainty then or speak of it in such an elevated way, but Tuum recognizes it as one now and believes it is on the list in his father's office.

There are many deaths not just the one to come. The one that came before this one and the ones before that and so on and so on. Then there are the deaths yet to come after the next one. *Future deaths*, his father has called them. They are trickier because they haven't happened yet. The others are easier to know because they've already occurred. They are part of the mix even if he only ever learns a little about them. His father has told him of a time he'd chanted and saw much blood. That meant that either he'd killed someone in a past life or someone had killed him.

We live in this present moment and mistake it for *always* and ignore that there is no *always* only *ever.* But as precarious as any given life is, they are the only moments of awareness.

After freeing the mosquito, Tuum can't sleep so he lies on the narrow cot and listens to the occasional light footstep outside his room and wonders who is about at this hour but doesn't get up to investigate.

He meditates for an hour but still can't sleep so gets up and turns on the light and goes to the desk against the wall and sits in the narrow bamboo chair with a very upright back. It is not comfortable nor is it meant to be. At the back of the desk he finds a small stack of blank papers and a single sharpened pencil. This is meant for him to make study notes, but instead he writes a letter.

*May 5, 1970*

*Roong my sweetest love:*

*A mosquito has woken me in the middle of my first night here, so, my love, I begin my first letter to you. We didn't talk about writing to each other, but I feel such a desire to be near you that I must get my thoughts down on paper. I do not wish to be here. I wish to be with you. I feel like a fraud and worry that my father senses that. The more I am near him the more I recognize the debt I owe to him for his love and devotion after the accident to say nothing of what he has done on your behalf. The debt I owe him seems impossible to repay. Yet I will do my duty and do as he asks. Strangely when I am near him, I wish to hurry away. I don't know how to repair the damage between us. Yet I don't yet see a way back to you if I don't. But do not despair at the sound of that as it is my way of getting my bearings tonight. Before the mosquito woke me, I dreamt of us riding a bus through the greenest of mountains and hills.*

*To be a fraud is one of the sixteen causes of sorrow. Missing you is another. How am I to do this? And why? I should be with you my love. Lying with you and listening as you sing to me in that lovely lilting voice of yours. Instead just minutes ago I hurried a mosquito out of my room. As I did that I thought of the old man I met a year ago on the Chi River and who took to living in his boat after his wife died.*

*He was 92 when she died, and he was over a hundred by the time I met him. Still, twice each day he went fishing in his narrow boat and sold his fish in the market and kept some to eat. He would not accept any help from anyone. When I tried to give him twenty baht, he refused it. He spoke so lovingly of his wife and how much he missed her. He lived so fully through that love that not even her death could take that love away. It ran so deeply through him that it must have brought him to enlightenment.*

*So must our love bring us to enlightenment for I live in you just as you live in me. That is how it is meant to be when love is fullest. I will fulfil my duty to my father as I have promised, but my love for you will not waver one bit from me being away from you.*

*I fear that what my father expects of me is impossible. I am not like him and nothing he does will make me so. I hope he comes to that conclusion soon.*

As he writes this last part, he feels a stab of pain down his left arm and then down his back. He takes the pain as a physical manifestation that he may be lying to her and to himself more than to his father. He stops there and signs it.

*Phom Rak Khun (I love you)*

*Tuum*
*xxxxxxooooo*

He folds the letter in half and then in half again making it as small as possible so he can hide it in his room until he is able to secure an envelope later tomorrow.

He places the note, now folded to one-inch square under the mattress of his cot in case the monk who attends to his room later decides to snoop. He then turns off the light and lies on his cot and is soon asleep.

He wakes a few hours later and it is still dark outside. He lies in the heavy heat in the room and thinks: *Here I am.* And then: *Now what?* He can't answer that. The heat causes him to sweat at the wrists. He is used to this now and traces it back to the accident. It never happened before then. To distract his mind from that past, he turns on his side and thinks of the sixteen causes of sorrow and then mentally checks off those he has already eliminated. He knows without his father saying it that his first step on this journey is to eliminate as many of the sixteen causes of sorrow as possible.

*Am I equal to such a task?* he asks himself because Tuum the mathematics teacher isn't the son his father helped to walk again. He hasn't been that for a long time.

All of this is *yak,* too difficult. Maybe he can manage most of the causes of sorrow but not all sixteen. Not even his father has eliminated all of those in this life. But the point is not to eliminate them permanently but for a day, or week, or month will suffice. He runs through the list again and knows which ones he will stumble with. Many are easy but a few like *Stubbornness* and *Intoxicated with life* he is not so certain about eliminating.

"You are too humble," his father said to him yesterday afternoon before they left the house for the temple. This statement had taken him aback and he'd thought about it all the way to the temple. How could his father have said that except as some form of provocation and why would he wish to do that? Besides it isn't a fault to be humble and in fact humility is to be cherished and nourished. Even as he thinks that he realizes that he is indulging in one of the causes of sorrow right now and the pain of that knowledge drives home exactly what his father was likely doing by saying that. *It is always a test.*

He closes his eyes and counts to ten and tries to think of nothing at all. What comes hurrying back then is his wish to hold Roong as soon as possible. He remembers then that Buddha says: *Desire is the root cause of all sorrow.*

# Chapter 6

## *Chum Phae*
## *Present day*

FOR THEIR BREAKFAST, Ed cooks on the propane burner the eggs and sausage patties that Nan brought with her from Khon Kaen. He adds cardamom, cilantro, a hint of lime, and cinnamon just for her.

She looks up from her plate and says: "Song says you smile more now than when you arrived here." She pushes a small portion of patty with her fork toward her spoon. "He likes your kindness."

Until he'd married Nan, he hadn't considered kindness one of his better qualities nor did he necessarily nurture it. When he'd been married to Teresa, they'd both considered kindness a weakness and didn't go out of their way to help others. Instead they always claimed that selfishness and hard work were necessary for success. After the divorce, he began to shed those beliefs, and since marrying Nan, he's learned just how dangerous they are.

Not long after they married, he'd asked Nan if a tree or insect or frog is kind? He understands now that to ask such questions means he didn't fully grasp what she meant by kindness. She told him then that every being is capable of kindness and to connect with his kindness he must recognize kindness in a tree, in a blade of grass, and even in a mouse or rat.

"You must be kind at all times," she's told him. Kindness is the most important of Buddha's teachings and the most elusive. Nirvana may be the extinguishing of suffering, the extinguishing of heat and torment, the extinguishing doubt and anxiety, and the extinguishing of the self. But it is only possible through kindness.

"Sutum's ghost requires our kindness," she says, between bites of scrambled eggs. This is her way of letting him know that she senses his thoughts. He looks down at his plate and realizes that he's stopped eating and that his fork and spoon are resting side by side on his plate.

She's told him this before, but this time he asks how they can be kind to a ghost, and she says the same way they are kind to the living.

For Nan a ghost is an energy source, like a radio signal, that only a few people like Run can tune in. Now and then someone may hear an unfamiliar noise in a room or outside. That will be a ghost or angel trying to get their attention.

She tells him that he can't leave food for Sutum like he might for a mouse or help him out of the house like a mosquito that he's cupped in his hands. The kindness Sutum requires involves the deep thinking only possible during meditation.

Nan finishes eating before he does and slides her empty plate to one side and sits with her hands folded on the table. He chews slowly mindful of each bite. The flavours expand in his mouth and don't fade when he swallows.

"Sutum is resting right now," she says. "Ghosts continue to maintain the same habits and routines they had in life. There are many layers of worlds and his world and our world are like two pieces of paper one on top of the other. We are on our paper and he is on his. The pieces of paper may touch but we can't be on his paper and he can't be on ours."

Nan walks her dishes to the sink and then returns to the table and folds her hands in front of her and smiles.

He pushes a bit of egg onto his spoon with his fork and then places it in his mouth. He chews this, slowly thinking about what she's said. He understands what she means by the sheets of paper but realizes that she likely knows much more than she is telling him.

"We have to harvest rice for an hour longer each day from now on," she says.

This shift in topics catches him off guard as he is still thinking of about Sutum.

She says that there are still more than ten rai of rice to harvest and given that it is just the three of them, it will take them close to another month and they don't have another month before the quality of the rice will diminish dramatically. She says that would put Song at risk of a considerable financial loss.

"Song needs a bumper crop this season to get out of debt," she says.

A half hour later, they join Song out in the rice paddy. He stops working and Nan approaches him and wais him. They talk for a few minutes, their voices lowered, and neither of them laughs as they usually do.

Eventually she joins Ed and they work more quickly than usual, but it still takes them all morning to harvest less than a quarter of a rai of rice. When the sun is overhead and too hot for Ed, they break for lunch. He's sweated through his t-shirt. They sit in the shade of a tamarind. Aom has ridden a bicycle here and she and Song eat lunch under another tamarind out of hearing distance.

Ed asks Nan what she and Song talked about earlier and she says that she's told him about Sutum's ghost.

He asks if Song was surprised at the news and she says no.

They don't quit working until it's almost too dark to see what they are doing. The sounds of frogs and crickets grow louder the closer they get to the hut.

They leave the door open to air out the hut and sit on the porch before fixing their evening meal. The crickets stop earlier than usual, perhaps disturbed by a noisy breeze that pushes in from the north. It cools his face and hands and allows him to settle more deeply than usual. The frogs sing louder after the crickets go quiet.

Nan pushes back slightly in her chair and that sound gets his attention and he opens his eyes. He realizes that he's slouched a bit and sits up in his chair.

She pulls her knees to her chin and smiles, and he takes that to mean she's thought of something pleasant.

"When my father was a boy his family owned only one bicycle, and everyone shared it. Few people had cars then. Now most families have cars. My mother's family had a car and a water buffalo, and she had a bicycle all to herself. She rode it to school and to the market."

"What made you think of that?"

"Today Song told me that Sutum's bicycle was still at his house and he wondered what he should do with it. I told him to take it to the temple as they can give it to a family who needs it."

"How did your father's family manage with just one bicycle?"

"It's not as bad as it sounds because at that time many families couldn't even afford a bicycle and so my father would pick up fruit or vegetables from the market for those families. The bike had a large basket in the front, so he could easily carry things. It seemed a simple thing to be kind before everyone had cars."

Ed's great grandparents hadn't had a car either but relied on horses whenever they needed to go into Victoria. They'd lived in Sooke and used a horse and wagon to fetch supplies from Victoria. Mostly they lived on the water, his great grandfather a fisherman. The horses had been a pair of brown Clydesdales that measured eighteen hands high, his father said. *Those horses really knew how to work*, his father had been fond of saying. Ed has only seen photographs of them. In one, his grandfather is about twelve or thirteen and is standing to the right side one of the Clydesdales. His grandfather isn't smiling, and his hair is messed up and he doesn't look at all ready to have his picture taken. He is lifting the horse's head slightly with his right hand for a more dramatic pose. Ed came across the photo when going through his father's things at the nursing home after he died. Ed remembers his grandfather best by that photo. It's one of the personal items he's brought with him to the hut.

"My father still had that bicycle when I was a girl and I rode it to school until my last year of high school. My parents still have it and my father rides it now and then to the market because it's easier to park. They save the car for driving on the highway."

"Maybe we can take Sutum's bicycle to the temple for Song," he says.

"I've already suggested that and he's said that he wishes to take it himself."

Ed wonders if that bicycle is one of the unfinished details keeping Sutum here and he asks her.

She says no and then perhaps sensing his deeper inner wish, she says: "We can't leave here until Sutum has moved on."

"What if he doesn't move on?"

"He will. It could be tomorrow; it could be weeks, months or years from now."

"We'll have to stay here that long?"

"Maybe. But Run will help to make it happen sooner. We don't know where Sutum is meant to go to next until he goes there. He might go to Ethiopia and have to deal with hunger, he might go to Russia or Germany or Canada even. Souls go all over the world. Sometimes a soul might jump to the body of a blind man and another time to the body of a girl with a limp. That is the law of action.

"Every soul has an expiry date so if someone dies when they are young like Sutum when they are meant to live until they are ninety, they are stuck in limbo unless someone who shares their blood or someone like Run connects with them. He can see where they are and where they are supposed to be, and while he chants and prays at the temple, he can help Sutum go where he needs to go.

"You and I can't falter because, if we falter, Sutum's soul will falter. There is some karmic reason he's here. Buddha guides it."

She explains that Buddha has said that every life is like a pin pressed into the sand. Next to it is another pin and next to that another pin and so on. All of them so close but they never touch. No one can pull out a pin or move it. They are where they are. They are where they're meant to be.

"So is it with you, Sutum, and me. We are meant to be here. I love you and that is why it is so important we get this right. Our love and all our lives that follow this one depend on us not making a mistake with Sutum."

The hut has cooled enough that they go inside and eat a light dinner. Later when they meditate, the details of his dream of Sutum this morning come back to him.

After they finish meditating, he tells her all he remembers of the dream. "I was riding in a *tuk tuk* in Khon Kaen and Sutum was driving it. We went from temple to temple and at each temple Sutum carried a dead and cleaned chicken inside to give to the monks. At the last temple he had run out of chickens and asked me to follow him. He stopped at a young monk who sat cross-legged in front of a small statute of Buddha. They spoke in Isaan briefly and the young monk pointed to a set of stairs behind him. When Sutum reached the stairs, he told me in English to wait there for him and he ran all the way to the top, without stopping once, even though there were more than thirty steps. At the top, he opened the door and disappeared. I waited for him to come back but he never did."

Nan says: "That is a good dream. It means we are making progress." She then grips a handful of her hair and inspects it. "See these grey hairs." She pulls up several long strands from just above her forehead.

He nods.

"I can't stop my hair from turning grey or keep my nails from growing. This body is where I am now but not where I have been or where I will be. There is much about it that I don't control. Nor can Buddha control it, just as Sutum can't control being here. Every day he runs up those stairs and goes in that door in your dream but when he opens that door it always leads right back to this hut."

She says that if he'd run after Sutum and gone through the door after him, he would have ended up here. Maybe he would have even encountered himself and Nan already here perhaps at the table as they are now and there would be two Sutums here as well.

She says that the stairs and the door don't matter. They aren't really there unlike her grey hairs, which do exist.

She then says that there are two categories that everything falls into. What is here and what isn't here. The second category is every bit as important as the first one and is not a fabrication, but just as real as the first category. Thoughts can be linked together by one or the other, or both. Thoughts are larger than a body even though they appear at first to be contained by a single body and limited to it.

"I am not really talking about grey hairs," she says. "Just as you were not really dreaming about Sutum. You might think you were but in fact you were dreaming about yourself. Perhaps you were here in another life and Sutum is just the catalyst to connect you with that. We are only ever dreaming about ourselves. Everyone in our dreams is a version of ourselves even when we dream about our parents, children, or lovers."

He wonders how she can know such powerful things but understands that she does.

He asks her if he is dreaming not about Sutum but himself how does that mean they are making progress?

"Because of the chickens in your dream. You are feeding monks and feeding monks is making merit. A good thing."

He scratches his ear and says: "Should we chant more?"

"Yes, that would be a good idea and after that we must call Run and tell him about your dream. We should chant outside though so that we get fresh air and more oxygen."

When they are sitting out front an animal, the size of a rat, scurries from the tall grass and straight across a patch of moonlight. It doesn't stop long enough for him to recognize it but vanishes with scurrying noises in the grass. He wonders if it is the same rat that has been burrowing in the roof but doubts it. That rat stopped as soon as Nan arrived. There are no coincidences. He closes his eyes and chants.

He wakes at first light the next morning. They'd made love late into the night and at one point a sliver of bamboo scratched his leg and he yelped. She'd covered his mouth although there is no one nearby to hear.

Earlier when they'd called Run, he'd chanted first and then prayed silently for a half hour as Ed held the phone. The only sound on the phone's speaker was a continuous static.

Several times, he'd wondered if Run had hung up or the call had been dropped but Nan shook her head whenever he went to end the call. After a half hour Run's familiar chanting started again and he ended ten minutes later with: "*Satu, Satu, Satu.*"

Run then told Nan that he'd learned more about Ed. He'd lived in Thailand near the end of the last century and his father had many other enemies in the lives before that one and those enemies had wanted to hurt both of them. Some of those enemies have now gathered around this hut and he suspects that Sutum in a past life was one of those as well.

It rains now, lightly at first and then two loud claps of thunder shake the ground and wake Nan. She smiles at him and a few minutes later there's a heavy downpour.

"That's too much rain. We'll have to wait for the rice to dry before working," she says and slips from the covers and goes to the sink for water. She brings him back a full glass.

"I didn't dream about Sutum last night," he says.

"I know," she says.

He believes her and wonders again about all those outside the hut. Once he might have wondered why they can't just come inside, but now understands that ghosts see different walls than the living do.

Sutum could come inside because he'd most recently died, but he can't go back outside. The logic of that evades him but he's learned to set aside his western reliance on the physical evidence for every truth. He understands now that truths are not bound like that. They simply exist and are. There is much that isn't readily perceived. What Nan knows extends beyond the senses.

Run can see the ghost world but can't describe it. Knows it and who is there and can even communicate with them but he can't speak very specifically about it.

The layers of time are significant and bend and weave. They join and then snap apart again. None of this is recorded or made real in the ways he's considered matters to be made real before now. But even if all this is new to him, they are ancient truths passed down through generations.

An hour after they eat their morning meal the sun comes out, but Nan says that it is still too wet to harvest today, and they'll have to wait until tomorrow.

"Let's go for a ride instead," she says.

When he asks where she'd like to go, she says to the caves near Udon Thani. That is over an hour away but he says okay even though it means he must ride there on the back of her motorcycle.

He's nervous at first but soon adjusts to it and takes in the passing rice fields between uneven rows of trees. Most fields are deserted today because of the rain. He sees a few huts similar to theirs and he suspects that each of those has ghosts too. Until now he hasn't known the responsibilities that the living have to ghosts.

Hot, moist air blows around him, and as it does, he realizes how little of this world he really understands, how much he's simply taken for granted without taking the time to think deeply about it or to truly inspect all that requires inspecting. For most of his life, he's lacked spiritual curiosity.

After a half hour, he closes his eyes and meditates which he's never done before on the back of a motorcycle. As he meditates, he sees a kaleidoscope of colours in his head. This is new and perhaps triggered by the motions of the motorcycle in the bright sunlight. The colours collide and blend in his head and briefly he hears colours and sees sounds.

He keeps his eyes closed and but senses Nan lean into each curve and how that alters slightly the steady vibration and noise.

Much later, the motorcycle slows up a hill and she shifts gears abruptly. He opens his eyes then and it's too bright at first. When his eyes adjust, he sees that they are on an oiled road and that is causing the motorcycle to vibrate more. He grips Nan's waist tighter and she lifts a hand off the handlebars and squeezes his arm.

Riding here with her, he wishes he could see more the way she and Run see. He used to think that such visions weren't possible, and that any such perceptions were beyond his limited command of his senses, but on the back here he understands for the first time the full impact of their karmic predicament.

Nan parks the motorcycle at the front of a large paved parking lot that is less than half full. The caves are not as busy this time of year. At the entrance they pay for a guided tour and the female guide is close to Nan's age and speaks Thai to Nan who then translates for Ed. The main entrance to the cave is noisy with bats and that noise is amplified when they step into the cave. A million bats exit the cave at exactly this time each day. When the guide tells them this, he realizes that Nan has made sure to arrive in time for him to witness the magnificence of their exit. Inside, the cave smells of bat guano and reminds him of his grandparents' barn.

Before they make it even 200 metres in, Nan gets down on a knee and says that she can't go any farther. She turns around and runs back outside. He's close behind her, and she stops next to her motorcycle and heaves into the tall grass. Then she belches loudly five times and vomits more into the grass.

"Too many ghosts in there," she says. "And black magic. Did you notice how the tour guide waved her coffee cup and touched the charms around her neck? Those are black magic tricks to attract business. Many people use black magic." She takes out her cell phone and calls Run. She talks to him for a while and then she holds the phone close to Ed so he can listen to Run chanting.

He closes his eyes and focuses on Run's voice. Most of the words sound familiar by now even if he doesn't know their precise meanings. Run ends with: *Bowel Mai Krup.*

Nan puts the phone into her purse and then hugs him for a long time.

"Run said that two women attached themselves to me and would not let go. One died horribly, he said. Someone murdered her in the cave and she's trapped there." Nan shivers then and belches loudly twice more.

"That's the bad energy leaving me," she says.

He feels several sharp jabs in his side but doesn't tell her about those nor does he ask her if Run saw anyone attached to him. She would have told him if he had.

On the drive back they are in full sun the whole time and he's thankful for being on the motorcycle as the wind cools him. She drives so expertly he closes his eyes for longer durations. In time, he sees Sutum sitting at the table in the hut as he walks in. Sutum turns toward him and smiles and waves as though he can see him but likely he is waving at someone else.

Nan parks next to the hut but doesn't go inside right away. Instead she sits in a chair out front. He joins her and it is soon raining again, the clouds forming quickly. They are under the protection of the overhang and thus stay dry although it rains so forcefully that many rice plants are flattened.

When the rain lets up, she leans toward him and whispers: "We have to be good signals so we can help Sutum."

Later as they eat dinner, he realizes that he met Nan exactly five years ago today. He'd been on his way to Udon Thani to visit a monk that he had heard many good reports about in Bangkok. He took the bus but got off at Khon Kaen, deciding to explore it before going on to Udon Thani. On his second day in Khon Kaen his cell phone stopped working so he went to Central Plaza to get a new one. Nan had a cell phone kiosk on the third floor where there were many such shops. He liked the phones she had. He tested a number of them. Her English was so clear that they talked for more than an hour.

She told him how every night she packed up her most valuable phones and brought them home with her. She owned a Honda Wave motorcycle then and had a safe in her apartment and locked the phones in it every night. In the mornings she'd retrieve them and drive them back to her kiosk.

She would tell him after they were married that some days she sold one or two phones and other days she sold none. But every day she sold a case or set of headphones or a charger, so she was able to get by. She never brought those accessories home and didn't worry about them being stolen.

She started the kiosk with money her brother lent her but never dreamed it would be where she'd meet her husband. "You can't plan that," she's said. "That is proof of the law of action."

In all the years she had her kiosk she always dealt honestly with people. She would buy phones from those in need of cash and sometimes paid more than the phones were worth.

That first day they met he'd stopped at several other kiosks first, but she'd had the fairest prices and knew more about each phone. The one he'd settled on had lasted for the first three years they were married. He never did make it to Udon Thani. Today at the cave has been the closest he's ever been to there.

As he eats, he thinks about how, until he met Nan, he'd mostly journeyed sideways in his life. Now he understands how to bend and not break, how to sense what lingers in the gnarled centre of his being. His soul contains all his journeys tightly packed together and it goes on collecting them life after life.

Five years later he is grateful for that broken phone but believes now that there are no coincidences and that the phone had been destined to break on that day so that he could meet her.

She doesn't say anything about any of that now but instead tells him a story about a monk that makes him think again of that day five years ago and also more about today. The monk had gone into the countryside outside of Ayutthaya to chant and meditate. It started to rain so he looked around for shelter and spotted a cave nearby. He hurried there and arrived just before a heavy downpour. He sat on a large rock just inside the cave and continued to chant and then meditated. In all that time it didn't stop raining. He waited until nightfall expecting the rain to stop but it didn't. He looked around and decided he'd have to spend the night there. While he sat cross-legged on a rock listening to the rain, he heard animal noises behind him in the cave. He listened closer to determine what animal it was. At first, he thought it was a mouse or rat or very large gecko. Soon after, though, a cobra slithered very close to the rock where he sat. The snake took more than a minute to pass by, which meant it was very long.

The monk thought how unfortunate it was that he'd taken shelter in this cave, but he then reminded himself that there are no coincidences.

The snake didn't stop near him nor attack him but moved to another part of the cave and curled up. The monk decided that meant that he and the snake didn't have any karmic grievances between them so there didn't need to be any karmic balancing. He returned to his chanting and meditating. He stayed on the rock, though, just to be safe and slept there in the lotus position. It continued to rain all night and when he woke in the morning it was still raining. His legs were numb, so he had to unfold them slowly to let the blood flow properly to them again, and at the same time, not to disturb the snake, which had spent the night curled up in a corner of the cave. It didn't budge when he got up to stretch and had his morning pee.

It rained all that day and the next. He spent seven days in the cave with the snake. Not once did the snake approach him or attempt to harm him. He knew by then that they truly hadn't crossed paths before in any other life and this was likely their very first encounter.

On the eighth morning it stopped raining and, when he rose, he didn't move as cautiously as he had the first few days. By now he and the snake had grown accustomed to each other and had always maintained a safe distance from each other. He gathered up the small bag he had brought with him and hurried on his way before the rain started again. The snake slowly moved from its corner as he left but didn't come to the edge of the cave to look out. To the snake it was just another morning and the cave was its home.

The monk soon caught a bus and was back in the city in a mere hour. He was very hungry by then and ate two bowls of warm rice. He didn't think of the snake as he ate or for a long time afterward, but years later, he thought of it nearly every day for he'd learned a very powerful lesson during those seven days trapped with that cobra.

After telling Ed this story Nan says that was the first time the snake and monk met. They met many times after that in various future lives but not as a monk and snake and not in a cave. In time they fell in love and married. And that love carried forward into other lives. Love has many origins, she says, and many agents including the rain and caves.

He recognizes this story as her way of assuring him that what happened to her in the cave today was very real.

# Chapter 7

## *Chum Phae*
## *1970*

A HEAVY RAIN wakes him at first light and his room is muggier than earlier. He lies in his cot and feels so lethargic in that stalled air that all he can manage to do is listen to the rain slap against the tiled courtyard outside his window. When the rain slows and then stops, the room finally cools, and he slips from the cot and puts a cushion on the floor and sits there in a lotus position. But the heat soon swells back in and makes it difficult for him to meditate.

He closes his eyes but his mind flits from thought to thought. Soon many voices in his head are speaking at once. In this gibberish his father's voice rises louder than the rest. *What is the hurry? Rushing will ruin you. You need to let go of selfishness and impatience, if you are to have any chance.*

He snaps his fingers and counts to twenty and that quiets his father's voice. His head stays quiet for a few seconds, but his father's voice returns. *Think of me and this busyness, this chatter, your noisy thoughts, as a monkey mind. You must give it a simple task to distract it. Do that and you'll quiet all the noises in your head. It will get very quiet in there.*

He remembers his father saying those exact words, as he lay in bed unable to move his legs. His father had then said: "Look at your toes and concentrate on moving them. The more you imagine them moving the more likely they will move. Remember how easily you once controlled them, without even needing to think about it. They just moved when you needed them to move. So it will be again. And soon after, your legs will move just as your arms do now."

Tuum had done exactly as his father instructed and in time, he could move them. He remembers that first morning vividly. A loud clap of thunder and a noisy rain woke him and he sat up in bed as he did every morning and tossed off his light sheet and stared at his bare toes. He propped himself up against the pillows and without realizing what he was doing, his toes wiggled. And so it progressed.

His father's voice stays quiet in his head and he finishes his meditation and unfolds from the lotus position and stretches. Two hours have passed and outside his door he hears the shuffle of many feet as the day is underway. Some hurry past and others move more slowly, each footstep hisses on the tile as they pass.

It is the time to join the other monks as they line up out front of the temple for morning alms. He grabs his alms bowl and hurries to join them at the main gate of the temple. He stands with Pon, Win and A who are lined up behind Kay and twelve other novice monks.

More than thirty villagers have come to give alms to the monks. Many are women Roong's age or slightly older. The oldest ones are close to his father's age and they smile often and their outward display of happiness improves his mood. He doesn't make eye contact with any of the women for to do so would be to break one of the five rules he must live by while in the temple. His bowl is filled with warm rice first and then large chunks of pork and chopped broccoli and onions.

All the monks return to the main dining area and none of them speaks as they eat. Tuum is one of the first to finish and he goes to the porcelain sink at the back of the room to rinse out his bowl. Pon joins him there. Tuum dries his bowl and carries it with him back to his room. He angles the hardback chair away from the desk and sits in it and keeps his back perfectly upright, his head straight in line with a dot he imagines on the plain white wall.

He recites a different chant from the one he did first thing this morning and this one begins with "*Phen Dukkang Aniccang Anatta.*" (It is suffering. It is impermanent. It is uncontrollable.) He repeats this chant many times to himself. This is to ward off any evil spirits lingering from the food he just ate. Although those who brought it for morning merit came with good intentions, sometimes, they may have unwittingly brought dark forces with them. The chant nullifies those.

An hour later there is a soft knock on his door and, when he opens it, his father is there. He is wearing a white robe.

"We must begin," he says and then hurries away, his bare feet making no sound as he walks. Tuum follows him down the wide hallway to a teak door and his father opens it and steps inside and makes room for Tuum.

The room is small, no more than three metres by three metres, and there's no window in the room, which makes it feel even smaller. There's barely enough space for a small bamboo table and two teak chairs across from each other. His father sits in one and motions for Tuum to sit in the other.

His father folds his hands on the table and closes his eyes. Tuum does the same and here his mind magically slows and soon he floats in an internal silence that has no time, no dimensions, no moment. He is everywhere and nowhere at once.

A sharp pain in his right foot brings him back to the present and this room. He realizes that his breathing has slowed to the point that he counts nearly to seventy between breaths. He's only managed to do that once before today, many years ago when he was first learning to walk again. He stays focused on his breathing until he senses his father moving across from him.

He opens his eyes and moves his foot up and down and the pain dissipates. His father is looking directly at him and so intently that Tuum shifts his gaze to one side to avoid the scrutiny.

His father slides his hands along the table's surface as he did on his desk at home but here this means that his father is waiting for him to say: "*Pa Choi Noi Eh Krup.*" (Father help me please.)

After Tuum says this, his father nods and says: "It is time I tell you about the Trinity of Buddha and the four bases of mindfulness."

Tuum sits upright in his chair and firmly clasps his hands in front of him to keep from responding. How can his father begin with the lesson all school children learn before they are twelve? He has expected his father to set out convincing arguments and not start with an insult. Does he truly believe that his son hasn't yet mastered such basic principles? This is the second time his father has chosen to insult him like this.

"Mastering the four bases of mindfulness are crucial before one can understand Buddha's trinity. You will already know this and know what those bases are, but you must forget all that you have learned because there is a deeper truth that I will share with you today. Few people know this truth and it is protected from all but the most senior monks. But you need to learn it too. This is your first step."

Tuum is certain that his father is purposefully baiting him and he sees an opportunity to speak.

"Father—"

"It is not your time to speak. Here I wish you to call me Jan."

"Jan—"

"Not now. Not until I finish."

His father places both his hands on the table and Tuum focuses on how each knuckle is bulbous and each finger crooked, some turned in and others turned out, depending upon how he's utilized them in his daily life. Tuum hadn't noticed that yesterday and it is as though his father has aged more overnight.

"When your grandfather was dying, I wanted above all for him to stay alive. I went to the temple three times a day and prayed to the Buddha bone, and then I went to the hospital to sit at his side. His breathing had become very forced by then and I asked the doctor and nurses to make his breathing easier and they did the best they could but nothing they did improved his breathing very much. The doctors reminded me that he was over ninety and there was little they could do. In fact, whatever treatment they gave him only seemed to make him worse. He wheezed and huffed with each breath and coughed frequently between breaths.

"After a week of this, a doctor took me aside and she said that they'd tried everything possible to save him, but nothing had worked. The doctor said that I needed to be prepared because my father was going to die soon. Hearing that, I felt a jab of panic. I wasn't ready to let him go, but I also didn't wish to see him suffer by having the hospital prolong his life on my behalf. I meditated for a full day before I decided what to do. In the end, I asked the same doctor to please keep him alive as long as possible so I would have time to chant with him and ease him into his next life. With the hospital's help, he lived for another month.

"At the time, I felt I was given an extra month with him and in that month, I'd helped to properly send him to his next life. I would come to understand too late that in truth I had merely forced him to suffer a month longer than necessary. I had been selfish which was one of the causes of sorrow. I gained little in that month that the hospital kept him alive. Instead I had forced him to have a long and painful death. I also may have worsened his karmic future and caused his soul to be reborn in the wrong body.

"After he died, I could not stop coughing for a month. I coughed all day and through most of the night and rarely slept more than an hour or two at a time. The coughing continued with such intensity that most hours I felt in total agony and no matter how much I chanted or meditated I could not make it to stop. Then exactly a month later I stopped coughing. I know now that the coughing was caused by my asking the doctor to keep my father alive."

His father stops and shifts in his chair and lifts both hands and places each on top of a leg. Tuum watches his father but doesn't make eye contact. When he finally does his father's eyes are different, sadder and moist as though near tears. His shoulders are hunched forward. He looks in deep pain.

"Why are you telling me this?" Tuum asks. He barely remembers his grandfather and he'd been away at university when he'd died. His father sent word of his death but Tuum couldn't return home because of intense study obligations.

"This is your first lesson. It is your job to connect this to mindfulness."

"And if I can't?"

"You will. I am certain of that."

"I don't think I can."

"In time you will see that I am right and it will all fit together. Think of the trinity. Think of mindfulness. If you are truly mindful then you can have everything you want including a life with Roong. But falter now, let this slip away, and you will be running the rest of your life to catch up to her and yourself. There will be no chance for the two of you to be together if you fail now. Anything worthy is very difficult. That is the first lesson from Buddha. *Do not trust what is easy.*"

He recognizes the trick in what his father is saying but doesn't address it with him because to do so would be to fall for that trick. Tuum bites the inside of his cheek. It isn't his father's forcefulness or threats that catch him up now but the vulnerability in his father's story.

"Mindfulness is not as you have come to think of it. It is not how it has been taught to you before at school or in any temple. That is the story for children. First you must sit like me. Then close your eyes and think of my father as you remember him. It doesn't matter what day or what memory you recall as long as it is his face that you call forth. Hold that face in your mind until you sense him here. Find where he is now. Don't be fooled by those who come to you pretending to be him. There will be many of those. Don't let go. Don't break your concentration until you find him. When you do, you will know it is him with as powerful a certainty as you know that it is me across from you now.

"I failed to do that the final month he was alive. If I had, I could forgive myself now, but I can't because I didn't. Instead I chanted every day at his bedside and thought I was being the good and dutiful son, helping my father make his way forward. Instead I was forcing him to remain here as I foolishly fumbled around thinking I was being mindful.

"That is what I want you to grasp today. All you have thought you knew as mindfulness is not mindfulness. It is simply the mind playing dead for a while, going quiet. It is not breaking through.

"Now let us begin. Close your eyes. Think of my father's face. Concentrate on that face until there is nothing but that face surrounding you. This will be your first introduction to the true trinity. Forget all that's come before this."

The next morning, he wakes before first light and doesn't chant or meditate but gets up immediately. He hopes he has woken before everyone and listens at the door of his room to make sure that no one is moving about. When he's certain that all is quiet, he opens the door and hurries along the hallway to the main courtyard. The morning sun is less than a half circle in the east, but before he reaches the gates, he hears hurried footsteps behind him. The faster he walks the faster those steps get.

"Khun Tuum," Khun A calls behind him, but Tuum doesn't stop or turn around to answer. Instead, he increases his pace hoping that once he's in the street A will drop back.

When Tuum reaches the main gate of the temple, Kay is there. He nods at Tuum and says good morning. Tuum stops to wai him. Kay faces him with his back to the street. Tuum turns his head enough to see that A has stopped five paces back, his arms resting at his side. Tuum could return to his room now and he is certain nothing more would be said about this, but he's come this far and intends to go through with his plan.

"Buddha woke each day before sunrise and meditation-walked several kilometres before eating. He would walk straight toward the sunrise and only when the full heat of the sun was upon him would he turn around and walk back. Never once did he pick up his pace."

Tuum recognizes this as a pure fabrication and knows that Kay is testing him. It is a test he can't possibly pass and that is what Kay intends by this story.

In early morning's flattened light, Kay appears a decade younger. His robe is tightly bound and Tuum notices a sizeable knot at the shoulder. His hands are folded at his waist and he faces Tuum but doesn't say anything further.

He smiles at Tuum and he smiles back. Each of them stays perfectly still and maybe Kay is meditating on his feet. Tuum is certain that Kay, like his father, can immediately slip in and out of meditation. Tuum has witnessed his father doing that many times even during a meal or while walking beside him. He's tried to emulate it but so far hasn't managed it. Whenever he's tried to meditate while standing or walking, he either loses his balance or veers sharply to his right.

The streetlights go out behind Kay and this draws Tuum's eyes there, but he doesn't move in that direction. He waits to see what Kay does next.

"The mountains to the north are chilly at night," Kay says.

Tuum doesn't look north because he knows that is the direction Kay wants him to look because his father's house is that way. Instead he looks east over Kay's shoulder. The sun has risen enough to reveal the lush green mountainsides. Those detailed contours boost his nerve and he steps around Kay and hurries through the gate into the street.

Kay is right behind him and moves much quicker than Tuum expects given his age. He soon catches up to Tuum and says: "I will walk with you"—and falls perfectly in step with him.

He realizes that even breaking into a run won't deter Kay. Tuum nods and slows his pace not wishing to put strain on the old monk's heart. He looks back at the temple and A hasn't moved.

Although the sun has yet to fully rise, there is a heavy heat in the air and any slight coolness from last night has already burned off. As he walks his robe loosens and he stops to tie it tighter. Kay stays back a step as he does this.

When he's secured his robe, he quickens his pace again. All of the shops he passes are closed and nearby vendor carts are still wrapped in blankets for the night. In another hour the streets will be bustling with vendors preparing food and drink for those on their way to work.

But, for now, he and Kay have the street to themselves. When he reaches the first corner, he turns west toward the bus station. He can see it two blocks ahead and a line has already formed there. He quickens his pace a little but Kay keeps up.

At the next corner he stops to allow the first arriving bus to pass. Kay stands beside him at the corner. Despite how fast Tuum has been walking, Kay shows no outward signs of exertion.

"These streets look cleaner in the dark," Kay says. "The litter, mud, and blown leaves are hidden then. I prefer to walk through the village at night, as I am less likely to lose my way.

"My father was born in a rainstorm, and because of that, he was connected to water his whole life. He became a fisherman and, if he spent more than two days away from the water, his mood became dark. When I was a boy, we lived near the banks of the Mekong River. Sometimes that's how Buddha works. What happens on the day we are born determines the rest of our lives. Every day of my father's working life, he fished on the Mekong River, even on the day he died. That day he carried a heavy basket of fish into the house like he'd done each day for years. He gave the basket to my mother and said he felt a little tired and needed to lie down. He didn't undress but lay on top of the sheets and stopped breathing.

"My mother sensed something was wrong and checked on him a few minutes later and he was laying on his side. He never slept on his side in all the years they were married, she told me later. He wasn't snoring like he usually did. She knew without getting any closer that he was dead.

"She then immediately tossed all the fish he brought home into the street. They slid every which way when they landed and neighbours hurried to gather them up and burned them out in the open because they'd brought black magic into the village. She always insisted afterward that it was the black magic in those fish that had killed my father. The next day, neighbours carried his body to the temple. For three days afterward, she walked around the house shooing away spirits. She was doing that when I arrived from Krung Thep a day later."

They have walked halfway down the second block and Kay has stayed beside him the whole time he's been telling Tuum this story.

The bus station is straight ahead, and the front doors must have already opened because those who were lined up out front have disappeared. Tuum doesn't yet know the point of Kay's story except to get him to pause and listen, which he does now even though the bus station is only steps away.

"The Mekong River has tides. Not this far north but near the delta in Vietnam. There the high tides cause flooding in the rainy seasons. My father fished all the way to the delta when I was a boy. He'd be gone for days at a time but always returned with enough fish to sell and leave extra to last my mother and me until he returned two or three weeks later. We ate well when I was a boy, even if it was fish for every evening meal. I was well nourished and so I didn't have a reason to complain but I did. I remember coming home from school when I was ten and telling my mother that I was tired of eating fish.

She told me that was all there was to eat and I either ate that or didn't eat. I went to my room without eating but by morning I was hungry enough to eat a heaping bowl of rice and fish.

"I was thirty-seven when my father died but every day after his death I made of point of eating fish for at least one meal. That changed of course when I became I monk. I'm vegetarian now. That haunts me at times but a monk must obey his vows."

Kay stops speaking.

*There's a hint.* Tuum recognizes that plant but ignores it. Instead he looks down at Kay's feet and wonders how such tiny feet and thin legs can carry him so effortlessly.

The street is busier now and everyone who passes stops to wai Kay. He nods and they continue on their way.

Tuum turns slightly away from him and advances through the main doors of the station and joins the long line there.

"After my father died, I moved back to that village to be with my mother. I discovered through meditation that my father's spirit was still in his fishing boat. My mother and I travelled to the Mekong and had his boat pulled ashore and raised onto rocks. Every evening we sat beside it and chanted. It took a full week before we drew my father away from his boat and guided him to his next life and we could then return home.

"Afterward, my mother missed him constantly. She would speak of him at dinner as if he'd just died. She worried about him and if he was being properly fed and clothed in his new body. Had his soul jumped to a good life? I would find her sobbing in a chair after dinner, and when I asked her if she was okay, she'd say that she was and that I wasn't to pay attention to her tears as they didn't mean what I thought they meant. What they did mean she never said except that she was simply an old woman prone to tears. I chanted and meditated about those tears with a dedication I'd never shown before. For hours in the morning and again for hours after dinner and late into the night I chanted. Row upon row of chants from every book of chants I could find. But her loneliness only grew worse and a year later, not more than a month after the anniversary of my father's death, she told me before dinner that she was feeling tired and needed to lay down for a nap. I left her alone and made dinner for us as I usually did by then. When it was ready, I knocked on the door to her bedroom to let her know but she didn't answer. I knocked three more times because she was hard of hearing, but she still didn't respond. I went inside and she was already dead and had been dead for several hours, the doctor told me later. Likely she died within minutes of lying down.

"For three months following her pyre, her spirit sat in her favourite chair looking out the window. When she was alive, she'd sat there nearly every day hoping my father would return that day. I sat across from her then and chanted for her daily until her soul too became shiny and jumped to its next life. Months later I saw during meditation that they were both back on earth, in other bodies. They were in different parts of the country from each other and had been born into different families. But I took comfort in knowing that they were both back on earth. It was then that I decided that I was meant to stay in the northeast. Not in that village but farther south at this temple. I sold the house and all the contents within a month and moved here and have lived here ever since."

Kay stops talking now and Tuum notices that the line for tickets has shortened considerably. Directly in front of him is a rather large man holding two suitcases in one hand and his son's hand with the other. His hands are so large that the boy's hand is completely hidden. The boy is no more than seven or eight but doesn't fidget or say a word. He stands perfectly still at his father's side. He looks up from to time to time at his father who ignores him and stares straight ahead likely watching the progress of the line.

Tuum is impressed by how well behaved the boy is. As soon as he thinks that the boy tugs at his father's hand until his father stiffens his arm and draws the boy closer to him. The boy stops tugging on his father's arm then but kicks back once and his father turns in his direction and the boy drops his head.

Tuum wonders then if all of this is under some master influence of Kay and that what he is witnessing between the boy and his father is meant to illustrate the state of matters between his father and him. He shrugs off that thought because he senses the chirp of his own ego in it, because plainly these are simply two strangers who happen to be in front of him in line.

The clock above the ticket window indicates that it is 6:30 AM. Arriving here on the half hour unnerves him, and he doesn't like to start a journey on the half hour. He prefers the top of the hour. For a second, he considers that too as part of some master trick of Kay's but dismisses that thought. Whatever Kay is doing now, it's not in as plain sight as that.

Kay takes up his story again. "When I joined the temple, it was much smaller than it is now with only the main temple building and two outbuildings and a small garden, not large enough to provide for everyone living in the temple. It didn't have a Buddha bone yet either. Soon after I came, we raised enough money to build the gold Pagoda out front. Everyone who lived at the temple, and all those who visited, meditated for a Buddha bone. Despite our efforts nothing happened for many years. Then your father began to attend the temple and within a month we had a Buddha bone. They only come to those worthy of them. Such a gift requires a great man like your father."

How could his father have made such a gift without his knowing it? He does remember coming to the temple often with his father shortly after his mother died.

Tuum hadn't been so keen to go because he worried that he would miss her more there. But he wasn't old enough yet to consider disobeying his father. But on the very first visit he'd liked the smells of incense and the noisy swish of the monks' robes as they passed. That sound triggered happy memories of kneeling at the temple with his mother.

That first time he came there with his father images of his mother came to him. They weren't memories but new images of her from where she was then. She didn't look like his mother and dressed differently, so she appeared a stranger to him, but he knew with complete certainty that it was his mother.

He'd told his father this afterwards, and his father had nodded and said: "*Dee.*" (Good.) And then he said he'd seen her too and that she would have been stuck at the temple a long time if they hadn't been there. They must return every day until she is no longer there. That had been the very first time he'd fully understood his duties to the dead.

For months after, they returned to the temple every afternoon and stayed for three hours to chant for his mother's soul. He remembers how much effort it had taken.

He's certain that there had already been a Buddha bone in the temple during those months after his mother died. He assumes now that his father must have arranged for that right after his mother's death. Perhaps it was something they had agreed upon in those final days or something his father insisted on himself.

There are only three people ahead of him in line now but the woman at the very front is buying tickets for a large group traveling south to Hat Yai. The agent writes out many tickets and hands each one to her as he finishes it. If anyone behind her is feeling impatient, no one shows any outward sign of that nor is a single word of complaint uttered.

"When your father brought the Buddha bone to the temple, we arranged for 500 monks to bless it. Many of the monks came from as far away as Nan and Loei. Your father set the Buddha bone where it is now. In the years since, the Buddha bone has brought much prosperity and good fortune to the temple and the village. Word of that good fortune has spread and every year more people travel from farther away—"

"Where to?" The ticket agent asks Tuum as he's now at the front of the line.

"Khon Kaen," he says.

"Twenty baht."

He hands him a folded bill from his closed fist.

"It leaves from gate five." The agent points over his right shoulder to where three buses are parked.

Tuum nods and the agent writes out the ticket and hands it to him.

He walks to an empty bench and sits at one end and Kay sits at the other end leaving a wide gap between them.

"Many novice monks passed through our temple each year and

only Buddha knows which ones are destined to stay. No one knows what is intended of them, not even Buddha. The only evidence of what is planned is what occurs. I have come to understand that what is, is what is. Buddha says: *To climb up a hill is also to walk down it.*"

Tuum doubts that Buddha said that and assumes that this is another parable. He also suspects that the only time Kay has veered away from parable today has been when he's spoken about the death of his parents.

Tuum doesn't respond to Kay and they sit in silence. When Tuum's bus is called over the PA, he joins the queue of boarding passengers and Kay remains on the bench. Once in line, Tuum glances in Kay's direction, and he's sitting upright with his eyes closed, meditating.

There are five people in line ahead of him including the father and son from earlier. They are at the very front of the line and the boy is more active now and runs up and down beside his father, who laughs loudly once at something the boy must have said or done but Tuum doesn't see or hear. The father then turns around and scans those in line as though waiting for someone to join them. He turns back and stays perfectly still. He doesn't stop his son from racing to the front of the bus and back.

Tuum doesn't fidget or sway but maintains perfect posture. He keeps his arms stiff at his side and hears the jangle of a gold bracelet behind him but doesn't turn around to locate the source.

The driver opens the front door and steps out of the bus and says something to the father who reaches in a pocket and pulls out two tickets. The driver does a cursory scan of each and then waves the father and boy past. The father hoists his son up the first higher step and the boy easily bolts up the rest of the way and then and runs out of view inside the bus. The father moves much slower and keeps his head up, likely not taking his eyes off his son.

Behind them is a man in a suit and behind him is a woman Nong's age. Tuum suspects she's been visiting her family here but lives in Khon Kaen.

The old man behind her is completely bald like Jan and Kay. He holds a cane in his right hand. He doesn't lean on it but swings it back and forth in front of him and in the other hand he holds his ticket high enough for even Tuum to see it. He passes the ticket to the driver and he checks it quickly and waves him past.

It is Tuum's turn now and, instead of handing over his ticket, he steps out of line and turns back in Kay's direction. The woman with the noisy bracelet behind him smiles as he passes. When he reaches Kay, he stands in front of him until Kay opens his eyes and acknowledges him with a nod.

Kay sits a minute longer and then stands and turns in the direction of the temple. Kay walks slightly ahead for a few steps but Tuum catches up and then they walk side by side. Tuum crumbles the ticket in his hand and forms it into a ball without opening his fist. He holds it firmly there and slightly swings his arms as he walks. Kay and he walk beside each other the whole way back but don't speak.

A is still standing inside the main gate when they arrive back at the temple. He wais Kay and the two of them remain there while Tuum continues to his room.

Once there, he unfurls his fist and raises the balled-up ticket to eye level and studies it briefly and then tosses it in the trash.

He sits in the lotus position on his cot and concentrates on the inner dark of his head. Shadows appear and vanish so quickly he barely registers them. *A disturbance of the mind,* he calls it later when he opens his eyes and can't comprehend why he's back at the temple. His decision to not board the bus had felt right the moment he made it but now back at his room he's no longer certain. Then he'd thought the decision was all his to make because of what his father had said yesterday and had nothing to do with Kay's presence or anything he'd said along the way. In fact, the more Kay talked, the more certain Tuum had become that he'd leave for Khon Kaen. But when it had been his turn to board the bus, all he could think about was that boy bolting ahead of his father and the father charging after him. He didn't wish to share the bus with them and the fragile reminder of all his earlier years with his father. Then as soon as he was standing again beside Kay that feeling was already dissipating and it took all his will to resist the urge to turn around and board the bus.

He's the one who chose to come back here but the more he thinks about it now the more certain he is that not a single act he did today was of his own doing.

If he were to leave again, Kay would tag along. No matter how many times he attempted to leave, Kay would always know and accompany him. And each time he would tell Tuum a completely different story, not a single word of it the same. It is that realization which makes leaving now all the more impossible. He's no match for such mastery.

He goes to his desk and writes to Roong.

*May 8, 1970*

*My dearest Roong. My angel of angels:*

*I attempted to leave today but only got as far as the bus station. Kay has managed to keep me here without so much as a word of cajoling. I see now that forces beyond my grasp or control hold me here. I am certain in time I will understand that influence and be free of it and be able to return to you. But until then I can't leave. That may sound impossible, but I assure you it is true. My time here will be longer than I'd anticipated. Be patient my love because we have a most happy, glorious future awaiting us. I've already gotten sweet glimpses of it in several dreams.*

*Phom Rak Khun*

*Tuum*
*xxxxxxoooo*

# Chapter 8

## *Chum Phae*
## *Present day*

Many swirls of stars weave around the full moon tonight. Nan and Ed sit outside and he shifts his gaze to the night sky. It appears even more otherworldly and distant than it has other evenings, even the one after Sutum died. The stars are in flux as Nan and he are in flux, as everything is in flux.

He's not sure why but thinks of gravity tonight and how it keeps the planets in place. It's the only cosmic glue he knows of for certain, but Nan knows of others. She's turned away from him and is meditating. He meditates now too.

They remain outside and talk and at one point she says that there's an inner balance and an outer balance. The inner balance is our gyroscope and is what keeps us from spinning out of control.

He asks her what an outer balance is, and she says it's the necessary balances in the physical world—like right balances left, hot balances cold, light balances dark, and good balances evil.

Clouds have formed overhead, blocking whole swaths of the night sky. He thinks then of how words ripple and ideas flow from one to the other. She doesn't elaborate on this and instead tells him that Song wishes to visit Sutum tomorrow night. He will light incense and sit and chant with Sutum and then later the two will visit.

"He must do this alone," she says.

The next evening, Ed prepares dinner. He cooks sticky rice, cabbage, chopped garlic, onions and eggplant. Nan naps as he lets the eggplant simmer in the frying pan in a thin layer of water. Standing over the single propane burner, he realizes that love comes in stages and in the middle of love it is possible to believe that love has always existed, that the beloved has always been the beloved. Love is more constant than most other emotions. Anger and fear are the most transitory, the most impulsive. They may come and go quickly, but love endures. Once love is declared it feels permanent. And thinking about his love for Nan, it is possible to believe he has always loved her exactly as he loves her now. Dealing with Sutum's ghost has only intensified that love and allows him to sense for the first time that this love has carried forward for the both of them, that it is larger than this life.

He's always thought of love as being confined to a single life but sees no reason why now. He accepts that any given life can have residues or latencies of past loves from past lives and those carry forward into this life and the next. The first time he met Nan he had felt different although then he hadn't been equipped to think that way. But he does now and likes the idea of cascading love, and that love requires many attempts. He senses what they have now is deeper than what any one life can provide. In this moment he likes the idea that he loved her in the past and will go on loving her into the next life and the one after that and after that. What he's believed before seems cruel by comparison.

At the same time, he must accept that everything is impermanent and yet as he cooks eggplant it's possible to believe that love is a permanent element that spans beyond all else.

He places chunks of tofu into the frying pan and then adds coconut oil. He shakes the frying pan over the burner and watches the tofu brown. He derives joy from these tasks and feels the air lighten around him. He glances at the corner where Sutum's ghost likely is. From here it is merely a bare corner of the hut, nothing there to catch his eye except trapped shadows.

After he finishes cooking, he wakes Nan and they eat in quiet.

Song knocks shortly after they've finished eating and have cleaned up and put the dishes away.

Ed opens the door for Song and wais him. Song nods and enters and goes to the table and slides out a chair noiselessly and sits on it in a lotus position.

"We should go," Nan whispers.

They walk to the highway, and the night air is light and dry. It hasn't rained for nearly a week. At the highway they sit beneath a tamarind tree and watch the traffic. It is so noisy here that they only speak during the lulls. In between Ed sinks into the sound of traffic and lets it tug him along, a noisy counterbalance to his quiet heart. The steady stream of traffic makes the passing of time more tangible.

Later Nan takes his hand and they kiss. She moves away at some point as even here it is important that they not be too demonstrative as someone might see. Traffic thins to a few noisy trucks that shake past, jammed to the top with fruit or eggs. The loads are tied down with blue tarps like the ones they use to collect rice.

Nan says then that there are many words that mean *sad* in Thai and there are many words that mean *happy*. He tells her that there are more words in English for *sad* than *happy*. She asks if that's true or he's just made that up. He confesses that he doesn't know that for certain and isn't sure why he's said it.

"*Mai Pen Rai*," she says and then adds that it isn't possible for him to know everything about himself, but it is important to know when he's about to be angry, or when he is already angry.

"If you see yourself getting angry, then stop. Buddha says you may not be able to hold all the leaves on a bush, but every leaf is the same as the one you are holding. That sameness is a clue. Nothing stays in the world for long. Everything is impermanent. Everything is uncontrollable. Every life contains suffering."

Three motorcycles rumble past, likely Harleys or big Hondas. Each bike has only one rider and is headed away from Khon Kaen, going north toward the mountains. He follows their shaky headlights briefly and then turns back to Nan. In the limited light he watches her mouth open slowly and then close before she starts to speak.

"Those bikes, all that noise," she says as though to say *what is the point of it* but instead says: "Buddha mostly walked. He didn't even ride an elephant. Imagine how big the world feels when we walk? The moon must have seemed even farther away then. But now people have gone there. Walked on it. Slept on it. To Buddha it had simply been the brightest object in the night sky."

He'd never thought of people sleeping on the moon before. Apollo 17 spent three days on the moon so they must have slept. He can't imagine what that had been like. Where did they sleep?

"Are their ghosts on the moon?"

"Many."

"Are there ghosts in space too, on other planets?"

"Yes, and so on."

Until this moment it hasn't occurred to him that ghosts would exist beyond the Earth. He's assumed that they are confined to Earth. But it makes sense that they ripple farther and farther away.

"Space is dry with no food, so the shapes of those ghosts are different. Made up mostly of the material in space."

"What does that mean?"

"It is what is and what is adapted to. All must be included," she says and abruptly adds: "Time to go back."

They stand together and she kisses him longer now that it is dark, and they are more invisible to passing vehicles. They kiss under a full, yellow moon.

When they return, Song is sitting on the front steps. He stands and speaks briefly to Nan and then she and Ed wai him and he nods and goes to his car. He backs the Yaris a long way before turning it around and driving slowly in the direction of the highway.

Ed stands out front until Song's headlights disappear into the night. He's curious as to what Song said to Nan, but at this moment, he still can't get the moon out of his thoughts and the notion of the ghosts that inhabit it.

He goes inside and Nan is sitting on the edge of the bamboo cot with her eyes closed, chanting. He sits quietly at the table and waits for her to finish.

She stays that way for a half hour, and in the candlelight, he can see her lips moving at times, but she utters no sounds.

When she finishes, she unfolds her legs and tiptoes barefoot from the cot and joins him at the table.

"Song said that Sutum is happy here. That he doesn't wish to leave. Ghosts can't stay where they are even if they are happy there. That would be very dangerous. They must leave, must be made to move on. If they don't leave then a karmic chain is in jeopardy. Sometimes ghosts need coaxing. They get too comfortable where they are just like the living do and see no reason to move on. Song says he would like to visit again, that he has further progress he needs to make with Sutum.

"I told him that it is okay if he comes for a visit or two, but anything after that would be dangerous for him, for Sutum, for us. We are Sutum's way out now. Neither Song nor Sutum know that, only we and Run do."

Ed briefly wishes they could just get on her Honda Click and drive away. But he knows they'd only get a few miles before Nan would start to vomit, might even choke and he might not be able to save her. The karmic consequences of them leaving would be so catastrophic for her and he would lose her.

Both their futures are now dependent on their succeeding with Sutum.

A dream wakes him and he hears noises at the sink. The cot is empty beside him so he knows that Nan is already up. Hints of morning light are visible in the window. He lies there replaying the dream as he will need to tell Nan all the details he can remember. It is not Sutum in his dream but another man that he doesn't recognize. He is with a woman that Ed has also never seen before in any dream.

"We're digging a grave in our silken finery," the woman says to the man. She says this in perfect English. Ed knows instantly that it's a dream because of the clarity of her English. The man is digging with a small shovel and as soon as the woman says *grave*, Ed's dream self knows they are not in Thailand.

She dances as though to *Mor-Lam* rhythms, but there's no music playing in the dream. Still she dances. The man sets the shovel to one side and takes her hand and she stops dancing. They kiss and Ed feels uncomfortable watching, but they act as if he isn't there and likely he isn't.

"What shall we do?" the woman asks, after they stop kissing. Again he hears this in English.

"Perhaps we should light a fire," the man says and it is immediately snowing. A few flakes at first and then a heavy driving snow as though in the dead of winter in Canada. The snow falls on palm trees and rice plants and mango trees so they are now back in Thailand. The woman reaches out a hand and says: "How lovely, look what we've done."

A horse gallops past kicking up a cloud of snow behind it. As soon as it vanishes from view, another horse gallops past and then another and another. The man and woman join hands and dance as more and more horses bolt past. The horses are all sorts of colours and sizes and some are a mix of white, brown, and black. They run at full gallop, and none of them has a rider or loses their footing in the snow or are even slowed by it. For a moment it appears that the snow has turned to rice, but quickly it is snow again, and growing deeper. The horses continue to pass one at a time with a significant gap between each one.

He wants to know what has spooked the horses, and he turns his gaze in the direction they've come from but like a TV screen he can't see past the edge of his dream. When he turns back to the man and woman, they are gone but their fresh footprints are visible in the snow and lead in the same direction as the horses.

Ed turns again in the direction the horses have come from and walks that way. As he does the snow disappears and the heat rises significantly. It's the rising heat and absence of snow that wakes him. The last thing he hears as he wakes is the man saying: "Yes my angel of angels, we shall go in our silken finery."

In the press of morning heat, he hears Nan noisily rummaging in the cutlery drawer. He feels a tight fist of pain in his back from the uneven bamboo and stretches until it subsides.

Nan returns to the cot and her arms are cool from running a damp cloth over them, something she said her mother taught her to do. She lies beside him and he tells her about the dream and he asks her what it means.

"Our silken finery means our morality, our goodness," she says. "What comes from good must also be good."

He thinks about that for a moment, and traces that notion back to his dream but all he can think of is that in Thailand it can only snow in a dream. Then the man says my angel of angels so clearly at the end. He wonders now if she and the man are simply an invention of his dream, or if there's something more to it. He'd read somewhere once that dreams are *unopened letters from eternity.* Her voice as she'd said *our silken finery* sounded unfamiliar and yet very familiar.

To him the phrase sounded like a warning, but he prefers Nan's interpretation.

"The best way to make lips beautiful is not by lipstick but by having them speak beautiful words," Nan says. "Kind, friendly eyes are shiny, beautiful eyes. Makeup won't turn cheeks beautiful the way receiving a complement will. This is the meaning of *our silken finery.* The snow, horses and grave are from you, so to me they are a mystery."

She hugs him.

"He woke me," she says and runs a hand along his arm.

"How?"

"At the sink."

"Is he there now?"

"No."

"Here at all?"

"Yes. In his usual corner. Run says he sits in a lotus position there most of the time. He looks very comfortable."

"What else does the dream mean?" he asks her.

"That your connection to this hut is more than just your connections to Sutum. That means mine must be too.

"We should chant now while there are still traces of that dream swirling around in you. The more we chant the more likely some of the details in the dream will stay with you. Those details will be important for you."

He drifts away and then returns again from a feeling of nothingness to his breathing first and then his internal words and realizes that he's been chanting the whole time.

In this pilfered dark he listens for any sound of Sutum somewhere in the room. Is that even possible? Nan has told him that ghosts don't make sounds like they do in movies. That the disturbances and noises he's taken to be coming from Sutum are all in his head. They are his mind's way of communicating the connections he feels with Sutum. His version of Sutum's ghost is not Nan's version nor Song's nor Run's.

He thinks back to all that has transpired these weeks and realizes that most of what he has been calling Sutum is his own fabrication giving shapes to forces he doesn't fully understand. Nan and Run don't use the word *ghost* when referring to this presence. They use *spirit* and each time Nan has said *spirit* he has heard *ghost* but now feels a shift in his thinking as he adapts. Their word is the better choice.

He knows that the dark inside and outside is molecular and ever expanding and contracting. He, Nan, and Sutum are participants in that molecular dark.

She stirs and he can't tell if she is still meditating or asleep. He opens his eyes and the room is as dark as his head until his eyes adjust. Then he can make out vague details in the hut. He considers reaching out to touch her but doesn't wish to disturb her. He's learned from her the importance of lying still and settling firmly in the moment and floating with it and allowing himself to be carried along. Where he's going isn't as important as allowing himself to go there.

He remembers again what she has already told him about *spirits*. "They don't test their strength for they don't have strength. They are exposed souls in limbo, that inhabit neither air nor bodies nor even space and time as you and I inhabit space and time. They are a collective history that they must forget but can't forget. It is their inability to forget that keeps them here."

He slips out of the cot and goes to the table and sits in a chair facing the cot. He senses Sutum somewhere near him but doesn't know how he senses that or even what to do with that sensation. But he now senses other remnants too, as if his dream has opened a door to different kinds of perceptions. Are they lingering memories from a past life that have somehow rippled here? He doesn't really sense anything physical about any of this like he does Sutum. But the convergence is real. What exactly manifests to him now he can't identify except energy beyond his own. Those energies have changed around him and that means a presence of some sort.

He closes his eyes and speaks in his mind to Sutum and who or whatever else may be present. *Tell me what you want? What do you need?*

He doesn't sense any response. But asks again for he must keep asking. His head stays silent. It is not possible to speak directly to a spirit except through someone like Run. Still he believes he is doing the right thing and that this is making a difference.

Run doesn't speak to a spirit in the way Ed thinks of speaking. It is more akin to a chant. One chants to the other and keeps chanting until the spirit becomes shiny like a diamond. Spirits are like a fly that enters a great house when the door is open and can't find its way back out.

It isn't good for spirits to be trapped like this as the body waiting for Sutum's soul may have another soul jump into it instead and then the karmic timetable may be dangerously altered, possibly for the worse. No soul can stay out of the karmic cycle, indefinitely. Each needs to return.

He looks in the direction of Nan on the cot and at first it appears to him that she is not there, that she has slipped away. Finally, his eyes adjust, and he can better make out her shape. He rises and as he does, he senses another powerful energy shift in the room. Sutum has shifted. But to do what?

He tiptoes to the cot and slips under the thin sheet. He is shaking from what has just happened.

"You okay?" Nan asks and turns towards him.

"Yes, I am very happy," he says. He tells her then about what he has discovered.

"Yes," she says. "That is how it works."

*Child O'Child. You are breathing.*

Sutum somewhere in the dark is noiseless but present.

*There are no walls. There are no walls.*

Until that moment last night when he sat at the table and sensed Sutum near him he'd always felt his self as being intact, fixed and permitted only small changes. Then later when he came to the cot and lay with his back next to Nan and Sutum was somewhere in the loose distance he sensed his self slip away, move, fragment, become disconnected from the chain of memories that had held it until then. He sensed others here too, from before, shadowy shimmers. Sutum, he is here to help, but he's beginning to feel a closeness to others too, as shadowy and partial as they are. The others have departed, jumped again and again to other bodies, but what remains, Ed realizes, may be soul memories, and those matter too, although he hasn't determined how yet.

Today the heat is especially sweltering as Ed and Nan walk to work. They must walk much farther now that the harvesting is nearly done.

Song is not working yet so they go to where he left off last night. When Ed bends to grab his first fist full of rice stalks and slice through with the scythe he feels how intermittent his self is. His body attends to the repetition of the work but his mind struggles with all he has learned in the past day. He realizes that attached memories are not what matter most because as Nan has explained it is the clean self, the core that he has had since birth that is sacred and gets carried forward from life to life. It is the centre of the circle that is bound by the dirt and clutter of this life. By meditating he can shift all of that out of the way and get a clear view of his true inner self, not bound by the events of this one life or any life—the molten self, an amalgam of all past lives.

Nan is within reaching distance but engrossed in her work as he sets his fourth bundle of rice in the pile with the others and stops. He watches her work and basks in his love for her, realizing he hasn't known a magnitude of love this great before. This is the first time he's fully understood the implications of all she has been saying to him for five years. How can it have taken this long? The completeness of love he feels now is due partly to all he has learned from Sutum's spirit being trapped in the hut.

Something in her impeccable grace and rhythm seems more familiar to him today and maybe that dream wasn't really about the man and woman but about Nan and him. Or maybe they are one and the same. The horses and all that snow may have been from a past life they shared in Canada. Whose grave had they been digging? Were they burying someone they both loved dearly? A child or parent?

Nan stops and turns and smiles at him and he smiles back. She comes over to where he stands and whispers for him not to stop work because they need to harvest as quickly as possible before the day gets unbearably hot. It already feels too hot for him. He tells her that watching her today makes him very happy.

"In an hour we will shake the rice onto the tarp," she says, and points to the large pile started yesterday by Song.

He nods. That is her way of saying she is happy too. She then says: "Tonight, Song will visit Sutum. It will rain."

It is dark and already raining by the time Song arrives that evening. He goes to the corner where the gecko died. He kneels facing the corner and wais again and stays kneeling.

Ed and Nan leave then and stand for a while in the porch waiting to see if the rain lets up. She takes his hand and grips it firmly at her side. When the rain doesn't lighten, she lets go of his hand and runs to Song's car and gets in the driver's side. He follows after her but trips in the slippery grass and grabs the door handle to keep from falling.

She drives them south to the Tesco Lotus mall seven kilometres away and on the outskirts of Chum Phae. Inside, the mall is similar to those in Victoria and many of the shops are the same: Mr. Donut, Starbucks, McDonald's, and KFC. But there are Thai chains too like Pizza Company and Power Buy.

They eat at the food court which has many stalls selling tasty meals. They look around afterward but don't buy anything. He wonders how such places fit into Nan's notions of enlightenment and *Samadhi* (deep meditation).

When he asks her, she says that the world is the world. He takes that to mean that this is all a façade and the same invisible forces swirl here too. All of it always changes and nothing stays the same.

What changes is part of a greater self, made up of all the lesser selves including his. The connective tissue between people changes but some form of practical commerce is always necessary.

The rain has stopped when they return to the car. They've purchased Pad Thai for Song and a large package of rice noodles and a bag of bean sprouts and a packet of dried tofu. The one luxury beyond toilet paper and paper towels are two chocolate bars for him and a bag of roasted almonds for Nan.

Song is sitting out front of the hut when they return. He comes inside with them and eats the Pad Thai, distributing the contents evenly between three bowls and insisting they join him. They eat in silence, and when Song's dish is empty, he walks it to the sink and rinses it off and then comes back for theirs and does the same.

After he has washed and dried them and put them away in the cupboard, he says: "*Kop Khun Krup,*" and leaves.

She tells Ed after Song has left that he's said nothing to her about Sutum today.

## Chapter 9

# *Chum Phae*
# *1970*

It is afternoon and Tuum returns to the small room and enters without knocking. His father is already at the table with his hands folded, his eyes closed, his lips moving as he chants to himself.

Tuum sits noisily but his father continues to chant. When he finally opens his eyes, Tuum expects his father to scold him for what has happened earlier today at the bus station, but his father simply nods and Tuum wais back.

Tuum folds his hand on the table and waits for his father to speak. He doesn't have to wait long.

"During the school holiday months when I was twelve, I used to take daily walks to the nearby hills that overlooked a shared rice field. I would be gone from noon to sundown. I don't know what drew me there the first time, but I guess I was curious like most boys that age. Partway up the closest hill, I found a ledge above the rice field. From it I had a view of both my village to the north and the rice field below. From there I could easily locate the tiled roof of my parents' house and all the neighbouring houses. It was there that I practiced meditating for hours at a time. As I sat with my legs crossed, the afternoon heat on my face was unbearable but I persisted. The hotter I got the more determined I became.

"When I'd finally open my eyes again it would be late afternoon, the sun and heat already waning. No matter how many times I went there I'd be transfixed by the view of our village in the distance. Each time I would count adjoining rooftops until I found my parents' house.

The more I did that the more easily I could locate it without counting. I learned then the importance of knowing exactly where I am.

"I returned to the ledge every day to watch all the activities below. I was most struck by how remarkably still it all was. For long periods of time not even a blade of grass or stock of rice moved. The only movements were those of the few farmers who laboured in the shared field below me. They worked slowly but purposefully and from my ledge I could identify a few of them by what part of the field they worked but most remained a mystery to me beyond the common rhythms to their work. Occasionally, I would spot people walking on the main road beyond the field. Those were either approaching or leaving the village. From my vantage point they were mere vague moving shapes. Their lives and purposes were also vague to me. Yet when I closed my eyes and meditated, I sensed some connection to all of them although I was much too young to know exactly what I was connecting to.

"I found my calling on that ledge although I wouldn't know it until decades later. Looking back now I see a clear pattern to all of my life and how every event in it fits with all the others. In time you will be able to do the same. It is not for the young to know such matters as too much is still missing. Back then I only thought in terms of myself and I thought every event happened by accident without purpose or reason. Later I would learn from the teachings of Buddha that the law of action drives all we do.

"Those afternoons on that ledge I was a boy foolishly toying with powers I didn't understand yet. What I had learned, I did mostly out of boredom. I mistakenly thought that the world was as simple as that view.

"One day I went there earlier than usual for reasons that escape me now, but there I was. A water buffalo and a farmer worked directly below me, and I watched them plough short furrows for the second rice crop of that year. They completed three full furrows and when the sun was directly overhead the farmer tied the water buffalo to a large tamarind tree and walked back to the main road. I assume he was going for lunch because at the main road he turned toward the village.

"The buffalo was below me but off to one side. I watched it pace for a while and then drink some of the water the farmer had left it in a large bowl. Then in the brutal midday heat it slowly lowered its hind haunches and then its front legs and lay in the shade of that tamarind tree. I was amazed by the gracefulness of it as it settled on the short grass there. It chewed the available tuffs in front of it and now and then it flicked its tail to shoo away flies.

"I expected once it cooled off in the shade it would rise again to tug at the rope in protest not because I knew the way of water buffalo even then but because that is what I imagined myself doing if I was the water buffalo. Instead it stayed in the shade.

"The heat got to me and I inched deeper into the shade of the mango tree on my ledge and was now directly above the buffalo. It stopped chewing and appeared to go to sleep although its tail continued to flick every now and then. I nodded off too and when I woke some time had passed but the buffalo still hadn't moved, although the shade had shifted, and its hindquarters were now partly exposed to the sun.

"From that height I saw the awkward curve of its spine, and the outline of vertebrae beneath hide. I wasn't more than ten metres above it, and if I had dropped straight down from the ledge I would have landed on its back.

"I glanced around at the stillness of the midday heat and except for the swaying of distant grass and trees nothing moved. As my gaze returned back toward the water buffalo, I noticed a stirring in the grass behind it. The buffalo must have sensed that too as it raised up on its front haunches and then hoisted up its back. It walked away from the movement in the grass as far as the rope allowed. When it reached the end of its tether, it then pulled forcefully on that rope, but the farmer had secured it well to the tamarind.

"The king cobra lifted its head briefly and then hurried in the shorter grass in the direction of the buffalo. When the snake was a few feet away it rose up and lunged forward and struck a back leg of the buffalo and then recoiled. This all happened so quickly that I barely registered the movements. The buffalo raised its head and bellowed louder than I've ever heard a buffalo bellow. It then moaned and cried in ways a child might cry. Its hind legs buckled first, and it listed backward and then the front haunches gave out too and its head slapped against the ground and bounced several times from the initial impact. I heard a slight thump followed by two loud grunts. The cobra stopped a few feet off and raised its head long enough for me to see it and then lowered it again and continued away from the village. When it was farther into the taller grass, it stopped to look up again.

"The buffalo now lay in full sun and rolled from one side to other and kicked at the air as it rolled. It grunted repeatedly then each time a little quieter. It then pushed its front legs into the ground and tried to stand. It managed to lift its head and the front half of its body but dropped again.

"I didn't leave my perch until I was certain the snake was far enough away that it wasn't likely to circle back. I then scrambled down to the buffalo, and I had to jump the final metre. When I reached the buffalo, its head was already flat on the ground and it was panting heavily and snorting. It raised its head slightly when I touched its hindquarters and its eyes flicked open but swirled so dramatically that it closed them again right away.

"I took out the pocketknife I always carried with me and cut the rope but I was too late. I searched both hind legs until I found the bite marks halfway up the left one. I considered cutting into it then but already knew the animal couldn't be saved. It took another half hour but in time it stopped breathing.

"Then I believed I had done all I could. I thought that I had no part in that karmic drama. I'd simply been a bystander, a distant observer. I hadn't caused the buffalo's death nor did my being there hurry it along in anyway. Nor could I have saved it.

"But I was meant to learn from that drama the strictness of the Dharma way. I chanted for the soul of the buffalo although I was too young to really comprehend the true purpose for what I was doing or to really accomplish what I was required to accomplish. I was a mere boy playing with forces beyond my command or comprehension. I simply did what I'd seen my parents and monks at the temple do.

"No images came to me when I closed my eyes. But I chanted all the same and it felt right to do that. I don't know if I helped that buffalo's soul or not. My mother later taught me the importance of assisting the dead. I have no idea where the soul of that water buffalo ended up.

"When the farmer returned from his lunch, he scolded me and accused me of bringing him bad fortune and black magic and said his buffalo would still be alive if I hadn't been there. I pointed out to him that he was wrong, although I don't know where I got the nerve to say that to an adult. But I did. Then I said there wasn't anything I could have done to save the buffalo that he'd been the one who tied it up and left it behind. I said that that resulted in its death and not my being there. I didn't see then how harsh my words were. If I'd been older, I would have been humbler and accepted that I did play a role in it all whether I wanted to believe that or not. There are no bystanders. Everyone is a participant and, in some way, responsible.

"The farmer didn't reply but looked at me with such anger in his eyes that he had to look away. He didn't speak that anger or let it manifest. He controlled it and I am thankful for that now and realize that, despite any error the man may have made in leaving his buffalo, he was a good man. He likely had left his buffalo tied up like that many times in the past without incident. He couldn't have allowed it to simply wander off. His silence then allowed me to say with some impertinence that I'd been able to comfort the buffalo in its final moments as I'd chanted for its soul.

"The farmer wept then and thanked me and said he was sorry for being angry with me. He said the snake was not an agent of Buddha but some dark angel or dark power. He said he'd been troubled all week by terrifying dreams and now he knew why. He didn't say what those dreams were. He curled up beside the buffalo despite the overwhelming heat. I didn't have any idea what he would do with such a big dead animal. I was just a boy and didn't know yet how such responsibilities were handled.

"I left him and hurried home. I had no desire to go back up to my ledge and never returned to it again: not the rest of that summer nor any summer afterward. As I ran home, I didn't look back even when I reached the main road. Instead I kept running, eager to put as much distance as possible between me and what had happened. I realized then that I had escaped something although I wasn't quite sure what it was and didn't know until many years later.

"After that incident, I stayed close to home until the school year started again. Miraculously from that day forward, I could meditate with little effort. The flywheel of events traps us, shapes us, and carries us forward yelling and screaming if it has to, taking us to exactly where we are supposed to be. There is good in it all that I recognize every day. So little of any of it is of our doing and our lives are determined by events that occurred a long time ago. We arrive in this present day because of our parents and their parents and their parents. I claim to be in possession of powers but most days I am merely an obedient participant.

"Still I have never forgotten that cobra and buffalo and what I witnessed that day. All that I've gained, I've gained because of what happened then."

This is a parable like the ones Kay told him earlier today. Tuum supposes too that it is as close as his father will come to talking to him about what he did today. He also senses that his father believes that all powers, great or small, have traceable origins. Just as whatever happens between Roong and him have traceable origins that may arc across many lifetimes. All is not what it seems. Once he couldn't walk, and now he can, and that too has a karmic origin, just as his being here with his father does. His father believes knowing the origins is important. Tuum doesn't yet.

Today it didn't rain and tomorrow it likely won't rain but on some future day it will. That is for certain. His knowing that fact doesn't make him any closer to a day it will rain. It is merely not this day. He is here with his father on a hot, dry day. How distant he is from a future day of rain does not change where he is now. What was certain and what will be certain doesn't change where he is. He is here.

His father stays sitting with his eyes fixed on the surface of the table, exactly what he sees there Tuum can only speculate. He scans the polished dark wood several times looking for a clue but only notices how easily it hides blemishes. Tuum closes his eyes and waits, considers again and again his father admitting to being afraid.

His father eventually stands and says: "Tomorrow, we will start earlier. Now you know why."

Later that evening after a small dinner and his usual evening chant and meditation, he writes a second letter to Roong.

*May 8, 1970*

*My loveliest angel:*

*This afternoon, my father said nothing about my going to the bus station. Instead he told me about seeing a cobra kill a water buffalo when he was a boy. He clearly intended his story as a lesson to me about going to the bus station. But I don't see it that way.*

*Later, he leaned over the table and I sensed his desire to be my father again. We have yet to speak in detail about the accident. I am waiting most for that. I can't yet broach that with him. And he does not bring it up. I can only speak of it to you. That is the conundrum.*

*From his parable it is clear that my father believes that in a past life I was a snake. In his story he chose a cobra, but I am certain I was a garden snake. I don't understand yet what it is he hopes to accomplish in these daily sessions.*

*I am eager to be with you, for the noises and fragrances of you. As I meditated this evening, I glimpsed us aboard a large boat on a placid river and we were not in a hurry. We had days to get to where we were going.*

*Phom Rak Khun*

*Tuum*
*xxxxxxxxoooooo*

Once again in this small room in the temple, the heat intensifies the smell of his father's garlicky sweat. Tuum catches, too, a hint of cinnamon likely from his father's lunch.

His father sags in his chair as the afternoon progresses and looks older at times than Kay. When he leans forward, his shoulders slouch. His eyes are narrow slits and Tuum notices how puffy and pockmarked the skin on his face is. Deep wrinkles criss-cross his cheeks, forehead and chin. The bags under his eyes are getting progressively more pronounced each day. His shaved head has many brown spots, some as large as a thumb. Beads of sweat form below his bottom lip and on his forehead as he chants.

His father hasn't shaven today and his face and head have white stubble that is noticeable even in this diminished light. Tuum can't take his eyes away from that stubble and is not used to his father not attending to his hygiene. His eyes are even redder than usual and Tuum wonders if he slept well last night but doesn't ask.

His father folds his hands on the table as usual and says without any preamble: "There was another woman before your mother."

Tuum squares his feet on the floor in front of him and briefly looks down to check on their positions and then braces for what will come next. The glib way his father has stated this makes him prickle.

He is okay with Nong and any others who came after his mother but the notion that his father loved someone before his mother also indicates how precarious Tuum's place here is. Would he have found Roong? Certainly, his soul would have found a different body from this one. But where and when that would be is impossible to know.

"Her name was Sarah Pee and she came from a neighbouring village. When I came back from university, I met her in the market of my parents' village. She had the most sorrowful eyes and they compelled me to say hello. She said hello back but then continued on her way."

Tuum is troubled by the similarity to how he met Roong. There are no coincidences so where is this leading?

"In the days afterward, I didn't think of her and I imagine she didn't think of me. A week later, I was hired by the agricultural department to travel from village to village and take inventory of rice crops. I was provided with a place to live in her village although I did not know yet that it was her village.

"It so happened that my job took me past her family's rice field most mornings and that's where I saw her again, working close to the road when I passed. In the weeks to follow I would stop my bicycle at her farm and watch her work. I could always spot her from a distance because she was shorter than everyone else in the field and yet worked the fastest. She never once stopped to acknowledge me."

His father stops now and clears his throat and scratches under his chin. Those actions make him seem most like his father. He remembers those very mannerisms from when he was learning to walk again. Each time he'd passed his father in the open field, his father would scratch under his chin and then clear his throat. Sometimes he'd offer words of encouragement or praise and other times he'd just nod.

Tuum has the urge now to reach across the table and take his hand but doesn't and can't really say why he doesn't except that the past is impossible to gain back.

"We met again in the street a few months later and talked for more than an hour. I can't recall a single word we said but do recall how very happy I felt. A thick crowd hurried around us but I felt as though we were alone in the street." His father's voice breaks, and he has to clear his throat several more times before he can go on.

His father tells him that at some point Sarah Pee said she must hurry home and he said he would walk her there. She lived in a small house with her parents and brother on the northern edge of the village very far from his accommodations. At her house, she took his hand and suggested he come over that evening and meet her parents.

That evening he sat with her and her parents and her father asked after Jan's father and then he asked, as was required, what Jan could offer in the way of a marriage gift. Jan had come prepared and although his means then had been meagre he'd managed to save enough that what he offered her parents pleased them. He and Sarah Pee agreed to marry after the harvest.

Tuum takes in the weight of the news that his father was married before he married Tuum's mother. His father goes silent and Tuum considers telling him that he needn't go on today and that they can continue tomorrow, but before he has a chance to say this, his father begins again.

He tells Tuum of how that year the rains came more heavily than usual and it rained so much that many farmers in the village had already lost their crop and were waiting out the rains before they tilled and planted again. Her father's land was on higher ground, so his crops had fared better than most but there was still an urgency to harvest it as quickly as possible. So she worked long hours every day. This meant that the only time his father and Sarah Pee got to spend together was when he'd stop at her farm at lunchtime on his way to one of the northern villages he was commissioned to inspect.

Each day they ate lunch under the protection of the same tamarind tree. They didn't eat much, a bit of rice and vegetables, a bit of egg for protein, no meat.

"Under that tamarind tree, we spoke of the children we would have and where we'd built our modest house and raise our family. We agreed on everything. We laughed often during those lunches. I remember us laughing so hard at times that we rolled around on the ground."

The notion of his father rolling around on the ground laughing fascinates Tuum as he can count on one hand the number of times he's seen his father laugh. He remembers his father and mother singing together more often than laughing.

"Our lunches would be over too soon, and she'd have to hurry back to work and I'd have many miles to pedal. When I would pass by on the way home in the evenings, she'd still be working in the field. I'd stop to watch her and would pedal the rest of the way home in the dark.

"I got to know her family's house and her family very well. They were always welcoming me, and they would bring us bowls of food to eat as we talked. Her brother was much younger and in school so didn't help with the harvesting. Her mother was often busy for hours in the kitchen and her father would kneel to chant in front of their altar table for an hour or more after dinner. I felt a happiness then that I wouldn't feel again until you were born.

"As our wedding day approached, we both grew excited and our lunches in the field usually turned into planning sessions. We were eager to make a show of it. Our families weren't large on either side and so that made it all the more important that the wedding be substantial."

His father pauses again and coughs into his hands several times and then he takes out a cloth he's kept hidden in a hand until now and wipes around his nose and mouth with it. It isn't the first time his father has coughed recently but today it is the deeper and raspier than before and the sound of it concerns Tuum.

His father circles the cloth with his fingers and hides it again in a closed fist. He then continues his story.

In the last week of October, a typhoon devastated the coast of Vietnam and continued inland as a monsoon. By the time it reached his village, the wind and rain hadn't abated much. The thunder and lightning were worse than any he'd experienced before. Sarah Pee had gone to the field that day to work and didn't heed the darkening clouds. He rode his bike west that day so didn't pass her field. He'd gone to a more distant village in the morning. When the heavy rains came, he took shelter in a small restaurant. He ate a bowl of tasty dark rice and when the rain didn't let up he ordered a spicy papaya salad, and after finishing that, he sat and talked with the owner who was a very pleasant woman.

"The sights, sounds and smells you remember from a disastrous day in your life are arbitrary but stay with you all your life and in time it is possible to understand that they are not at all arbitrary. I remember this woman's face as vividly now as if we had just recently passed in the street. I don't remember her name, or the name of her restaurant or even where it was. I have tried to find it many times but never have. I vividly remember her raspy voice.

"She spoke of her daughter who had gone to Krung Thep. She worked fourteen hours a day as a maid for a wealthy family and every month she mailed home the few bills she managed to save from her meagre pay. The envelopes she sent were never thick, but they made a significant difference to her mother's life. She told me how she'd become very worried recently because the envelopes had stopped coming. She asked me what that could mean. I told her it couldn't be good news. I wish now I'd been gentler with her and hadn't been so honest. On one of the worst days of my life I failed to show kindness when it was needed. I have no idea what happened to her daughter, but Krung Thep is a large city with many dangers. That detail haunts me to this day. Not as much as everything else that happened that day but all the same that woman and her daughter are now a part of what I am unable forget."

His father says that the rain finally let up and he was able to ride home before dark. He hadn't been home long before there was a loud knock on his door. He'd expected it to be Sarah Pee but it was her father. As soon as he saw him there, he knew. Her father didn't say a word at first but simply shook in the doorway.

"I'll never forget how much he was shaking. He opened his mouth to speak but nothing came out but a creaky whisper."

His father pauses and stands and Tuum assumes that he is going to stop for today, but this far into the story, Tuum doesn't wish for his father to stop. He wants to know all there is to know about Sarah Pee. His father may never have the momentum for this story again. His father goes to the door and opens it halfway likely to let in cooler air. He stands there for a moment fanning the door with both hands and then closes it and returns to the table and sits down.

Tuum sees tears in his father's eyes for the first time since Tuum's mother died.

"I helped him to the only chair in the small living room of my apartment. He slumped in it and stayed quiet. Perhaps he was chanting or perhaps he was just too grieved for words yet. I boiled water for tea and brought him a warm cup of jasmine tea. By then he'd recovered enough to sit upright in the chair and his eyes alertly followed me with new energy. He took several long sips of tea and that perked him up. He finally set the cup down and told me how he'd found Sarah Pee lying face down in the rice field. She'd been struck by lightning and looked as though she were resting on the ground. When he got closer, he saw the burns around her neck where her gold necklace was. There was nothing he could do. She must have been standing in the open, but the lightning hit her anyway despite all the tall trees around her. 'That's how Karma works,' he said. Otherwise why hadn't the lightning hit one of the tamarind trees instead? In that moment his pain erupted in me too and I couldn't speak of it.

"He said he would like it if we chanted for her, so I sat in the lotus position on the floor beside him and we chanted aloud doing many lines from memory. Then he stopped all at once and I stopped too. He stared ahead and didn't say anything for a long time. I closed my eyes and I was shaking all over.

"When he finally spoke, he said that his legs were cramping up and he got out of the chair and shook each one a couple of times."

His father's hands are shaking now too and Tuum reaches across the table to steady them and at first his touch does nothing but in time the trembling stops and Tuum takes his hands away and his father continues.

"Her father told me how it had been dark by the time he brought her home in his rice wagon."

His father stops again and leans a little closer to Tuum. He sips from the glass of rose water someone has left there today. It is the first time there has been a glass of water here and Tuum wonders if his father had requested it. He watches him take two long swallows of the water and then lifts a hand to his forehead and rests it there briefly though Tuum has no idea why. He's never seen his father do that before and wonders if it is a habit he had when Sarah Pee was alive.

His father adjusts his position in his chair so he is more upright and closes his eyes but opens them again immediately and tells Tuum how the normally obedient buffalo stopped well back of the house and refused to advance any farther no matter how many times Sarah Pee's father coaxed it. He eventually gave up and went around back and tossed aside the blanket. He'd laid Sarah Pee on her back but somehow, she'd turned onto her side on the trip home. He wrapped her in the blanket again not wishing Sarah Pee's mother to see her like this. He then lifted her onto his shoulder and carried her inside. Her mother screamed and ran outside and then fell to her knees just outside the door chanting at the top of her lungs. She was still there when he left to come to Jan's house.

"He told me then that he'd lain Sarah Pee on her bed and that he wanted me to sit with her. We left immediately and rode our bicycles side by side. Neither of us had headlights, and the night was so dark that we kept having to swerve at the least second out of each other's way. The monsoon rains had passed by then and the streets had mostly dried, but broken branches and pieces of boards and other debris from the storm riddled the streets so we had to frequently avoid that too.

"When a street became too clogged with debris, we got off and walked our bicycles until we reached a leeward street. I remember the whoosh of air as her father passed me once going down a slight hill. He stopped soon after because the way ahead had become clogged again. How he saw all that debris in that dense dark I don't know. From there we walked our bicycles the rest of the way. I'd been winded enough that I gulped and then sucked in the damp air and it soothed my burning throat. I was sweating profusely by then, but her father wasn't."

When they reach the house, his father went immediately to her tiny bedroom. That had been the first time he'd set foot in it. The room was only large enough for a single bed and a plain, wooden chair next to it. He sat in it for many hours and couldn't take his eyes off Sarah Pee and from that angle she could have been sleeping, except for the scarf her mother had wrapped around her neck. He never touched her but this close he felt her linger, felt her there and the love they shared. None of that had changed.

"I learned years later that lightning kills you on the inside and doesn't touch your outside except where you are wearing metal like her necklace. I couldn't get over how she looked exactly the same as the last time I saw her only her eyes were closed. I wondered for years: *Why lightning*? But sometimes Karma gets so entwined, so compressed it is difficult to sort out exactly what is playing out. That is what I came to accept with her. *Lightning killed her* because that was how she was meant to die this time."

Most of the time his father spent with Sarah Pee that night, he didn't speak and when he did it was to tell her that he loved her and how much he would miss her. He also chanted and prayed for her soul to travel safely. As he chanted, he saw Sarah Pee standing far in the distance. She waved in his direction. Whether she was waving at him or someone else he couldn't tell. She then ran toward him but didn't stop when she reached him but kept going. He turned in his mind and watched her continue along a road and then turn suddenly to her right and vanish into a thick stand of trees. She was in a different body, younger too, the setting unfamiliar, there were snow-capped mountains in the distance so it looked like she was in Switzerland or France, the trees pine and spruce. Trees he only knew from pictures he'd seen in university.

"I realize now those images were from a future life we have together. I loved your mother very much. I don't want you to think otherwise, and sometime in the future I will be with her again too, but that will be a different life from the one I will have with Sarah Pee. In that life we will get married."

Tuum accepts the karmic truth to what his father says but his father's certainty disturbs him. His father may be able to see in the future, but Tuum doubts he can see it that precisely, so he takes these predictions to be his father's wishful thinking.

What is certain is that in those lives his father will be someone else's son and someone else's father just as Tuum will be someone else's son and father. Or maybe a mother, or daughter, or sister. The possibilities aren't predictable or knowable in the way his father claims they are. It is true that love spans many lifetimes, and to limit love to a single life would diminish its power.

"When I finally said good night to her parents and rode my bicycle home it was very late, well past midnight. I had to avoid the debris again and halfway home I gave up and simply got off the bicycle and walked. I stumbled several times and tripped once and the bicycle slid along the gravel street. I picked it up and kept walking. By the time I got home I was so exhausted I fell asleep on the bed with all my clothes on despite the heat and humidity.

"I slept until noon the next day and woke too late to go to work but that didn't matter to me by then as I understood from my nighttime vigil that I would soon be leaving there for good. I've never been back to that village.

"The very next day I returned to my parents' village and their house. For the next three months I hardly slept at all. I had so many dreams. I don't recall them now only the impression that they tormented me, and most mornings I felt as though I hadn't slept at all. I also remember waking a few mornings with an inexplicable sense of joy that meant that I had dreamt of Sarah Pee. On such mornings I would lie awhile in bed and feel such lightness that I believed I could float away into thin air and never come back.

"I was too young to have a proper understanding of what was

really happening to me. In this life, that was my first deep love and then it was a lost love. Six months to the hour after she died the dreams and visions stopped. At the time I felt great relief at being free of them. Only when I was much older would I fully grasp all I had lost and exactly how long a journey love is. I'd foolishly longed for dreams and visions thinking they would allow me to find Sarah Pee again, but they didn't.

"When the dreams stopped my life returned to normal and I had the urge to study law. My father was delighted at the news and within the year I was attending law school in Bangkok. The rest you know. How I met your mother and then later you were born."

It is hard for Tuum to think of his father different than he is now. He senses too that although his father doesn't say as much today that it was the accident and teaching Tuum again to walk that allowed his father to accept what had happened to Sarah Pee and gain the powers he has now. Before the accident, it seemed to Tuum that their life had been ordinary, but he realizes now that it was far from that and always had been so.

Tuum assumes his father is finished for the day, the story about Sarah Pee having been so exhausting to tell. But his father leans forward, even closer this time, and holds Tuum in his gaze for a moment and then slides a hand back and forth along the table to indicate he's not yet finished.

His father stops his hand directly in front of him and places the other flat beside it. He says that a year before the motorcycle accident he started to dream about Sarah Pee again. It was usually the same dream, where she was at the reins of a buffalo cart. She came up behind him and stopped beside him in the street and said hello. It was clear in the dream who she was but she didn't recognize him. She always asked him if he knew the way to the river. He always gave her the same, detailed instructions. She then thanked him and he always realized at that point that she was the same age she was when she died but he was a much older man.

The dream would always end with him watching her ride on ahead of him and turn at the next corner as he instructed her to. He didn't move from where he stood in the dream although he wanted more than anything to follow after her. The dream would not permit that.

The dreams worried him because he didn't know why they had begun. He didn't tell Tuum's mother about them and each day he'd wake from such a dream and his first instinct would be that he should tell her, but he couldn't bring himself to do it. The dreams stopped after the accident and he came to understand what they had been warning him about.

"I didn't seek this gift nor was it offered. It had been there all along, but I had to accept it and acknowledge it, as you must. Sometimes we must lose those we love so we can gain the love of those we have yet to meet."

Tuum thinks about Sarah Pee and the power of rain and lightning. He sees his father for the first time as a man in love. He admires him for accepting the life he'd eventually settled into without Sarah Pee. Tuum sees it as a good life whether his father sees it that way or not. He is a man of power because of losing Sarah Pee. But maybe he would have been happier and many miles away from here if she had lived.

His father stands and says: "That's all I have energy for today." He nods at Tuum and then backs to door and opens it, all the time facing his son, perhaps trying to gauge how his story has been received.

His father stops briefly in the open doorway and nods a second time and turns to leave, closing the door behind him. Tuum stays at the table and rests his hands on it. In the half light, he listens to the noises outside for hints of his father's presence there but hears no trace of him. It's as though his father has simply vanished on the other side of the door. Tuum feels for the first time that it is his father who is changing in these daily meetings not him. His father had looked so frail standing in the door just now as though any word Tuum uttered would have erased him from being.

It was as though his father had lifted the façade he'd lived behind for years and allowed Tuum to see his true self. As his father told him his story, the wrinkles on his cheeks and forehead became more pronounced.

When Tuum first arrived here, he'd been determined to leave as soon as possible but he wouldn't have heard this story or sensed how much his father needed to tell it. He also senses that there is more that his father is leading up to.

He has been willing to give up everything for his love for Roong including any chance to regain what he lost with his father. Now he knows that all of this is for his father's sake more than his, so how can he leave? It is his duty to stay. Once his father spent every waking hour helping him to walk again, now he must accompany his father to the very end of whatever this is.

He has focused on how much he is not like his father, but after hearing his father talk about Sarah Pee, Tuum realizes that he is much more like his father than he has believed.

When he finally gets up and leaves the little room, he doesn't close the door but hurries to his room to chant. He's already decided what he must do.

Later, he writes a short letter to Roong.

*May 15, 1970*

*My angel of angels:*

*Today my father told me of the origins of his gift, his mindfulness. It was a winding story and it surprised me with the many twists I didn't know about until now. My father loved someone before my mother. I don't know why that surprises me, but it does. I know he loved my mother but his first love was different. His story was powerful and sad, and that sadness tore at my core. There is too much to it for me to put in a letter so I will tell you in person when we are together again.*

*Forgive me my love but I must stay here a little longer. My father is leading up to something and it is my duty to hear him out.*

*I will be with you so very soon my love.*

*Phom Rak Khun*

*Tuum*
*xxxxoooooo*

# Chapter 10

## Chum Phae
## Present Day

Ed is simply awake and not due to any outward interruption. It is not yet daylight but there is enough vague light through the window to indicate morning is not far off. He practices stillness. Nan as told him that he must master this if he is to reach *Samadhi* like Run. When all movement stops, the false self falls away leaving only the inner self, the conscious, enlightened self—light and airy.

*Be still and know*, Nan has said. So has Run.

He tries to focus on each part of his body one by one and willing them to not move, not to even twitch or lean. But his mind remains a gaggle of thoughts that flit, collide, and careen. The more he focuses on his breathing, the more new thoughts are spawned. *This is love; this is not love. This is expansion; this not expansion. This is contraction; this is not contraction.*

"Be a conduit," Nan has suggested when trying to explain how she has learned to stop her mind. Become the outside rather than the inside. Deep in the heart of him is the outside; inside is everything else. He is everything but who he claims to be. *Samadhi* is the gateless gate, the pathless path, the edge of the bound self, the separate self, and means joining to the wider, greater self.

He gives up and slides out of the cot careful not to wake Nan. He tiptoes to the front door and opens it slowly and stretches in the early morning heat. The sun is a vague halo over the mountains to the north and east. He doesn't sit in a wicker chair but on the uneven wooden deck and crosses his legs. He closes his eyes and soon there is only his breathing in and out.

Images flash by and he stops those and goes back to his breathing, but more images appear and then others. The images are random and disconnected from each other. Some linger and others hurry past before he can make out what they are.

He is determined today to make a breakthrough, but try as he might, he can't get his mind to co-operate. It simply won't go still, and only slows down for a second or two and then speeds up again. At times the images come in such rapid fire that his mind glows even with his eyes closed.

There is a tap on his shoulder and he opens his eyes. Song is there and Ed wonders why he is here so early.

"*Gin Khao,*" (Eat) he says, and Ed realizes by how high the sun is that it's nearly noon.

His legs are numb when he tries to stand and has to lean on Song. They go inside and he expects to see Nan sleeping on the cot, but the cot is empty and made up.

He goes to the door and sees her working in the distance. He realizes that she has sent Song to get him. He gathers up some vegetables, rice, and water and takes them out to where Nan is working. Song walks beside him. They don't speak. The heat forms a tight pocket around him. He feels an internal stillness, calm—pure nothing.

His mind is always telling him stories, lying to him, creating cohesions he wishes to rip apart but fears that to do so would be to rip himself apart. He must let it all flow, become fluid. That sounds simple. He should have an easy time of it, but he isn't having an easy time. Part of him resists but what part is that? Or is it in his nature to resist? To be sceptical?

*To lie to oneself is to deny the self, to distance the self from the self and others,* Run has taught him.

He closes his eyes and Sutum is there. Not the *spirit* or even the once living Sutum but the figure he saw falling in the distance. Sutum falls and then the gunshot sounds and from a distance the two events occur in reverse order.

Then he and Song are kneeling beside Sutum, except now Sutum is not dead but is still breathing, his chest rises and falls rapidly as though he has been running.

Then Ed is Sutum and is running away. He hears the shot and waits to feel the bullet enter his flesh, but it doesn't, and he keeps running and believes by some miracle he can outrun the bullet. He runs until he is out of breath and collapses on the ground and feels around for a wound but there isn't any.

A week later, at the end of Song's nightly vigil, Song tells Nan: "*Set leaw,*" which means finished and then says: "*Dee.*" And she wais him and Ed does too, and Song nods and turns to leave and then turns back and speaks quickly to Nan in Isaan.

She nods a number of times, and when Song stops speaking, she speaks for several minutes. Ed tries to catch key words but they speak Isaan so he doesn't recognize many of the words until Song says: "*Pope gun my proong nee.*" (See you tomorrow.)

After Song drives away, Ed asks Nan what Song said and she says that the harvest will be finished in four more days.

"He also said that the police visited him today and informed him that Sutum's murderer has turned himself in. He has confessed to the killing and said he did it because Sutum had been in love with his wife. Song said that to himself tonight and it seemed to help Sutum to settle. Later Song sat with Sutum in the corner and when Song meditated he saw Sutum get up and dance and later he was riding his bicycle down the main street of a large village. Song didn't recognize the village. Later Song went to the window and prayed until the moonlight covered his hands. That is a good sign."

She lights a candle and puts it near the sink.

He doesn't ask why she does that or why the moonlight on Song's hands is a good sign. She lets the candle burn for an hour before she blows it out and they go to sleep.

The next day the long walk to the field tires him more than usual and as he works his back aches for the first time in weeks and stiffens significantly by the time they stop for lunch. Perhaps it is the knowledge that he only has four days of this left that causes his body to buckle. Whatever the cause, he aches more than usual and wonders if he has caught a virus.

At lunch, Nan and he discuss how best to conclude matters with Sutum before they finish harvesting the crop. He suggests that they call Run after dinner and stay on the phone longer than usual, as in the past week, Run has made significant progress with Sutum.

She agrees and says that Run told her a story last night that he wanted her to share with Ed today. The story is from the time when communists from Vietnam, Laos and Cambodia settled in the jungles of Northeast Thailand. Run hadn't explained the significance of the story to her but she says it will either make more sense in time for her or it is actually meant for Ed and not her.

It hasn't occurred to Ed until now that communists would have settled in Thailand but that idea intrigues him. He asks if there are still communist villages. She says the villages remain but the communists either died of old age or left.

"This isn't a communist country," she says. "Run told me how in one village a monk liked to carry around a gun and grenades. He felt it fashionable like the communists who had recently passed through his village.

"In that same village there was a good and wise monk who meditated by walking up and down the same seventy-metre path at least twice a day—in the morning and again just after dark. He walked very slowly, putting one foot in front of the other and saying *Put Dho* (Buddha) with each step. This was the same monk who had years earlier taught himself to stay alert while meditating by sitting in the lotus position at the very edge of a steep cliff. He would sit there for an hour or more without nodding off. If he ever had nodded off, he would've fallen to his death."

She describes how the communist monk had taken a disliking to the good and wise monk because the good and wise monk's goodness interfered with his communist goals. Events took a nasty turn the morning after a major earthquake struck Japan. The communist monk was one of the few in the village who owned a radio and the next day he'd told the villagers in great detail all the news about the earthquake that he'd heard reported on the radio, including specifics about damage to buildings and loss of life.

He went around the village asking everyone he met if they had heard the news about the earthquake and whenever they said they hadn't he'd proceed to relay to them all he'd heard on the radio. The good and wise monk said to the communist monk that he shouldn't focus on an earthquake so far away because there were earthquakes much closer that he needed to worry about. The good and wise monk said he could see that a quake had occurred inside the communist monk and that his good and bad side had split and his good side lay in rubble and his bad side remained intact. He said to the communist monk that he must attend to his personal split before it's too late. *Wherever you go you have a gun and grenade. That is far removed from the ways of a monk. Do not be seduced by fashion and political values. They are as transitory as the wind and rain.*

The good and wise monk often spoke in the village about how the law of action must guide each person in their lives and not any political doctrine no matter how enticing. He said that the world had not been made fairer by political ideologies. This angered the communist monk even more because to him the communist doctrine was more powerful and truthful than any religious doctrine.

For the good and wise monk, the journey of each soul wasn't confined by the demands of any political system. All souls are on a journey to *enlightenment* and that journey has no political objective.

Because of these powerful differences, the communist monk decided that action was necessary. The good and wise monk had become his spiritual adversary. He knew of the monk's daily practice of pacing as he meditated so that made him an easy target.

On a hot and muggy May evening as the good and wise monk meditated, he heard a grenade go off a hundred metres to his right. He wondered who had caused that explosion. He closed his eyes and focused very deeply in his meditation as he walked. This allowed him to see in his mind's eye that the communist monk had thrown the grenade and that he was now hiding in the grass and was creeping toward him with another grenade. He watched the communist monk approach, but the good and wise monk continued to pace and ignored him as he was protected by the power of his meditation. When the communist monk was close enough, he threw the second grenade, but it didn't explode. The good and wise monk reached down and picked up the grenade and withdrew an elastic band from his robe, and with his free hand, he tied the elastic around the grenade to hold the striker lever in place and keep it from going off.

The good and wise monk said: "A child has left a toy here. To whom does this toy belong?"

The communist monk ran off, and the good and wise monk held the grenade and continued his meditation until he was done. He took the grenade home with him that evening and left it on his table as he slept.

The next morning after practicing *Sati,* he took the grenade from his table and walked it to the temple where the communist monk lived. He knocked politely at the door to the communist monk's room. When the communist monk opened the door, the good and wise monk handed him the grenade and said: "Here is your toy back. When you were playing you dropped it. It is not my business to return toys as I have much to do, but here is yours this one time."

The communist monk shook violently and would not accept the grenade at first, but the good and wise monk thrust it more insistently and forced him to take it. The good and wise monk then turned and walked back to his own temple.

The communist couldn't stop shaking. His face turned yellow with fear and he took to bed. Within an hour he had a high fever, which lasted many days. He didn't speak to anyone, not even to the young novice monk who brought him water and food each day.

After the sixth day of much meditation, the fever finally broke. When it did, he sat up in bed although it was the middle of the night. In the dark he did more *Sati* hand exercises to calm himself. That evening he returned to the good and wise monk's temple and waited for the good and wise monk.

When the good and wise monk had completed his meditation, the communist monk asked him to forgive him for what he had done.

The good and wise monk said: "I forgive you, so for us, person to person, the karma between us is now completed. However, if you continue in your way and do bad things to others this will not absolve you. Nor does it absolve you from any evil you have already done to others. Do not forsake Buddhist practices to gain political advantage or upheaval. You must not lose sight of religious discipline. The law of action binds you and me and all others. Having a gun and grenade doesn't improve your lot in that regard. Every day you must be a good monk and act only with kindness."

Despite the good and wise monk's willingness to forgive the communist monk, he had already done so much harm with others that he soon took sick again and was confined most days to his bed. He couldn't walk without the help of others. He spent his last decade being sickly and eventually died at home. By the time he died, he could no longer leave his bed or do more than sit up. Young monks had to feed him every meal.

After he died, villagers asked the good and wise monk how high a level of heaven had the communist monk gone to.

The good and wise monk said: "Don't ask how high he went or to what level of heaven but ask how low."

Villagers then asked him to what level of hell the monk had gone and the good and wise monk said: "Those who are mentally restless, like a runner with a torch, will only stop when the torch goes out."

Nan says: "Run told me that the good and wise monk is still alive today and never makes any mention of the communist monk and what he did. That story has been left for others to tell and read about."

Run and Ed have never spoken about the Vietnam War and Ed was born after it ended. But his father had marched in antiwar protests in Stanley Park and years later showed Ed pictures he'd taken of the crowd holding placards.

When Ed had asked his father about the purpose of the protests he'd said: "Most wars are unnecessary and are based on lies. They claim to be about freedom, but most are not. They are about doctrine and exaggerated differences. Wars have aftermaths. That is their true and crucial context, their legacy."

Ed had never shared any of this with Run, so this makes his story all the more significant to Ed.

Run has somehow discovered another of Ed's cogs. But he also suspects that Run's story means that matters with Sutum are drawing to a close. He gathers that from the clue of the elastic band. The smallest of items is able to stop mighty calamities.

Nan returns to work and he joins her. From where they are cutting, he is only metres now from where Song's land and crop ends. When he glances back, he sees the openness of the trimmed land. He sees too the spot where Sutum fell, now far in the distance. In a week or so, Song will plough all this under, including there, and get ready for the next crop.

Later when they shake off the rice tops onto the tarp, the wind picks up and the corners of the tarp flap about forcing him and Nan to secure them with heavy stones.

After they have shaken enough rice on the tarp, they fold it from each of the four corners and tie all four lines in the middle. Later, Song will come with his tractor and wagon and lift the tied tarp into the wagon.

That evening, when they return to the hut, their footsteps sound extra loud on the wooden steps. Nan goes in ahead of him and he remains at the top of the steps, his back to a slight breeze. The jagged grains of the wooden door appear enhanced, oddly highlighted by the angle of the afternoon sun. He feels better than he did this morning. The work has energized him.

Nan opens the door and asks if he is coming in. As soon as he crosses the threshold, he senses a significant change inside.

## Chapter 11

## *Chum Phae*
## *1970*

His father meets him in the little room as before but says that today he prefers to do a meditation walk. Once on the main courtyard, his father lifts one foot on the intake of breath and places it down a short distance ahead on the exhale and then does the same with the other foot. His intakes are longer than his exhales and it takes Tuum several paces to adapt to this rhythm. When he catches on, he keeps pace with his father, but stays two steps back.

It takes them nearly a half hour to make one full circle of the temple grounds. On the way they pass the largest of three gardens where five novices are busy attending to rows of vegetables. After that garden, they walk on the brick lane alongside the high cement wall on the north side that separates the temple grounds from the three-story row houses in the street beyond. At the northeast corner, they pass the temple toilets and showers and then progress along the east side where two smaller gardens catch morning sun. One monk works in each of those. The second of those gardens is dedicated to flowers and currently lotuses and morning glories are in bloom.

When they arrive at the front gate, a woman and her daughter offer baskets brimming with rice to A. Tuum stops to watch, and when he turns back, his father is now five paces ahead, but he soon catches up.

Thick bushes line the west wall and in front of that are a few cement benches. He expects his father to pick one and rest, but he continues around a second time. Tuum feels an ache in each calf from the slow pace. His hands swell as he walks, and he opens and closes them to improve circulation.

The third time around his father stops at the toilets and uses one and Tuum uses another. When he emerges, his father is sitting on a nearby bench. He joins his father and suggests they move to the main gate where the breeze will carry the odours of fresh flowers.

"Here will do," his father says. He pulls his legs up into the lotus position and closes his eyes.

Tuum does the same except he drops his head slightly. While he has his eyes closed and his head lowered for better concentration, his father speaks.

"We think of the sun and wind as eternal, but they are not nor did Buddha ever say they were. Each day is perfect in that it contains only what it can contain, nothing extra. There's nothing missing nor is anything superfluous. A day is as perfect a whole as there is and each day that follows is equally perfect. That is what Buddha teaches us. We must accept each day for exactly what it is, and what happens during it and to expect nothing more. Like an egg is whole so is a day whole. Still that perfection is not to be taken for granted. You can open your eyes now. We're here." He says this as though they have been walking rather than sitting on the bench.

"So far I've told you my stories but now I will tell yours."

"Mine?" Tuum asks, for how can his father tell his story? It isn't his to tell.

"We had you later in life and now you know why. When your mother was pregnant, I worried that I was too old to be a father but your mother was much wiser and said that I was a fool to entertain such thoughts. I am thankful now that she set me right. You were not an easy child. Every night for the first six years you woke your mother and me with your cries after some nightmare. Years later I came to understand that those nightmares meant that my gift had also manifested in you. When I discovered this, I said nothing to you or your mother and I should have.

"When you were seven, the nightmares stopped or at least you stopped waking us because of them. Before then, you would recount your nightmares and ask us what they meant. I would always be unsure what to tell you, but your mother would come up with a positive interpretation for each of them. Her explanations calmed you and you were able to go back to sleep. I then believed her interpretations were necessary parental fabrications but understand now that she'd been right. I thought then that she was too easy on you and allowed you to believe that the world is a good and kind place. If left to me, I wouldn't have been so gentle or positive with you because I thought you needed to know the harsh truths. Your mother understood better than I, the deep roots in each life."

His father unfolds his legs and refolds them again and shifts his position so his back is straighter. He then inches back in the bench until he is nearly touching the cement wall of the building. His father's breathing is louder at this angle and Tuum notices how raspy and clogged it sounds.

"Your mother loved you more than she loved me. Until you learned to walk again after the accident, she would encourage me every day to do more, to try harder and she kept me motivated even on those days I was ready to give up. At first, I doubted that you would ever walk again, but she always believed that you would and insisted I never doubt that.

"When you finally were able to walk once more on your own, I foolishly thought all of our past karmic feuds and curses had been settled. I know now that such a state doesn't exist except through enlightenment.

"In the first year after the accident, she doted on you and chanted many hours every day. When you finally walked again, her disposition sweetened even more than it had been after you were born. I know those final three years she was truly happy. I was happy too and thought that we could finally put that accident behind us. That was my ego letting me foolishly pretend. I felt such complete joy seeing you hurry downstairs and out into the street. On those afternoons you would go to the field across the street and run around it, following the same route you could barely walk a year earlier. I'd watch you and believe that your mother's and my chanting and daily efforts had paid off.

"In the weeks after you could walk on your own, whenever I meditated, I would see this most gorgeous blue light. I took that as a sign that the days were made whole again. But the wholeness of a day means that it also includes the events and outcomes we would prefer it not contain. We don't make the days whole nor does a day's wholeness rely on what we wish or do not wish for."

His father tells him that the first day that his mother's illness manifested he'd been called away early in the morning to help a rice farmer who'd lost half his crop due to heavy flooding from a recent monsoon. The farmer needed his advice on what to do to save the rest of his crop.

"I suppose I should have blamed that rice farmer and the monsoon for calling me away on that day. Not that my being home would have changed any of it. Still in the months afterward I convinced myself that if I had been home that day that I would have been there to block evil from entering her. By the time I got back it had already fully taken hold of her."

His father tells him how all that morning he walked the rice farmer's last unharvested field and assured him that his best course of action was not to harvest the crop now as he had planned to do but to wait another week. He assured him that in that time the crop he had left would be of premium quality and he would in fact receive more money than he would have for the full crop otherwise. The farmer thanked him and gave him five bags of fine rice from the previous year's harvest.

On his way home, he'd allowed himself to feel pride in helping the farmer and because of that pride he hadn't hurried.

"When I reached home, my throat tightened on the first step, and by the time I'd reached the top step, I leaned over panting to catch my breath and thought that the pork I'd eaten at the rice farm had been spoiled. I waited for your mother to open the door as she usually did, sensing my arrival in advance. But not that day. I thought then the two of you had gone out so I opened the door and, as soon as I stepped inside, I was hit by a blast of heated air. Your mother always found a way to keep the house cool even on the hottest days. I began to feel uneasy.

"I heard you say *help* even though you assured me later that you hadn't spoken. Then I heard gasps mixed with even louder sobs that appeared to be coming from the living room. I hurried there expecting to find you both. I thought perhaps you had fallen and injured your legs again. But the living room was empty. I called out but got no answer and decided that, as I had thought before, the two of you had gone out. I went to the kitchen to wash my hands and noticed that the dishes from breakfast were still in the sink. That's when I knew I was wrong. I returned to the living room and went upstairs. As I neared the top, I heard more gasps."

Tuum remembers his father appearing suddenly in the doorway. He was sitting in a chair next to his mother's bed and had placed a damp cloth on her forehead as she'd asked him to. He'd looked up from his mother and his father was there.

His father asked what was wrong and his mother told him not to worry that she'd felt a bit tired and hot and had come up to lie down and rest. She said that she'd be fine in a few minutes. His father asked about the cloth and she'd said she'd felt a bit feverish.

Later when she attempted to get out of bed, she lost her balance and his father caught her just in time. He carried her downstairs and Tuum followed behind. He remembers now how tightly knotted his stomach had felt.

His father laid his mother on the couch in the living room and hurried into the street. He reappeared a few minutes later with several men and someone improvised a stretcher from a closet door. More people came into the house and a large group helped slide her onto the door and his father held her hand as others carried her outside and set her gingerly into the back of a truck that someone had backed up nearly to the front steps. His father got up into the back with her and Tuum too.

At the hospital his mother perked up and she sat up on the emergency bed and talked cheerily to the doctor and nurse that attended to her. His father and he sat with her, each on opposite sides of the narrow bed. Tuum remembers how noisy and confusing the hospital had been.

"I sensed then holding her hand that the news would not be good. I didn't say that to you or to her. I made eye contact with her often, but I couldn't look over at you. I had no idea what you were thinking, nor did I ask.

"I'd realized at that moment that all the feuds in past lives weren't settled or mended after the accident as I had thought. This was another continuation. She whispered in my ear then that all three of us should chant and that then I should to take you home. She didn't want you to be there when the doctors delivered their diagnosis. I didn't realize it then and wouldn't figure it out until much later that she'd known for months that she wasn't well. She'd hid it from me. She could be very stoic. We chanted as she'd asked and then you and I walked home."

Tuum doesn't remember the chanting or the walk home. What he does remember is his father standing in the living room as he sat on the couch and his farther saying that he needed to return to the hospital and asking if Tuum was okay on his own. He remembers feeling a thrill of pride at his father's words and answering that he would be fine. His father had then assured him that he'd bring his mother home in a few hours. He didn't return until the next morning and came alone.

"It took doctors a full day to find her cancer. It had started in her breast, they said, but by the time they saw her, it had spread to her liver and kidneys. I asked how someone so young could have cancer. The attending doctor said cancer grows faster in the young. He didn't say anything about karma and the law of action, but I knew he was likely thinking about that too, but it wasn't for a doctor to speak that way. He said it was best that your mother stayed in the hospital, that she would get the around the clock care she needed. He warned me that her decline would be rapid.

"I sat with her at the hospital every day for a week. She said she didn't want you to visit because she couldn't bear for you to see her that way. I insisted that you should. We chanted about that and after two hours she agreed to let you visit once more."

Tuum remembers that visit vividly because it was the last time he saw his mother alive. He rode there on the back of his father's motorcycle. He hadn't done that since the accident but did so that day. He expected the ride to trigger more memories of the accident, but it didn't and all the way there he held onto the flimsy hope that his visit would help his mother get better and she'd come home.

His mother waied him when he arrived. She'd never done that before and he'd thought that peculiar but waied her back. His father did the same. She was propped up in bed by pillows on both sides of her. When he sat beside her bed, they were at eye level.

Her face looked drained of blood and her eyes were puffy and red. He remembers her saying: *Listen to your father.* He doesn't remember anything else she said. He didn't stay long and by the time he left, she had slipped from the sitting position and lay on her back. She attempted to raise her head to say goodbye but couldn't. Her voice was so weak he barely heard her.

His father returned to the hospital that evening and he remembers wandering the house alone and how empty and scary it felt. He was fifteen and he felt older than that most days but not when he was alone in the house.

"She was lucid the day before she died and made me promise to be a good father and never to ask for an explanation as to what happened to her but to accept that karma was more powerful than any of us. She was much wiser than me but despite her wishes I want you to know now what I learned after she died. A hundred and fifty years ago, she and her husband had grown coffee on a steep mountainside plot in the far north. She had two children a boy and a girl and twice they successfully hid in the nearby forest and escaped invading armies from Burma as they passed near their farm. However, a retreating Burmese army surprised them a few days later. They killed her husband but left her and the two children alive. After the soldiers killed her husband, they slept that night in her house. During the night, she snuck out her children and then set fire to the house and padlocked the doors from the outside. The soldiers woke up too late and each screamed terribly as they died. All those years later, they'd finally found her and exacted revenge. I don't doubt that sometime in the future she will do the same to them again. I've decided against her wishes that you need to know that. I am sorry now for not telling you sooner and I ask for your forgiveness."

Tuum takes a large gulp of air and he feels his chest swell and then tighten. The anger he has felt all these years towards his father had risen up again when he was forced to come here even though his father had done the near impossible for Roong.

But it is not in him to deny his father forgiveness and says he forgives him. The words come easier than he's ever imagined they might. As soon as he says them, he is unable to move, can't feel his legs or arms.

His lungs go on filling up and emptying, but his whole body feels at a complete standstill.

Tuum takes a deep inhale and finally says: "On the day she died, I had been chanting for her at the dining table and when I finished I heard her call my name so clearly that I looked around expecting that she'd somehow snuck into the house and was standing behind me.

"When I saw she wasn't there, I thought I had simply imagined her voice. But then a moment or two later I heard heavy thumps in the kitchen and then a loud snap followed by a dull smack like meat on the counter. That was followed by a long scream. It was her screaming. I am certain of that. I panicked and ran from room to room, but she wasn't anywhere. I opened the front door of the house and she wasn't there either. A woman laughed somewhere down the block. I closed the door and the house was completely quiet. I returned to the dining table and listened but heard nothing. An hour later you returned home and told me that she'd died.

"At the time your words sounded so impossible I didn't believe you and wanted to tell you that you were mistaken and that I had just heard her somewhere in the house. I only realized years later that all those noises I heard that day were in my head."

"I am sorry that I told you that news so abruptly that day. I'd only left her and was so emotionally rattled. I didn't know then what I would learn later. So, on that day, I'd been convinced that her death had been a karmic mistake and if I retraced everything that had happened in the past months I would find when the mistake had occurred and rectify it, and then she'd return as though nothing had happened. I didn't truly understand then how impossible it is to get free once you are trapped by a karmic feud. Nor did I understand yet how dark powers catapult forward from one life to another.

"Nobody is safe from such feuds and curses except through strict daily practice, and even then, it is at best fifty-fifty, as most often we learn the karmic consequences too late. Perhaps if I had been more focused on our karmic pasts than on developing and using my powers, I might have been able to break her karmic before it was too late. Since your mother's death I have done that very thing for many strangers.

"After she died, and I saw you sitting so expectantly at the table wishing for good news, I knew instantly that I had kept you in the dark too long. Perhaps that is why I told you the way I did. I thought I was coming clean to you, but I wasn't. I'd been too harsh."

Tuum hadn't thought his father harsh or cruel that day but he'd thought of Buddha as cruel. He'd blamed Buddha for his mother's death, not his father. His mother had been the kindest person he'd known, and she was dead, so he blamed that on kindness too. He didn't share those thoughts with his father then nor does he now. His father and mother had nursed him back after the accident. He couldn't betray that then or now.

The loss of his mother should have brought him closer to his father but instead it drove them farther apart.

"After she died, my powers grew exponentially, and I've often wondered if somehow that is her doing. Let us walk," his father says and rises from the bench. He circles the temple in the opposite direction from before, walking even more slowly.

Tuum walks side by side with him now. His shoulders and upper body feel looser and with each step his whole body lightens, and he barely feels the ground.

They circle the courtyard three times and don't speak until his father stops at the front gate of the temple and says: "Sorry"—and then wais him three times before he departs. His father has never said that before nor waied him three times.

Tuum watches his father go, and when he is ten metres from the temple, he stops. Tuum expects him to turn around, come back maybe to say something that he's forgotten. But instead, he remains standing in the middle of a crowd passing both ways. People have to weave around him to avoid bumping into him. They always stop to wai him before they pass. Tuum doesn't know if his father is in some physical distress and if he should go to his assistance. Just when he decides that he should, his father continues in the direction of home. As he walks, he favours his right leg a little and leans slightly that way as he walks.

Tuum watches him for a moment or two longer and then his father disappears from view. Tuum returns to his room and sits on his cot and thinks about the letter he'll write to Roong about all this. How exactly will he tell her about what has happened? He knows above all else that everything has changed between his father and him. They are again as they were after the accident. He isn't sure how that is possible and can't say fully all that has changed or what that change means. What he knows for certain is that everything is different now between them.

When he has thought all this through, he goes to the desk and writes to Roong.

*May 17, 1970*

*My angel of angels:*

*Today my father told me about when my mother died. I hadn't heard his perspective before and that version was devastating. He then asked me to forgive him and I did. In a flash all has changed between us.*

*This is not the end but merely the beginning. Now I am grateful to have come here even though it has kept you and I apart. I sense that next my father will talk about the accident. I must stay for that.*

*Then I will be truly free to return to you.*

*Phom Rak Khun*

*Tuum*
*xxxxooooo*

# Chapter 12

## Chum Phae
## Present Day

THE HARVESTING GOES well the next day and near lunchtime Ed stops working and his mind feels clear. Everything in view is more vivid and detailed. In particular, the afternoon sun enhances the mountains to the north. He notices that what he's mistaken for one mountain is in fact three and each has varying shades of green beneath the bluest of skies and billowing, grey clouds.

For lunch, Nan sets out two bowls of rice and two plates of stir-fried vegetables: broccoli, carrots, cabbage, baby corns, and cauliflower. She has chopped in boiled eggs too.

As they eat, she tells him that Run says that Sutum is ready to jump. "That means you've been a good signal and have attracted what you needed to attract."

An hour after lunch, a flock of chestnut-tailed starlings appears and they land on the piles of harvested rice on the tarp. They peck at the rice, feeding greedily.

Ed runs in their direction waving his arms to scare them off. At first, they ignore him but when he is close enough, they scatter into the air. In unison they circle overhead several times, and he expects them to land again somewhere nearby and feed more, but instead they fly straight north.

When he turns back to Nan, she stands watching him. Both her hands are behind her back. He approaches and she does not move until he hugs her and then she hugs him back.

"I love you and you are a good man," she says. "But those birds—"

He realizes now without her saying it, that scaring them off was not a good idea. The karmic ramifications of such an action are beyond his comprehension.

"Should I have left them?"

"Yes. They will eat for a little while and then fly away."

"Won't they just attract more birds?"

"We will have bagged up this rice before anymore show up. This is how it is. How it has always been. It is best not to disturb the birds. Let them eat. They will only take a little."

They return to their work. His body soon aches from the bending and cutting but the aches anchor him in ways they hadn't before yesterday. He feels oddly released and seeing the birds go he realizes too that Sutum has gone. The swiftness of that thought surprises him as does the certainty of it but he keeps it to himself.

He discovers that he has stopped working. In one hand he holds a fistful of rice, but his scythe remains still in his other hand. He has no idea how long he has been frozen like this. He admonishes himself for losing track and not staying focused on his work. Such inattention and lack of mindfulness can result in injury. The perils of living are not changed by *Sati,* but his attentiveness can be improved.

He senses Nan at his side and turns to watch her. She moves even more gracefully than earlier, and he notices a musical fluidness to her movements. She is as fully mindful as Song. Being so, makes her as completely human as the birds earlier are completely birds.

She smiles at him and continues to work, and he does the same, cutting through the bunch of rice he is holding. And then he grips another fistful and cuts through it with one slice of the scythe. He drops each bunch behind him in a row with the others.

They will collect those up later in a pushcart, and when the cart is full, they will wheel it to the blue tarp and beat the rice stocks there creating a fresh pile of rice next to the existing one. When that pile is large enough, they will bind up the tarp. There are more modern methods that other farmers use. But Nan says that Song has harvested rice this way his whole life and believes that the rice is not pure and special unless it is done this way.

More starlings appear but this flock is smaller. He lets them feed and they do so as greedily as the others. He tries not to focus on them as he works and waits as Nan has suggested.

The more he works the more he stops thinking about the birds. Later when he looks up from his work, they're gone.

A while later, more birds arrive. These are not starlings, and a breed he doesn't recognize. He lets them feed too. They eat more quickly than the starlings and are soon gone.

The sun is about to set so he and Nan gather up the last stalks of rice in the pushcart and wheel them to the tarp and shake those too and then wrap up the tarp. Song will collect the tarp tonight.

It is dark when they reach the hut.

He follows Nan up the steps and into the hut. The inside is thick with heat so he leaves the front door open. Nan turns around once in the room, and although it is dark and he can't properly see, he catches the reflection of her eyes in the limited light and recognizes that she too senses that Sutum is gone—must have known when he did out in the field.

He glimpses random images at first: A jeep rolls backwards down a hill and simply disappears from view. No one is in the jeep. A gymnast has a bad fall. Then a camel appears in a desert. The camel has no rider and he follows a few paces behind it. He is amazed at how tall the animal is and how quickly it moves through porous sand. His feet sink ankle deep into the sand with each step and he soon falls behind. The camel vanishes ahead of him and he sees flashes of snow and then a helicopter landing on a sunny day in the middle of a city but that disappears too, gone before he has time to recognize the city.

His head is empty then and he hears where he is in the middle of his chant and wonders how he managed to get there so quickly without hearing any of the words.

He sees a man standing under an umbrella in a hot sun and a young boy on the back of a motorcycle, a field in the hills with a water buffalo tied to a large tamarind tree. The man returns and is holding a bicycle but not riding it. This is the man in his earlier dream except now he is taller and thinner. He is in the middle of a rice paddy and judging by his clothes and the bicycle it is a different time from now. No one is working the field and the rice is young still, barely four inches high. His feet are bare, and he is swatting at flies or mosquitoes. He faces Ed and is speaking but there is no sound. Then he sits in the shade and Ed realizes they are now outside his and Nan's hut, but it's a different time. The man looks up at a flock of chestnut-tailed starlings, stands, and instantly vanishes. Ed walks up the wooden stairs of the hut but the entrance is now a large pair of mahogany doors that open and lead to jail cells. Ed enters one of the cells as it becomes a hospital room where the woman from his dream sits up in bed and is talking to someone behind him. He notices that she is wearing an ornate silk blouse and thinks how odd that is for a woman in a hospital bed. He turns to see to whom she is talking and is now entering a house. The house is cool and smells of jasmine and something else he doesn't recognize, perhaps food, perhaps not. He follows a short hallway to a study full of books and a desk stacked with neatly arranged binders. The study and house are empty, but now he hears people talking. He turns and sees the man and woman at a large metal table. There are other similar tables in the room and four people sit at each table. The woman is dressed in blue prisoner's garb. They face each other and the woman is crying and talking but Ed can't make out what she is saying. They sit perpendicular to Ed, so he sees them both in profile.

Ed becomes aware of his breathing and how slow it is and realizes he is still chanting.

He opens his eyes and Nan's eyes are closed as she continues to meditate. He doesn't disturb her but lies back and watches her and listens to the slowness of her breathing.

For another hour she meditates and does not move from that position. He stays motionless but doesn't chant anymore.

When he wakes hours later, it is still dark. If he has dreamed, he has no memory of it. The heat has dissipated a little, but he is sweating. He rises to pee and get a drink of water. His bare feet slap on the wood floor so he tiptoes so as not to wake Nan. He hears the rat burrowing in the roof. He accepts that there will always be a rat in the thatched roof trying to work a way inside.

He goes out into the night and sits in a wicker chair and studies the full moon. It is so full it looks swollen, even about to burst near the horizon. It is grey the way the moon is often grey but tonight it also has a yellow halo. He sits perfectly still with his eyes wide open and fixes on the moon as it slips bit by bit below the horizon. When it has completely gone, he gets up and goes in and back to the cot. He falls asleep right away and soon dreams that he is running naked in snow.

# Chapter 13

## *Chum Phae 1970*

His father doesn't appear at the temple the following day or the day after that. At first, this doesn't alarm Tuum and he welcomes a break from the intensity of their talks. Still he is keen to take up again from their last conversation, as clearly his father is working up to the accident. He meditates and sees a path through a thick bamboo wood. His father and he are walking side by side on the path. They are very far ahead from his vantage point and their backs are to him. He's not moving as they move and in no time, they are specks in the distance, surrounded by various shades of leaning green.

Tuum assumes that his father has been called away to help someone, so he uses the time to write more letters to Roong and explain in detail the breakthrough that has happened.

The more stories his father has told him the more difficult it is for him to leave without his father's blessing. His father now is not the distant father when Tuum's mother died but the caring, attentive father he'd been after the accident, the one who carried his son on his back until he could walk again.

His father has a truer heart than Tuum had believed before coming here and his father's sudden absence forces Tuum to examine his earlier feelings toward him and reconnect with what he'd felt as a boy for his father. He's still eager to be with Roong but is certain his father will allow that soon.

On the first afternoon of his father's absence, he meditates for a long time but that comes to nothing until the very end when he sees a little girl walking with a dog beside a road. It must be a long time ago because most people are walking, and a few ride horses and others are in wagons pulled either by horses or water buffaloes. The girl is talking to the dog but in a language Tuum doesn't understand although she is clearly Thai. The images don't last for long but near the end he sees a horse gallop by and the rider of the horse swoops down and grabs the dog by the collar and keeps riding ahead. The young girl waves her arms and screams after the horse but it soon vanishes around a bend in the road.

He breaks from this meditation and makes a note of what he's seen. He knows as he writes that it is Roong in another life. How long ago he can't say, nor can he say for sure if she is the girl or dog or the man on the horse, but she is one of them.

He considers describing that in a letter to Roong but decides it will be too difficult for him to fully convey in a letter the deeper meanings of what he's just seen. He decides that he will tell her in person.

Instead, he writes of his love for her and how it has deepened here and how the closeness he now feels with his father will make it possible for them to be even closer too. *It works like that*, his father would say. He tells her about his father's absence and that it will delay him a little longer, because he is confident that his father will be back soon. He urges her to be patient. Soon they will be together and this time they will be free to go wherever they wish.

On the third day of his father's absence, Tuum returns to the small room in the afternoon and sits across from his father's empty chair and places his hands flat on the table and lets the room's heat and stuffiness engulf him and hold him here. He sits for two hours and then stands and hurries to his room. He leaves the door open so that any breeze will air out the room and cool it. He can breathe more freely when he is in his room and sits on his cot and meditates easily despite all the daytime noises in the hall.

After the fourth day of his father's absence, he asks Kay if he's heard from his father and Kay says: "Your father is needed many in places, but I'll make inquiries if you wish."

Tuum tells him that that isn't necessary.

That afternoon in the small room alone he meditates and sees, after a time, a water buffalo walking along the side of a road. There are no people around it nor any traffic, just the buffalo. As soon as he fully senses what the image is, it fades, and his head stays dark. The water buffalo is likely his father in a past life. *That is my gift manifesting in you*, his father's voice says now in Tuum's thoughts.

When he finally opens his eyes, it is already evening and he has been meditating for several hours. It is fully dark when he returns to his room.

By the seventh day, Tuum has become quite concerned about his father's absence. He again seeks out Kay and finds him in a lotus position at the very back of the *Phra Ubosot* (ordination or main hall of the temple). He takes the same position behind Kay and waits.

Two hours later Kay stands and wais Buddha. Tuum does the same, and then he follows Kay to the main doors of the *Phra Ubosot*. Once they are outside, Tuum asks about his father. Kay says he has not heard anything more and is insistent that he will make further inquiries. Tuum says he would like that and thanks him.

It is already late in the afternoon, but he returns to the small room. It is so hot inside that he leaves the door open and sits in his usual chair but at first is unable to focus. When he finally does, he drops into a deep meditation and for the longest time has no sensation of his body except for his nearly stopped breathing. There are no sounds.

When the dark of his head brightens with a dim yellow glow, he sees a beehive, and a large swarm of bees circles above it. A boy stands perfectly still in the middle of the swarm. The bees flit and swirl around the boy but don't light on him. The boy remains perfectly still and doesn't raise his arms and flap them around in self-defence. A few bees land on his neck and shoulders but most buzz around him. The swarm swells in size and then elongates and drifts away from him for a time and then drifts back without breaking formation.

They then circle his chest and shoulders but none of them attack. Instead they frantically dive and dart close to him but veer away from him without touching him. Tuum expects the boy to run away, but instead he passes a metal object from one hand to the other. Tuum focuses on that object but can't make it out until boy turns to face him and he recognizes his father at ten. The metal object he is holding is a gun. Tuum opens his eyes immediately and without the usual slow return to consciousness. He stands and vacates the room without so much as a glance back.

That evening there is a soft rap at his door. When he opens it, Kay is there.

"You have a visitor," he says and waves for Tuum to follow. Nong is waiting for him at the main gate. She doesn't advance any farther into the temple. His chest tightens at the sight of her and he stops.

Kay continues until he reaches Nong and turns to face Tuum along with Nong. Tuum stays a moment longer where he is and then wais them and approaches.

"I'm sorry," she says. "Your father thought he only had a cold. But it turned out to be pneumonia and a very aggressive form. He caught it while on a vigil in a rice field in the northern mountains."

Now that she's talking, he wants her to stop. He wants to go back to that small room and find his father waiting there.

"He held on for three days and said he would be fine and didn't wish to worry you," she says. "He died an hour ago."

She then says in two days his father's body will be brought to the temple to be prepared. She wais him and leaves and walks away with her head down. His father never spoke to him of how he met Nong and he wonders if that was also one of the stories he was leading up to.

He doesn't return to his room but goes to the small one. Once there, he sits in his chair and doesn't move for the longest time. Then without really thinking about it, he closes his eyes and chants for his father's soul to make a speedy jump to a new body.

*May 26, 1970*

*My angel of angels:*

*My father died yesterday. It's hard for me to write those words and I have put off writing this letter for a whole day. I shake often and have to lie on the cot in this room to calm myself. When Nong told me the news yesterday my legs nearly buckled but somehow, I managed to hold myself up until she departed. Afterward all I could think to do was go back to that little room. I sat there alone and imagined him across from me. I chanted for his soul and later spoke aloud to him for nearly two hours. I have no idea where the words came from, but they continued to spill out unprompted. I told him stories, thanked him for all he'd done and told him how it felt when he carried me on his back on the field all those years ago. Then as quickly as the words started, they stopped, and I then chanted again. Not to myself, though, but aloud and for a long time.*

*When I finally finished, I was saddened to realize how easy it was to talk to my father now that he was dead and how easily the truth came to me then. I hurried back to my room. I know I passed people as I went but they were invisible to me.*

*The noises of monks coming and going outside my room seemed louder than usual. But those noises comforted me in ways they hadn't before. As I sat on my cot, I felt my father around me, in every litre of air in every noise and smell in the room—none of them his.*

*These weeks here with him have changed me for the good, I think. I can't yet articulate or explain the specifics of those changes, but I understand all the same that they have occurred, and I am sure you will notice too.*

*I remember your story of when your father died and only now do I understand the full extent of that pain. I chanted all morning for your father and my father, for your mother and my mother before writing this, and even then, I was unable to stop these words from stirring my thoughts.*

*I hope you will be pleased by the changes in me when I return. Much of what I know and feel now, I would have thought impossible before coming here. I am thankful for my time here even though it has kept me from you.*

*At least now I will be returning to you soon.*

*My father's spirit is here and has already made himself known. I don't doubt that he will travel with me.*

*I love you now more powerfully than I ever have and am eager to be with you, but I must remain here a few more days to make merit for my father. I am numb tonight and it will be some time before I can sleep.*

*I will write again a day or so before I depart to let you know that I am on my way. Your last letter reached me yesterday and I was happy to hear that you are thriving away from that house, even if the days pass slowly without me as you say. Once we are together again we will marry.*

*When I am in the deepest of meditations, I've had glimpses of us standing in the blue waters of the Gulf of Thailand. There are often many noisy gulls flying around us and sometimes I get a whiff of salty air.*

*Tonight, I will think of you often and that will strengthen me against what will be a long night.*

*My father was a great man with many gifts and now that he is gone I wish I had acknowledged that more and told him that, instead of just listening to him with wilfully deaf ears. There is much I would like to ask him now that I can't. I have his spirit to contend with and I will have much to tell him but that will be a one-sided conversation. There is much more I need to tell you but that must wait until we are together again.*

*Phom Rak Khun*

*Tuum*
*xxxxxxoooooo*

He wakes at first light, dresses quickly and sits on his cot in a lotus position to meditate. There are hurried footsteps in the hall. Those will be from Pin and Won attending to his father's body brought during the night. All night they and 21 other monks have sat with his body and chanted. They will chant for four days and four nights.

For the next four mornings he meditates for two hours before morning alms. On the fifth morning, when he wakes, he sits in the lotus position and meditates, but the noisy preparations underway make it difficult for him to concentrate.

At first, he sees a swirling light that shifts from blue to grey and then back to blue. That changes to yellow and then green and then back to blue, but this time the blue is the blue of sky on the clearest summer's day. Eventually that blue darkens, and he sees below him a water buffalo. *This too he takes to be his father in a past life.* It has stopped in the middle of a shallow river. The water flows around it and under it and is only as high as its belly. It raises its head to bellow but no sounds come out.

Tuum hears the noisy rush of water but doesn't hear any sounds from the buffalo. The current isn't strong enough to cause the animal any stress. The water quietly gurgles around it and the buffalo remains indifferent to the water. The opposite riverbank is steep and bamboo trees as tall as a house line the bank above. The very tops of those trees sway slightly, and he hears the hollow tap of bamboo stocks striking each other. The bank is steep enough that the buffalo couldn't possibly scramble down it or back up it so it remains a mystery how the buffalo got there in the first place. His meditating-self accepts that it has always been there even though it isn't really there. As soon as that notion registers, the backdrop fades to black and all that remains is the buffalo in the water.

It lowers its head and submerges its snout to drink but keeps its large nostrils above the water. The rope tied around its neck floats off at a sharp angle carried by the current. The end of the rope is frayed indicating that the water buffalo must have got lose from somewhere.

The buffalo finishes drinking and lifts its head and keeps it level, so it has a view of the bank on the other side. Tuum can't see what it sees. It flicks its tail several times and each time it lands on the water and its tip floats but the rest of it sinks. Tuum is able to pan around the buffalo and observe it from many angles including from overhead. From above, the buffalo looks like a roughly drawn rectangle, its head more misshapen and bulbous in places than the rest.

From above he also can see that one of its horns is twisted badly and the tip broken off, likely from a fight. As soon as he notices that, his head goes dark and he senses instantly that this image is not his but one projected by his father's spirit. How is that possible?

A half hour or so later he comes out of his meditation and unfolds from the lotus position on the cot and goes to the desk. He takes out a sheet of paper to write a letter to Roong, but before he can start it there's a light knock on his door.

When he opens it, Kay stands there, hands folded at his belly. "We're ready," he says.

Tuum nods and steps outside and closes the door. He waits for Kay to turn and walk ahead of him. At one point, Kay stops without warning and waits. It takes Tuum a second to realize that Kay has stopped to let a column of ants cross in front of him.

When Kay continues again, his bare feet move noiselessly along the tile floor. The *Viharn* (assembly hall) is packed with people. The senior monks sit at the front and the novice monks behind them and then the villagers. They all sit quietly waiting for Kay and Tuum. There are many villagers in attendance.

Kay and Tuum go to his father's coffin at the front and light incense sticks, each using a nearby lit candle and then wave scented smoke over the coffin and place the burning sticks in holders on each end of the coffin. Tuum places his at his father's head and Kay at his feet. Kay then nods to the crowd and they wai back in unison. Tuum wais them next. Nong faces him at the front of the crowd and she wais Kay and then Tuum and folds her hands in her lap.

Kay chants in Pali for a half hour and the crowd repeats each line after him.

Later Tuum, Pin, Won, A, and two others lift his father's coffin. Kay and Nong walk ahead of them as they carry the coffin to a waiting cart hitched to a water buffalo. Pin drives the buffalo cart while Nong, Tuum, and Kay fall in behind and then everyone else. They move very slowly and stop many times to chant or to rest. It takes them twenty minutes to exit the main gate and move to end of the block and then turn south in the direction of the small field where more villagers have gathered near a pyre constructed out of bamboo and teak soaked in coconut oil. Tuum smells that long before the procession reaches the pyre. The pedestal at the top has a gilded gold frame and the bier where the coffin will rest is constructed of dried bamboo and crepe paper, so that will easily catch fire. On the very top is a small windowed chamber where his father's coffin will sit. It is in direct alignment with the golden Buddha facing south from the temple.

When the procession reaches the pyre, six young men scramble up to receive the coffin as Tuum and the others lift it as high as possible. Tuum climbs up afterward to watch it being lowered into place. It fits perfectly on the bier with only a small gap on all sides. Through the four windows that surround it, the coffin is visible from many vantage points below. That is important.

Kay has worked his way partway up and Tuum goes back down to him and they stay together in the pyre while it is lit and, when the smoke billows up, Tuum scrambles down first and helps Kay back onto the ground.

They move away from the heat as the flames quickly shoot up the pyre. Nong moves to Tuum's left side. They watch the flames reach the windowed room and soon engulf it and the glass snaps and then melts in the flames.

The fire now engulfs the bier, and Kay, Nong, and Tuum take several steps back to be farther from the heat but still have a direct view of his father's coffin as it burns and exposes his head which soon catches fire and is blackened but remains joined to the rest of him. When the muscles in his neck and shoulders cook, they shrink, and his head turns to face them.

Tuum and everyone move forward then despite the heat and watch the flames continue to consume his father's body. Steam rises out of his eye sockets as the flesh on his head and shoulders melt more and expose jagged bone and vertebrae. Tuum reminds himself that little more than two weeks ago this had been his father sitting with him in the courtyard of the temple. But now he is turning to ash.

His father had insisted that Tuum attend his mother's pyre, but he'd been allowed to hide his eyes with his hands during the difficult parts, although he still heard the progression of the flames. His mother's pyre had horrified him, but this calms him.

Now, his father's legs and arms are exposed and rise up as tendons and muscles contract and succumb to the fire. Those movements are slow and purely mechanical so that his father's body erupts with spastic movements caused by the burning muscles and tendons.

His skull is now fully exposed and flames come out of his eye sockets and mouth and ear holes. Several times monks toss more pieces of oil-soaked bamboo onto the fire to speed it up. After two hours, the fire has mostly burned down but larger bones have dropped to the ground. A few villagers will continue to add wood until those too are reduced to ash or fragments.

Tuum, Kay, Nong and a few others remain, but everyone else has trickled away. Kay turns toward the temple and Tuum and Nong follow. Tomorrow when the fire is completely out Pin and Won and A will return to sift through the ashes for bits of bone. Those will later be polished and placed in small glass vials and put on display in the temple. Kay will likely offer him two vials as a remembrance of his father. Thinking of that, he feels for the first time the full impact of that loss.

Kay and Nong walk ahead and he stays back to watch a slight wind toss up ash and push it along the open field toward a row of trees in the distance. He marvels at how the world is never still even to honour the dead.

Without his father in the world, he feels time speed up. He wishes to linger but lingering wouldn't change what has happened or what happens next. It will all continue as it has always continued. His father had said the human cycle is short compared to larger karmic and cosmic cycles. He referred to all human life as the great expiration because everyone's time runs out.

Tuum leaves that all behind and hurries to catch up to Kay and Nong but by now they have disappeared down the block in the direction of the temple, so he decides instead to walk very slowly and careful like his father. He purposely doesn't look at the ground as he walks but stares straight ahead, sensing at all times where his feet are.

In time he gives up on this and hurries to catch up to the water buffalo and cart that carried the coffin to the pyre. Pin isn't driving the cart now but a stranger, likely a willing villager. The driver holds the reins loosely in his hands and doesn't tug on them.

Tuum walks next to the water buffalo staying even with its head.

He thinks of his visions of water buffaloes and then of this one. Although it is possible to think most buffalos look alike, they do not. This is the buffalo that pulled his father's coffin. That other buffalo is not a buffalo at all like this one but is a complex manifestation linked to his father's spirit. He can't yet say for certain what his father's life as a buffalo had been like or what his father's spirit wishes him to know.

He stays alongside this one as they pass Nong and Kay talking at the main gate. He doesn't stop to talk to them, only turns to wai them and Nong wais back. Tuum picks up his pace to catch up again with the water buffalo. He should have gone into the temple but continues alongside the buffalo and cart without the slightest idea where it is going, and that appeals to him at this moment.

The water buffalo has picked up its pace, likely because it is going down a slight incline. Its breath is laboured and it huffs so loudly that Tuum easily notes how short the time is between breaths.

Tuum slows then and looks into the back of the cart and sees the blankets that provided padding for his father's coffin and the two bright green ones that laid on top of the coffin to shield it from the intense sun. Those are now bunched in a corner where they landed when tossed aside. He grabs one of the green ones and pulls it out. It is surprisingly heavy, so he folds it and places it on his shoulder and sniffs it. It smells of buffalo and hay.

He leaves it on his shoulder and turns back toward the temple and the water buffalo and cart continue on. Back at the temple Nong and Kay are gone. He hurries up the steps and finds Kay waiting not far down the hall from his room. He is standing perfectly still and chanting. Tuum walks past him and continues to his room. At the door, he feels a breeze swirl around him and then down the hall. He thinks again of his father's spirit and knows it will be in his room waiting for him. This causes him to pause at the door without going in. Instead he slides the green blanket off his shoulder and folds it two more times so it is small enough to be placed under his arm. He isn't certain what possessed him to snatch it from the cart or what he will do with it.

He doesn't go inside his room to change clothes as he's planned but hurries back down hallway and leaves the folded blanket on the bench that he and his father sat on the first day he'd come here. He scrambles down the steps and walks in the direction of the main gate. Not long after he passes through it, Kay is alongside him. This time he doesn't say anything all the way to the bus station. When it is Tuum's turn to buy a ticket, he realizes then he hasn't brought any money with him.

Kay reaches into a bag that he carries over one shoulder and retrieves a hundred baht note and hands it to Tuum. He uses it to purchase a ticket and gives the change back to Kay but he refuses it. Tuum assumes this too is his father's doing.

At this moment, standing with Kay in the bus station, all he thinks of is that soon he will be re-united with Roong in Khon Kaen.

"Great people take a long time to die and even then they don't fully die because they live in all they leave behind," Kay says. "If not, imagine all that we'd lose." And then when Tuum doesn't respond: "We will keep your room for you for when you return. That is what your father wished."

Tuum wonders now what else has been promised on his behalf. He has no intention of returning but doesn't tell Kay this. He chooses to believe that Kay and his father both knew he felt this way even if they continued to talk as though he didn't.

All those stories his father told him—even about the day his mother died—he recognizes now had been more parables than true stories from his life. He certainly filled in here and there with just enough actual details but which parts those were only his father knew. Despite those mysteries he feels that much had been mended between them and he will continue to believe that no matter what.

There are only three passengers lined up for the bus. When it's his turn, he hands his ticket to the driver and Kay steps back out of line and Tuum boards the bus.

He chooses a window seat near the front and doesn't look out the window until he is settled. When he does, Kay is already halfway down the block. As he walks, the breeze fluffs out his robe a little and makes him appear to be bigger than he is.

The bus lurches back and then ahead as the driver grinds gears between reverse and first. Tuum pushes the seat back and closes his eyes. He senses his father's spirit in the empty seat beside him.

# Chapter 14

## Chum Phae and Khon Kaen Present Day

NAN AND HE board a *songtaew* (enclosed half-ton with two facing benches in the back—local bus) in Chum Phae and sit beside a young boy and his grandmother. The boy is sobbing quietly.

"*Yha Rong Hai,*" (Don't cry), Ed says to the boy at Nan's urging. She then suggests he give the boy a twenty baht note, and when he does, the boy flashes a broad, spontaneous smile. It is the pure smile of a child. The boy's grandmother smiles too, but hers is more worldly and cautious—the practiced smile of an adult.

"*Dee,*" Nan whispers in his ear.

He knows this is not the kindness that Nan or Run stress, but it is a first step. True kindness requires daily practice and discipline.

"Today is a Buddha day," Nan says later. When they were first married, she'd told him that every eighth day during the rainy season it rains, and every eighth day is a Buddha day. She'd then said: "Buddha says a rainy day is a good day to go to the temple and become clean."

Later she told him that *Dharma* means ridding his mind of all evil thoughts and making room for good ones. "Our brains work best when they contain good thoughts. Evil thoughts slow the mind and confuse it, put it off kilter. Think of the brain as a sewer pipe. Clear water flows best through it. The sluggish dirty water clogs it, even blocks it. Those are the evil thoughts."

Now on the *songtaew*, he can't yet imagine fully controlling his mind with such precision. Most of the time it seems his thoughts have a will of their own and he's never sure if the next thought will be a good or bad one. For periods of time, he can focus his mind but that requires paying attention and policing every thought as it occurs and rejecting the bad ones. Nan has also told him that kindness requires fast and true thinking.

"If your mind is full of evil thoughts there is no room for good ones. Chanting and meditation is the only way to clear your mind and make room."

He's never done a tally of his thoughts but knows that he has evil ones more often than he would like. He pushes those away as quickly as he can but isn't able to block or even anticipate them except when they are triggered by some conflict. At those times, he tends to even encourage such thoughts until he catches himself doing that.

From Nan and Run he's learned that bad thoughts are not organic but are merely the product of an unfocused, undisciplined mind. He considers his thinking as normal and typical as anyone's even if it is too often undisciplined. He's certainly never tried to police his thoughts until he met Nan. Now he understands that bad thoughts result from letting impulses direct him.

They get off at the Tesco Lotus mall and the boy waves as they leave and flashes them another smile. Ed is certain that the boy is free of evil thoughts. He can't remember his own thinking when he was two or three but is certain that they would have had been free of malice. A two-year-old is free of a larger context. All that changes as early as five or six. He knows that by then the ego takes root and is capable of feeling betrayed and hurt. That triggers thoughts of revenge and malice. Nan has said that evil thoughts impede all spiritual gain.

They stand in a warm rain and hold hands. Behind them the hut burns slowly at first and in time the flames engulf the bamboo and rise high above the roof despite the light rain.

"Good," Nan says, and closes her eyes, and moves her lips as she chants.

He hears only the crackle of the wood burning. His clothes are slightly soaked and that helps cool him.

He'd asked her earlier if she were sure.

"Yes Sutum's soul has moved on to its next life, so now we must burn the hut. Song agrees."

"So Sutum's soul won't come back?"

"Nor any of the others. They are lingering memories of what happened here, various times in the past including a more distant past. Run says that two hundred years ago there was a great house here and bad deeds were done in that house in the name of love. The house had many servants and many people came and went. They came to it for happiness but never left it happy. Someone cleaned up after. That was their mistake. You can't wipe away darkness and evil. The only way to prevent future tragedies is to burn the hut. The land must be allowed to go fallow and then be green for many lifetimes. Then it will be safe to build here once more. Otherwise any building will draw the evil back."

They move closer to Song's Yaris that they've parked a safe distance away from the fire. Song loaned them the car for their trip back to Khon Kaen. Later he will ride Nan's Honda Click into the city and visit his children and drive his Yaris back.

After a while, Nan gets in the driver's side, and Ed sits in the passenger side on one of the towels they set down earlier to keep the seats from getting too wet.

Nan doesn't start the engine right away. Instead she says: "We have to stay until it's just smouldering. Later the wind will scatter the ashes out over the rice paddy."

He asks if the ashes will carry evil with them.

"Once the fire has burned out, the evil will be gone."

The rain lets up just as the fire is reduced to embers. A grey, almost white, smoke rises from the humps of ash.

*All that ash,* he thinks.

"Song will sit here through the night to make sure the fire is completely out."

Ed thinks of the future and how broad it is and wonders how soon it will be before he can close his eyes and go there as Nan and Run go now. Nan has told him to be patient and that she's only gained that ability recently.

She starts the engine, backs up, and turns around driving slowly to the highway. She turns south and then east toward Khon Kaen. It is another Buddha day and the traffic is light.

As she drives, she tells Ed she loves him and takes his hand. He says he loves her too, and those words, as he says them, anchor him more than they ever have. She leaves the air conditioning off and his pants and shirt are soon dry.

"Two hundred years ago horses travelled this way, and this was a gravel road, but beyond that much of it is the same as it was then. In that past life, you and I were shyer and more reticent with each other and never got to stand in the rain holding hands like we did today."

He doesn't ask how she knows such details, but it comforts him to hear them. These bodies will run out of time and then their souls will have to jump to other bodies, and they will have to find each other all over again. That thought makes his head spin. Until he met Nan, he had no idea of such machinery. He understands now the true connection they have through all the lifetimes they have lived and have yet to live. He and Nan haven't spoken about that yet, but they will.

"You weren't as handsome then, and I wasn't as beautiful," she says.

Run has helped her with this, and over the phone recently, he's chanted for the two of them. These are ancient powers.

"It is fortunate for Sutum that you saw him die."

"Why is that?"

"Without you, he could have spent many years trapped in that hut."

Wouldn't Buddha have interceded? he asks. And she says Buddha has.

At first, he thought that he'd witnessed Sutum's murder because Buddha had wished him to but knows now that Buddha is not a meddler. He's but a recording of all that happens. Some of those recordings get played back later thanks to monks like Run, but huge chunks of them never get played again.

It is dark by the time they reach the city limits. The traffic thickens but she doesn't have to stop until a red light close to their apartment. They don't speak then, and he listens to the quiet idle of the engine. His clothes are completely dry and so is his hair and hers. They look like two people who got caught in the rain somewhere and are returning home.

In their apartment in Khon Kaen, Ed is amazed how it is exactly as he left it weeks ago. "It all looks the same," he says to Nan.

"Why wouldn't it?" she asks.

He's not the same inside and neither is she. He tells her that.

"That is how it is. Buddha says don't be fooled by what you see and what you hear. Proof is not necessary." She tells him of the monk and the hungry tiger. "A monk lived to be seventy years old and decided that was old enough. When he was twenty, he had been a bright man and had already learned a few valuable truths. When he was thirty, he knew even more truths and by the time he was forty and fifty he'd come to know the many truths that only a virtuous life of devotion reveals. At seventy he saw the good that he'd done throughout his life but understood that, even though he'd meditated more than ten thousand times, each time he did so he was meditating for the first time.

"Over the years the monk went many times to the forest to meditate and improve his practices. Each time, he would always arrive at the face of the same mountain, and whenever he did, he'd sense that a tiger had begun to follow him, a few paces back. The tiger never came any closer and if the monk stopped, the tiger stopped. If the monk drank water, the tiger drank water. If the monk stopped to chant, the tiger waited. After the monk had walked fully around the base of the mountain, the tiger would always part ways with him.

"By the time the monk was seventy he was ready for enlightenment. He again went to that mountain but this time there was no tiger. He waited for a half a day and chanted most of that time sitting in the lotus position on the forest floor. While he chanted, he got the notion to climb to a ledge that he could see about ten metres above him. When he reached the ledge, he sat in the lotus position and chanted.

"Later when he opened his eyes, he saw below him a mother tiger and heard somewhere in the thick greenery the hungry cries of her cub. He knew then that he was ready for enlightenment so he let his body fall to the ground and when he landed he broke many bones but didn't immediately die. He lay there waiting for death. To diminish the pain, he focused on the impermanence of his body. The mother tiger approached him and sniffed his dying body. He felt no fear as she did this and he told her that it was okay for her to do what was needed. She bit his arm to test him. He let her do that and didn't strike back. She bit his leg and when he didn't resist she griped an ankle in her jaws and dragged him to where her young cub lay whimpering.

"Her young sniffed at him too and then pawed greedily at his flesh and then tore through skin and muscle and tissue until he reached the monk's heart, which had stopped by then. As the young tiger tore away the monk's flesh and fed, the monk's soul reached enlightenment.

"Before he died the monk understood that he and the mother tiger had known each other in an earlier life, and by providing his body to her young, the monk was mending the karma between them.

"Sometimes enlightenment is beautiful and just like that, and what is needed is given and what is wanted is received. There are many stories of tigers following monks in the forest as they chant. The tigers never attack and the monks never stop their chants. But there is only the one story of the monk who jumped from the mountain and allowed the hungry young tiger below to feed on his body."

"Is this about Sutum?"

"No. It's about you and me.

"We were a tiger and monk in a past life?"

"No. The links are not that direct. The traces we get are at best intermittent. That hut for example. Something there ... But we aren't to know."

"The monk and the tiger?"

"That is about the traces. No more."

"The monk and the tiger?"

"Yes them. Now that we have burned the hut, Run says he can reveal to us that you and I had once been there and traces of us swirled around there. He sensed it in his meditations but couldn't reveal it before as that would have been too karmically dangerous.

"You and I?"

"Yes, but not at the same time. That's the key part. We were there together now and that wasn't a coincidence either. It is like a dream within a dream. Sunshine when it is raining. The two shouldn't happen at the same time but sometimes they do."

"We were passing through then?"

"No. We weren't."

# Chapter 15

## *Khon Kaen And Chum Phae 1970*

As soon as he steps inside his apartment in Khon Kaen, Tuum realizes that Roong isn't there. He calls out her name hoping that she is in the bathroom, but that door is wide open. His father's spirit steps around him and sits in a chair across the room from him and next to the window that overlooks the street. That window has been left open, which suggests that Roong will be back shortly.

He sits at his desk where the letters he's sent her are stacked in a neat pile on the left side of the desk. The letter on top is not the last one he sent but one from when his father was still alive. He scans through the stack and they are piled in the order he sent them. The last one is missing and likely hasn't arrived yet.

Besides the stack of his letters is a single sheet of paper not yet folded and laid flat. It is a letter addressed to him, dated on the day his father died, more than a week ago. He reads:

*May 25, 1970*

*My handsome Tuum:*

*Your last letter gave me great joy, and I am so happy to read that you and your father have made such glorious progress and are able to finally forgive one another. That is truly wondrous news. I am as hopeful as you are that soon you will be free to return. That thought fills me with much joy. After reading your letter, I chanted and focused on your face. I fell asleep easier than I have in recent days, and despite the heat lasting late into the night, I slept more peacefully than I have since you left.*

*I even slept through the noisy dogs that usually wake me at first light. I didn't dream once that I recall. When I woke, I lay in bed and I thought of how everything is getting better and better.*

*This evening not long after I finished eating my Kaeng Khe Hlek (copper pot curry) and sticky rice a policeman came to the door of the apartment. He said that my testimony was required at court tomorrow. I said I'd given my statement and he said that now that my mistress had been formally charged they needed me to give my testimony before a judge. He said that I was not to worry, as this was a mere formality to finalize the prosecutor's case and wouldn't take long.*

*He spoke highly of your father and how fortunate I was to have such a powerful benefactor. He said he would return in the morning to bring me to court. I told him that wasn't necessary and that I would do my duty and be there. He said that it was required of him.*

*I left the door open to let in the breeze and clear out any unwelcome spirits that may have attached unwittingly to him. There is more I want to say tonight but the fact I have to appear in court tomorrow weighs on me. I am sorry my love I will write more when I get back from court.*

The letter stops there. He flips it over to see if she has continued on the other side but it's blank. He sets her letter on the desk next to his and scans the room. Now that he is more attentive, he notices what's out of place. The bed is not made and several dishes have been cleaned but left to dry in the tray next to the sink. When he inspects those, they are completely dry and have a thin layer of dust on them.

He checks in the mailbox downstairs and finds his last letter. It's dark by now, but he rides his bicycle to the Remand Prison he'd visited only a month and a half ago. The guard on duty checks the records and says there is no Roong being held there. Tuum asks him to check again in case he missed the first time. He wais the guard when he asks this and the guard nods back and runs his finger very slowly over the lists this time. He doesn't find her name on it.

Tuum returns to his apartment building and asks his landlord on the first floor when he last saw Roong. He says that he saw her a week ago leaving with a police officer. They were talking friendly enough and he'd assumed that she was going to the police station to file a complaint.

Back in his apartment, he lies on the bed but doesn't sleep. He chants and after he finishes, he can't sleep so chants more. At first light, he dresses and hurries downstairs and collects his bicycle. The street is busy even at this early hour with people walking or riding bicycles to work. He pedals fast the whole way and reaches her mistress's house at precisely seven a.m. The guard at the main gate is asleep as he slips past and knocks on the front door five times. An older woman answers. She is stooped and her arms and legs are too large for her small round body. She smiles at him and doesn't complain about how early it is.

He asks if the mistress is still in prison. She says that her mistress has been free on bail for a week now but left for Hua Hin three days ago. He then asks if she has seen Roong and she says not for more than a month and a half.

He returns to his apartment and searches the closet, dresser, and desk for any notes she might have left, but turns up nothing. All he has to go on is her unfinished letter. He reads it again hoping that he's missed a key detail, but nothing new stands out. He makes the bed and sits in a lotus position there with his back against the wall and meditates hoping to connect with her and gain some idea of where she's gone.

His father's spirit causes Tuum to burp, fart and hiccup, with such regularity that it takes all his focus to stop them.

He reaches a deep inner quiet, and the water buffalo appears hitched to an empty, red cart. There is no driver and the buffalo has stopped on a road so narrow that the tall bamboo trees that line both sides arch over it and create a tunnel of green. He wills the buffalo to continue on its journey so he can learn where it is headed but it doesn't move. Noisy, mysterious birds circle the cart. These are loud and colourful birds that he has never seen before. Their singing is a most unpleasant racket and the powerful swoosh of their wings rock the cart from side to side, so violently that it looks as though it will tip.

As he concentrates on the cart, he picks out gouges and chinks and other signs of significant wear in the wood. The red has faded in some places to a vague pink but remains bright red on the under carriage. The cart appears older than the buffalo and likely other buffalos have been hitched to it before this one. As soon as he concludes that, the buffalo and cart vanish.

He opens his eyes, and when his brain properly adjusts, he sits on the edge of the bed and knows that the water buffalo means that his father's spirit is trying to get his attention. He asks his father's spirit to show him more and guide him to Roong, but he doesn't get so much as a hiccup or burp in response. He stands and pounds the table with his fists to get the spirit's attention, but that accomplishes nothing. He remembers his father's words: *Spirits aren't here to guide us. We are here to guide them*. How many years ago was that? He doesn't know except he is certain that it was after his mother died.

He walks around his apartment chanting until late into the night to break any bad karmic connections that linger and keep him from finding Roong. He wonders if in his time away, a dark force has attached to her in some harmful way like one did to his mother. If it is still here, he doesn't sense it.

He sits on the floor and leans forward until his head touches the floor. He slows his breathing but in time the burps and hiccups start again and he gets up and paces the room. But that doesn't stop them. He then opens the window and sticks his head out into the hot muggy night. He takes in a deep inhale and then makes a forceful exhale and the burps and hiccups stop. He worries that he is wrong and that the presence of his father's spirit may be hampering him from finding Roong. Eventually he rises and goes to the bed and collapses on it and sleeps briefly. When he wakes hours later, it is already light. He dresses and leaves without eating.

At the train station he purchases a second-class ticket to Hua Hin. Not long after the train leaves the station, he nods off and when he wakes a half hour later, the hiccups and burps have returned, and he sinks into deep meditation to get the disturbances to stop. Even then, he still burps quite loudly every ten minutes or so until the train reaches the outskirts of Krung Thep.

The main train station in Krung Thep is noisy and so crowded with travellers hurrying about that he gets lost twice before finding the gate for his train to Hua Hin.

He arrives there at 11:19 p.m. that evening. The three hotels next to the station are full, but the fourth hotel two blocks east of the station and closer to the Gulf of Thailand has a room available. The room is so small that there's barely six inches on either side of the double bed and the room smells strongly of mildew. He opens the window beside the bed to air it out. A rush of damp, salty air draws him to the window for greedy inhales and then he leans his head out the window until the room airs out.

Mayflies circle the nearby streetlight in a shifting mass. He studies the stray bugs that dart in and out of the light and then join the others. The mass circles the light with a building frenzy and then they drop to the ground one at a time and the base of the light is soon writhing with dying mayflies. He knows given the size of the mass that they will be at this all night and by morning the heap of dead mayflies will be a much bigger than it is now. Hotel staff will chant before they sweep the mass up and make several trips to the garbage. All those discarded bodies emptied of souls.

His father's soul could jump to one of those and would have to jump again by morning. Although Tuum isn't at all certain where his father's soul will go next, he it is certain it will not jump into the egg of a mayfly. This world is not his father's world anymore. This day is not his day. Other days await him but none of what he knew from this life will be carried forward with him. He'll have to start over and learn whatever he can. Will he ever get a glimpse of Tuum and himself in that temple? It isn't likely.

His father will start over in another life maybe in Cambodia or Laos or farther away in China or Japan. As long as his spirit stays with Tuum none of that will happen. For now, his father's spirit will keep his soul in limbo. A few mosquitos fly around him and he allows them to brush against a cheek or the top of his head. When their attention gets too insistent, he shoos them out the open window and shuts it and closes the curtains.

He barely sleeps for the third night in a row and is up at sunrise. He walks to the address the old woman scribbled for him. When he arrives there, the house is significantly larger than her house in Khon Kaen, and she must spend more time here, especially in the summer. Roong has never mentioned any trips here so likely she stayed behind in Khon Kaen to attend to the necessities of that house. This house is well positioned in the very middle of the town and must have a clear view east toward the beach and the shimmer off the Gulf of Thailand.

The house has no wall or main gate so he approaches the front door unaccosted. Despite the early hour, he knocks and a tall man much older than him opens the door immediately.

Tuum wais and says he is here to see the mistress. The man wais back and says that she isn't up yet but he expects she will be within the hour. He says that Tuum is free to wait inside. The man leads him down a long marble tiled hallway to a living room deep in the centre of the house. The man points to a leather chair in the far corner of the vast room which is lavishly furnished with antique Thai furniture. Much of it is made from teak and mahogany and there are many plumped, silk accent pillows. Tuum sits in the chair next to a large teak-framed window that affords a proper glimpse of the Gulf of Thailand. The chair is so plush and thickly padded that he barely collapses the cushion when he sits.

The man returns a short time later with a cup of jasmine tea and sets it on a lacquered coaster on the rosewood side table next to Tuum.

He sips the tea and the warm jasmine calms him and he nods off until cleaning noises down the hallway wake him. He sits upright expecting the mistress to appear at any moment but she doesn't. In time, he closes his eyes and chants quietly to himself asking any nearby uncles for help.

It's another hour before she enters the living room. She is older than he expects and wears a long black silk dress that is hemmed just above her ankles. She is barefoot and her silver hair has recently been cut to just below her ears.

"How is your father?" she asks after he stands to wai her.

"Well," he says, which is the right answer whether she knows he's dead or not.

"I assume you are here about Roong. I haven't seen her, and I don't expect to nor wish to see her at this point. She has caused me much difficulty but in time that will be sorted out. I've come to Hua Hin to put that behind me. This has always been my healing place. The weather is so agreeable and glorious especially in the summer. I am sorry you came all this way for nothing. A letter or phone call would have sufficed." She smiles when she says this.

He hears the scolding in her voice and detects it in her smile although she quickly masks that by smiling even more broadly. He feels an anger stir in him but keeps it in check to avoid saying or doing anything foolish. His father has reminded him many times that anger is a weak power. *Don't look in the sky unless you are expecting to see birds or clouds. There will always be one or the other.* He takes guidance now from those words.

"Your father has already taken care of her debt. She is free to go now and perhaps she has simply fled. I have no wish to help you but, for your father's sake I will not impede you either. I've told you all I know."

She nods and he wais her again. Custom and duty requires that of him regardless of what he may feel toward her. She leaves him and her feet are so silent on the floor that he hears nothing more until a door opens and closes out of sight.

He knows instantly that he has been impulsive and foolish coming here. *Do not hurry for there is always enough time. It may not seem like that sometimes, but there is. The amount of time given is the amount needed. That is an important lesson to learn from Buddha.* His father's words again calm him. He doesn't remember when his father said them or in what context but, at this very moment, they provide solace. His ego has allowed him to act in haste. He must not do that again. He admonishes himself for that and knows whatever has become of Roong, her mistress has had nothing to do with it. Nor does he believe, as her mistress has implied, that Roong has simply run away because her debt has been paid. Those words speak more about her character than Roong's.

He experiences a sudden series of hiccups and burps and his nose runs and he has to take several tissues off the side table and blow his nose three times. His father's spirit is trying to get his attention.

He sits down and closes his eyes and chants and the hiccups and burps stop. He continues to chant, and no one interrupts him or comes to see him out. He is allowed to stay as long as he wishes. He soon sinks into a deep meditation and seeks a connection to Roong. Instead he sees the water buffalo. This time it is grazing in an open field next to train tracks and is still hooked up to the cart. A train passes and the buffalo raises its head but doesn't move away.

He cuts that short and opens his eyes not wishing that contact with his father right now. The brightness of the room indicates that the day is advancing. The hiccups and burps return, and the burping gets louder and louder, so he meditates again to stop them. The water buffalo soon appears, and this time, it is in the mountains near Chiang Rai. He recognizes the two mountain ranges and the rushing river between them from when he was seventeen and went there with his father to help the leader of a nearby village sort out a series of thefts.

The water buffalo is no longer hooked up to the cart and walks alone on a gravel road and in a short while meets two elephants going the other way. The *mahouts* (elephant handlers) wave as they pass. The second mahout looks younger than the first and wears a straw hat, which he takes off and waves at the water buffalo.

With the hat off, Tuum recognizes his father in his early twenties. His father was never a mahout that he knows of and this jars him enough that he has the urge to open his eyes, but resists. *Why must I always be given riddles*?

*You aren't,* his father says now in his head.

"Then where is she?" he asks this aloud and hears footsteps somewhere in the house, but they are hurrying away from him.

*You are not asking the right question,* his father's voice says.

"What is the right question?"

*You will know when you ask it. Not before. Love can only take you so far, then you are on your own the rest of the way.*

He comes out of this meditation and the house is remarkably

quiet. It's large enough that he's certain that people are busy elsewhere in it but none of those sounds reach him.

He walks to the front door and the man who let him in is nowhere to be seen so he sees himself out. He returns immediately to his hotel, checks out and goes to the train station.

The next train to Krung Thep wouldn't be for three hours. The air in the station is so thick and salty that he waits outside under the shade of a substantial tamarind across the street. He senses his father's spirit nearby but experiences no hiccups or burps. He carries on a conversation in his head with the spirit although the spirit can't hear him.

He's certain his father's spirit knows exactly where Roong is and that is why he is sticking so close. There is no way for the spirit to tell him what it knows. The heat eventually drives him back inside and he stands below a ceiling fan to stay cool.

He doesn't sleep much on either the train to Krung Thep or later the one to Khon Kaen even though his father's spirit isn't with him most of the way. When the second train is an hour south of Khon Kaen, a rush of cool air from the empty seat beside lets him know that his father's spirit has manifested there again. Soon after the temperature drops, the hiccups and farting start. He doesn't reach Khon Kaen until four in the morning.

At his apartment, he flops on the bed and is soon asleep. Hours later he wakes to a faint jasmine odour he associates with Roong. Despite the urgency he feels, he moves with lethargy in the midday heat.

The smell of her persists and is so powerful that he rises from bed and searches everywhere in the room hoping that spiritually she's returned. He finds nothing and knows instantly that this is another trick of his brain and an indication of just how worried he is about her.

He realizes that the smell means dark forces have returned, and if he isn't careful, they'll enter him too.

If she were safe, she would have got word to him by now. The horrible truth of that forces him out of bed and he spends the rest of the day showing around the only photos he has of her taken in a photo booth the day they went to the lake. Everyone he asks hasn't seen her in more than a week.

He buys sticky rice and chopped chicken in the street and brings the bag upstairs but barely touches it. Instead he stares at the lumps of food on the plate for a full hour and isn't tempted even to eat a mouthful. Someone knocks and when he opens the door, he is surprised to see Kay there. How does he know where he lives?

"Your father came to me in a dream last night and said I should come here," he says after Tuum invites him in.

"Did he say anything else?"

"No."

He tells Kay then about the disappearance of Roong.

"Tomorrow we will look together," Kay says. He produces a mat that he's brought with him.

"You sleep in the bed," Tuum says. "I'll use the mat."

Kay doesn't protest and is up before the sun and wakes Tuum and asks him where his kettle is and then fills it with water and sets it on the burner. When the water boils, he takes tea leaves out of a second small pouch around his neck and adds it to the kettle. He lets it steep and then serves them each a cup. "This is a tea my father used to drink. I have been drinking it for years. Thanks to this tea I've rarely been sick."

It is a weak yellow colour and a little sweet but otherwise bland.

"Your father came to me in another dream last night and told me to ask at the courthouse. Upon waking, I remembered a dream your father told me about two weeks before he died. He said the dream caused him to worry about you and Roong because he'd learned that two of you were in great karmic peril if you stayed together. He'd had a dream where you were a viper and she was a Siamese crocodile. He said that isn't a good sign and that in his dream the crocodile attacked the viper and bit off a large chunk of its tail, but it was able to get away. It slithered into the grass and soon healed. The crocodile went back into the water. It was clear in the dream that this was not the first time they'd encountered each other. Nor would it be the last. Soon the viper would pass that way again and the crocodile would attack. Your father said that sometimes the viper kills the crocodile and sometimes the crocodile kills the viper. He also said that sometimes you are the viper and sometimes Roong is the viper. You and Roong have been killing each other for many lifetimes and that the karmic cycle has to be broken in this life because, if it isn't, you will continue to meet and die all over again. The chance to break the karmic cycle may not come again for many lifetimes."

It's only a dream, Tuum thinks, but then, Siamese crocodiles are so rare that its appearance in a dream is important. But in a dream any creature is possible even long extinct ones, or imaginary ones. To dream of any snake, even a viper, usually means good luck is coming to the dreamer so Tuum wonders why his father didn't view his dream that way. He also wonders why his father would dream first of Roong as a Siamese crocodile? If it were his dream, they'd both be either vipers or crocodiles, like creatures and not rivals. His father attached much significance to dreams and didn't dare cross them.

"He'd asked me not to say anything to you about the dream. I respected that wish and even forgot about it until last night. My memory isn't what it used to be."

His father wouldn't have lied to Kay about anything including a dream. To lie to an abbot is to lie to Buddha and, although his father could have left out vital details, he wouldn't have changed the essential meaning of the dream. Certainly, Kay could have forgotten some of the details. Why would his father have even told Kay about the dream except if he already sensed he would die soon or maybe he'd done that just in case something happened to him before he'd had a chance to alter that karma or warn Tuum about the dream.

Tuum is so certain that his father and he made a core breakthrough and that his father wouldn't have kept anything as dire as that from him, unless he hadn't worked up to it yet. He suspects now that there was more his father planned to tell him. Whatever details he'd left out when he told Kay about the dream has caused his spirit to be uneasy and so has found a way to contact Kay and send him here.

His father hasn't appeared in any of Tuum's dreams since he died, only in his meditations, and he now wonders why. When his mother died, he dreamt of her every night for months afterwards. When he finally told his father about those dreams, he'd said: *Dreams are just your mind making a mess of the day's events. Most often, they mean nothing at all.* That had been his father comforting a grieving son. A few years later he would contradict this and say that dreams were very powerful and must always be heeded. He admitted that he hadn't wanted to burden the younger Tuum with the duties that dreams demanded.

The courthouse is close enough that they walk there. Kay easily keeps pace with Tuum, and they reach there in less than ten minutes.

Court is in session, so they wait on a varnished bench just outside the main doors. Tuum studies the dark mahogany of the doors from where he is sitting. They are ten feet tall and each has a large carved elephant that takes up much of the door. Tuum rises and rests an ear against one of the doors but only hears muffled voices. He fingers the deep gouges in the wood that forms one of the elephants. He has a memory of fingering these same doors when he was a boy, likely while his mother and he waited for his father to finish for the day. They didn't do that very often, so they must of have been here for some special occasion that escapes him now.

He returns to the bench and sits beside Kay and waits. Kay chants silently to himself and Tuum does the same. With his eyes closed, he hears more clearly all the noises around him. The thick doors creak open three times, but he doesn't open his eyes to see who comes out until a fourth time. He watches six people exit the court together. They don't speak as they pass him, but they high wai Kay and he nods back.

The court remains in session until 2 p.m., and after the last people exit, a court attendant leaves the doors open. Kay and he enter, and Kay asks to speak to the presiding judge. She wais Kay and speaks only to him. She says that she recognizes Roong's name and the original case but knows nothing new about her or the case. There has been no trial as yet so she doubts that Roong would have been called to testify. The prosecutor, a woman no older than Nong, has nothing more to add.

They return to the bench outside the courtroom and sit on each end. Tuum now knows that Roong wasn't called here to testify. That must have been what his father meant in Kay's dream. He still has no clue where Roong has gone or who the mysterious policeman was. He doesn't sense his father's spirit here and there have been no disturbances from his spirit since Kay's arrival.

"Dreams sometimes require greater study to decipher exactly all that they mean and even then they seldom mean what they first appear to mean. We need to meditate here, and I am certain we will unlock more secrets of that dream and learn where's she's gone," Kay says and then slides a little closer to Tuum and closes his eyes.

Tuum thinks it might be better to return to the apartment and start over. But Kay's breathing has already slowed, indicating that he is deep in meditation.

The area is too noisy for Tuum to properly concentrate as more people leave work and walk past. He also hears a noisy conversation somewhere down the hall. He can't make out what is being said, only the back and forth between two different male voices.

He forces himself to persist and in time he sees himself sitting in the window seat of the same train car he rode back in from Hua Hin. This time he is in third-class and the details are accurate right down to the polished metal beneath the window. He has two bags with him, one much larger than the other. He stands and sets the smaller bag in the metal overhead rack and leaves the larger one at his feet. He pushes that closer to the window, so he has more legroom. He feels cramped and can't get comfortable. The seat beside him is empty and he could put his bag there, but he has a powerful sensation not to. The train pulls away from the station and soon after Kay appears from the car ahead and sits beside him in the empty aisle seat. He has no luggage with him. He nods to Tuum but doesn't speak and acts as though they don't know each other. He closes his eyes and chants.

"This is going nowhere," Tuum says aloud and forces his eyes open.

Kay opens his eyes too and says: "Why did you leave the train car? I only got seated beside you when you got up and left."

"You saw that too?"

"Yes. We have to take the train all the way back to here if we are to have any chance of finding Roong."

Tuum doubts Kay could know that for certain, but figures he has nothing to lose.

They try again and this time Tuum is not on a train but back in the small room at the temple and his father sits across the table from him. His father is speaking but he can't hear a word he is saying. It is as though he's gone deaf. His father is speaking so fast that Tuum can't read his lips either. His father points over his shoulder and when he looks there, he sees Roong's face in the window although there was no window in that room at the temple. Tuum stands and opens the door but Roong isn't there. Kay is.

"It's not the judge we need to talk to but the janitor," Kay says.

Tuum opens his eyes then and Kay's are open too.

"You said to ask the janitor," he says to Kay.

"You said to ask a street vendor outside. Perhaps we are both right."

He goes in pursuit of the janitor whom he finds in the second courtroom cleaning up. The janitor has heard of Tuum's father and is sorry to hear of his death but doesn't recognize Roong from the picture Tuum shows him.

He locates Kay out front of the courthouse speaking to an older woman selling Phad Thai and papaya salad.

"She says a policeman bought a papaya salad from her a week or so ago. She wouldn't have remembered him except that the woman with him looked familiar and she realized later that she had bought a papaya from her a few weeks earlier. The police officer and the woman didn't walk into the courthouse but went in the direction of the bus station. They didn't look in a hurry. The policeman gripped her arm not in a friendly way. That is another reason she remembers them. It bothered her the way the policeman gripped her arm."

Tuum shows her Roong's picture and the woman says it could be the same woman, but she was too far away to be certain.

Tuum and Kay take a *tuk tuk* to the bus station and he shows Roong's picture around, but no one remembers seeing her. One of the clerks suggests they come back tomorrow and ask those who work the morning shift.

They return to his apartment, but once there, he can't sit still. He wishes for morning to hurry so he can return to the station. He again suggests that Kay sleep in the bed. Tuum can't fall asleep on the mat and so he paces the small apartment while Kay sleeps but that doesn't help so he stops that after a while and sits in the lotus position on the mat and chants. He slips into a very deep meditation, but no images come to him. Later, he lies on the mat but barely sleeps an hour.

Kay wakes Tuum when it is already light out and offers him a cup of warm tea.

He takes a few sips and then sets the cup down. Not long after, they walk to the bus station and arrive at eight a.m.

None of the ticket agents recognize the photo of Roong except a young woman who remembers her with a policeman. He bought the ticket and handed it to Roong. She doesn't remember the destination of the ticket except she has a sense it was somewhere north like Chiang Mai or Chiang Rai.

Tuum thanks Kay now and they both agree that Kay has done as much as possible. Tuum buys Kay a ticket back to Chum Phae. They talk mostly about Tuum's father as they wait for Kay's bus to leave. Once it departs, Tuum realizes he will miss Kay. It has helped to have someone searching with him and in truth he wouldn't have got this far without his help.

Tuum returns to his apartment and meditates and pleads to his father's spirit for help in deciding where to go next, but there's not even a stray hiccup or burp.

*She is gone and I am alone*, he thinks later. No matter what pressure Roong felt to go where the ticket took her, Tuum is certain she didn't go for her safety but out of love for him. The most terrible feeling of all comes to him that the policeman, whoever he was, did this through his father's arranging. Perhaps his father called in a favour and that favour called in another favour down the line until it reached the policeman who'd then been sent to convince her that, if she really loved Tuum, the best thing she could do would be to disappear to save them both from the karmic peril awaiting them.

Likely his father made these arrangements weeks earlier after that dream when he'd been certain they were necessary to save Tuum and Roong from catastrophe. Tuum wishes to believe that, in his father's final days when he was terribly sick, he'd realized he'd misinterpreted his dream but by then it had been too late to stop it as events were already set in motion.

That would explain why he suddenly appeared in two of Kay's dreams. His father's spirit didn't know the most important detail. Where Roong has gone. Likely, the policeman never met his father and his father didn't know his identify. His father hadn't anticipated that a failsafe was necessary. When he'd realized that, it was too late and he had no way to call it off. Any chance of discovering who the policeman was had died with his father.

That would explain why his father's spirit has been so quiet now. It is up to Tuum to search from here forward. There is nothing more his father can tell him.

He packs a small bag and locks his door, having no idea when he will return.

First, he takes a bus to Roong's village which is only a few kilometres north and west of Chum Phae. He walks from the bus station to her father's rice farm. He recognizes the farm from the landmarks that she'd described to him. He stops at the bamboo hut she also told him about. It is at the southern edge of the rice paddy and is where she spent many nights during each harvest rather than return home in the dark. He goes inside and it is well swept and neat as though she has just left it. The new owners must be taking care of it. He goes to the double wide bamboo cot she told him about and then later sits at the crude table. His chair faces the wall and to his right are cupboards and a sink. He feels comfortable and at peace here as he imagines Roong must have felt also. The air thickens in the afternoon heat and he hurries out and walks a kilometre north, and then a kilometre west to reach the farmhouse.

He knocks on the door and a woman answers and smiles immediately and says that they don't get many visitors, so his arrival is a sign of good fortune. She invites him in and says that he's just in time for the evening meal. He sits at the table and she asks him how he happens to be in the area. He says that he is a friend of the former owners and has heard much good about the farm and has wanted to see it for himself. She says that's an even better omen.

Her husband sits at the end of the table and is spooning *Kaeng Nor Mai* (bamboo shoots curry) and sticky rice from a pot into bowls. He nods at Tuum but doesn't stop what he is doing.

The woman says that they have plenty and Tuum is welcome to have a bowl too. He thanks them and says he will. Two boys now come from another part of the house and sit across from each other at the table. The older boy sits beside Tuum and wais him and his parents before eating. The younger son also wais Tuum and his parents before eating. No one speaks as they eat.

When everyone has emptied their bowls, the husband says that they know little about Roong and her father and are happy to hear any stories he wishes to share.

He says that Roong's father is dead but doesn't tell them how he died because they may take that as a bad sign for future crops. He says the Roong is fine and that they will be married soon.

The woman smiles at this news.

It is getting dark by this time and Tuum helps the woman and boys clean up while the husband goes out to the shed for more rice. He then brings in a sack and empties it into a metal pail near the sink. He puts the tin lid back on the pail when it is full.

Tuum asks them if it is okay if he spends the night in the hut. He says that Roong has told him about it and he is pleased it is so well looked after. The husband smiles at this and says that workers stay there during the rice harvests. He then says that Tuum is welcome to stay in it as long as he wishes and can later help with the rice harvest if he is so inclined.

Tuum says that he would like that. Right now, he is on an important journey and must leave tomorrow but promises that he will return when it is time to harvest.

The man walks with him to the hut and they sit out front of it and chant together in the dark and then again inside. His wife has given him a blanket for the night, but it is warm enough and he doubts he will need it.

The farmer sets a small candle on the table and lights it and it brightens the interior enough that Tuum is thankful for it. The man leaves and Tuum sits at the table for a while in the same chair he'd sat in before. A slight wind makes the hut creak lightly. He listens to those creaks as they shift from one side of the hut to the other and back. He imagines Roong and himself spending nights here and then waking to harvest rice. If her father had lived longer, would Tuum have even met her? He believes he would have somehow even if he can't imagine how right now.

He slows his breathing but doesn't meditate or chant. Instead he goes on listening for other noises and yearns for any sensation of her having been here but gets none. Eventually, he blows out that candle and makes his way in the dark to the bamboo cot. It is firmer than he expects and lays out the blanket and lies on top of it and it provides just enough padding that he is soon asleep. Later a noisy rat in the thatched roof wakes him. He listens to its progress for a short while but loses interest and falls back to sleep.

In the morning he sits again at the table and then moves to the window. The glass has recently been cleaned so he has a clear view to the north where young stocks of rice bend in the morning breeze. Farther north of that is a green line of mountains misted by grey morning fog. All is still outside, *morning still*, at this hour and he spans the full view from the window not really certain what he is looking for or if he'll recognize it if he sees it.

She likely stood at this window in the mornings, the day set out for her without really having to think about it. He imagines that he stands in the exact spot she did. What did she derive from this view beyond the day's requirements? What future did she plan then? She has yet to share those details with Tuum. But he knows what to ask her now. Then her days must have seemed uncomplicated, the future no more than vague suggestions she got used to but didn't really think too much about most of the time even as she stood at this window.

He watches now as a flock of chestnut-tailed starlings land in the morning glare and hop about hunting for insects. Their presence makes him gleeful because she may have seen this very flock in the mornings.

She'd told him how the hut became a second home for her, a place of great comfort, and she enjoyed the nights she spent alone here. She could lose herself in the night and it didn't matter. She could meditate more deeply than she could at home and attributed that to having it all to herself.

He wonders what came to her during those deep meditations? Did she get a glimpse of the two of them or even of him here alone? He hopes not. She told him that she came out of those meditations with a powerful sense of being connected to all things, that she was exactly where she was supposed to be. He turns his back to the window and slides down the wall and sits in the lotus position to meditate.

Sitting on the floor allows him to get new sensations of her being here. Most are nothing more than shadows and odours that he hadn't noticed before. Not her odours or any odours he's previously associated with her but new odours that he now wishes to attribute to her.

He's not sure why those are the sensations he gets but assumes this is where she must have sat to chant and meditate. It makes sense to him that she would do that just below the window drawn here just as he has been drawn here by the angle of the morning light. These are mere traces but today any hint will suffice and gives him a place to start. He opens his eyes after he finishes meditating and takes in the hut one final time from this vantage point. The cot and table look bigger and the peeked roof is fully shadowed so none of the rafters or support beams are visible, only the vague bunching of thatch.

He imagines her moving from the cot to the table and then to the door. He can make out each place where she would have placed her foot on warped ridges of the uneven floorboards to take the shortest path to the door. He sees her hands moving through the stalled air as he has seen her do in Khon Kaen.

All the nights she spent here, he doubts that she had any sense of him, and the dark turns her life would soon take. She's told him, if she'd known her father would die soon, she wouldn't have spent a single night here but would have hurried home each evening to be with him. He imagines her happy here, finding in the demands of daily labour a powerful inner strength.

But what if he never finds her? He considers the farmer's offer again then and decides that it will be his duty to return here, as he can't think of anywhere else he can be without her.

He gets up then from beneath the window and goes to the corner near the cupboards and sits again in the lotus position. It is darker here and he doesn't get the same sensations of her. He closes his eyes and slows his breathing and in time he sees the water buffalo again. But this time he's the buffalo and is chewing on tall grass outside this hut. He tastes the grass, and its cool dampness in his throat blocks the air passage, and his breathing slows to faint breaths. In the distance Roong rides a bicycle toward him. She vanishes and he sees a large viper in the grass coming straight toward him. He abruptly comes out of the meditation then with such a shock as though someone has slapped him. He then has the dark sensation that he will die here and soon. Maybe that was what his father saw at some point and what he really was working up to. But how could he tell him something like that? He marvels at how this hut is so close to his father's village and yet practically on the other side of the world.

He bolts up now but, when he stands, his legs weaken and almost buckle, and he leans against the wall for support. He hears the hut creak in the wind and glances around and senses then that this hut will be here long after he has died.

When he leaves, he shuts the door slowly and thinks again of the lingering traces of Roong sealed up inside it. He thinks too of the kind family that owns it now and how both overlap through him. He makes sure that the door is properly latched and then walks quickly to the farmhouse eager to be on his way from here. He carries his small bag in one hand and has the folded blanket draped over his other shoulder. He thinks of the blanket that had been over his father's coffin. But that was a very different blanket. Was that only over a week ago? He arrives at the farmhouse in time to have breakfast with the family. The mother serves him a bowl of boiled rice with small chunks of chicken and ginger in it. The father drives him to the bus station in Chum Phae on his motorcycle.

At the bus station he buys a ticket for Chiang Rai via Chiang Mai. That is where he will start.

On the bus he closes his eyes and meditates. He breathes in and out in long slow inhales that he keeps silently to himself. In time, when the bus is well past Loei, he sees his father's spirit beautiful and shiny and knows his father's soul has already jumped to another body.

# Chapter 16

## *Khon Kaen Present Day*

THE NEXT MORNING, heat wakes him before Nan, and he leaves the bed and dresses and goes to the main window of their apartment and opens it. In between the traffic noises and bird-song, he hears the sobering hum of monks chanting somewhere in the mass of buildings to the north.

As he listens, he can't think of a single thing more that he wants than what he has right now. He's never felt that way before or been so fully himself. He wishes he could pause time and soak in this happiness for as long as possible. But such a thought is a selfish want and would deprive everyone else of their happiness. Instead he must take in every living dimension of this moment and then let it go.

Nan joins him at the window and they kiss and he knows that a year from now those monks will be chanting and the year after that, and, each time, heat will press in as it does now.

With Buddha the precariousness of each moment makes it inevitable. No other present is possible but this one. Whatever past lives they've lived are gone and where they are now is the only place they can be even if for the longest time they could have been somewhere else.

Ed lets go of that thought too for what good does it do to trace any moment to its origins? Neither steps away from the other and he rests a hand on her shoulder, and she smiles. Soon after she returns to bed.

Four floors below, pedestrians make their way in the street going to work or school. He watches a father and son hold hands as they walk toward the elementary school directly across the street from this apartment. As they near it, the boy runs a bit ahead tugging on his father's arm.

They reach the main entrance of the school, and the boy stops and lets his father cross the threshold first. When the father is a short way inside, he stops and faces his son. The father continues to hold his son's hand the whole time but now their arms have gone slack. The father waits for nearly a minute as his son stands in the doorway. Another boy unaccompanied by a parent hurries past them and into the school. The son lets go of his father's hand and chases after the boy. The father proceeds slowly after them.

Last night Nan told him about a father and son who'd carried the sickly grandfather to the river in a basket. When they got him there, they set the grandfather on the ground ready to roll him into the fast waters where he'd be quickly swept away. The father and son argued then over the basket as the grandfather shivered on the ground. The father wanted to leave the basket there seeing no point in carrying it back, but the son said they should take it home with them because he could use it later when the father got old. This shocked the father and he had a swift change of heart and asked the son to help him lift the grandfather back into the basket and they carried the grandfather home again. The grandfather lived many years after that, sitting out front of his son's house most mornings, his hands folded as he meditated.

He considers that story now against what he has just witnessed below. In that story the father had been selfish and hasty with his family obligations and in doing so had taught his son to be equally cruel. The father and son below demonstrated a very different dynamic, but each action produces good or bad ripples.

Two dogs stand now side by side in the neighbour's fenced yard beyond the car park of this apartment building. Both are mongrels, the kind he's got used to seeing here, with flat noses and small ears and mangy fur, their original breeds distant and vague and difficult to discern from their present features. One dog is white and the other sandy brown. They sniff each other and then lift their heads and bark loud enough to be heard over the morning traffic.

They sniff each other again and then the white dog goes to the front steps of the house and curls up under the shade of the front eves. The sandy dog hurries through the open metal gate and bolts toward the street. In the past Ed would've worried that the dog would then cross the street and get hit by a passing car but accepts now that every moment is impermanent and beyond his control.

The sandy dog doesn't cross the street but makes a sharp right turn and is likely headed toward the temple, whose rooftop is visible two blocks north. That is where he'd heard the monks just moments ago. He suspects the dog is one of the strays that lives at the temple. He turns his gaze back to the other dog still curled up in the shade. A woman Nan's age comes out of the house and places a bowl of food in front of the dog and then goes back inside. As soon as she is gone, the dog quickly gobbles up the contents of the bowl.

Ed thinks about the two dogs meeting and the haste with which they parted company. In the past he might have thought nothing of that and considered their behaviour simply what dogs do but realizes now that each dog has a karmic past as he and Nan and everyone has. Their meeting now is not by coincidence as there are no coincidences. Given how quickly the sandy dog went on its way, it is likely they have no karmic history and never crossed paths before, just as he and the father and son below likely didn't.

He returns to bed and lies next to Nan who is asleep again. Since burning the hut he's felt lighter and his thoughts less encumbered. He is able to quickly slip in and out of meditation and does so now. Somewhere in the middle of that meditation he sees the father and son and then the two dogs. Each image passes quickly, but not so quickly he doesn't recognize them. Later as he comes out of the meditation, his first tangible thought is that every day is like this, full of chance encounters, but none are coincidental.

When he is fully aware again, he remembers the powerful and mysterious images he saw last night while meditating. Nan has warned him that, whenever that happens, he needs to open his eyes immediately because he's connected to a black magic that can harm him.

He'd obeyed her warning despite being tempted by the blue light and the two figures framed in it. They sat on a beach with their backs to him. He recognized right way that they were Nan and himself in some past or future moment. That was all he'd allowed himself to see before opening his eyes.

He'd told her what he'd seen and she'd immediately chanted and then ended with "*Satu, Satu, Satu.*" He understood then the danger of that image. It wasn't that he risked being tricked by a false future, but that he very likely got a glimpse of their actual future and by doing so risked rendering that future impossible.

He remains still beside her now and knows how fortunate he is to be with her. He feels buoyant and yet on solid ground for the first time. Much of this is thanks to her and Run but also because of those weeks they spent together in the hut helping Sutum. That drew Nan and him even closer. He thinks again about what she's said about them being in that hut in a past life. *All is possible.*

She stirs beside him and smiles and opens her eyes.

"You're still awake," she says. She yawns and stretches her arms as far as they will go behind her.

"I've just come back to bed," he says.

She rolls onto her side to face him. "I just had a good dream. You were driving a new, blue Honda Fit and I was in the passenger seat. We were on a curvy highway in Canada that weaved around huge snow-topped mountains. An orange morning light glowed on each peak."

The dream confirms what he has been thinking for a while now that they needed to go to Canada. He's certain that she'd lived in Canada in a past life and they had been in love with each other there too.

We may be born in a given moment but that doesn't bind us to only this time. Time gathers up everything and everyone as it hurries along but who is to say what happens once can't happen again?

"Where were we going in the dream?" he asks.

"I don't know but it started to snow. I opened the car window and reached out a hand. It felt like I was reaching into a freezer. You said: 'Don't do that.' And I asked why and you said: 'That's how the devil gets in.' That made me laugh in the dream and that woke me just now. It's so hot already I wouldn't mind a little of that snow at this moment."

# CHAPTER 17

## Chiang Mai
## 1970

ROONG ENTERS QUICKLY, arms weighed down with bags of hot *Khao Soi* (Thai coconut curry noodle soup). She smiles, and sets the bags on the counter, and takes down two bowls from the cupboard. She sets the bowls on a round, amber dining table.

She spoons equal portions into each bowl and slides one across to him. She pushes small portions of noodles and chicken onto her spoon with her fork and chews slowly with her mouth closed.

The images always stop there. He senses that she is near, and if she'll go to a window and look out, he'll recognize a landmark and know where she is.

He returns to the bed in his hotel room and lies on top of the covers and closes his eyes and forces his mind to go blank but the images continue.

Soon he is asleep and has another dream about his father. These are more frequent now. In the dream, he is ten and his arms are draped around his father's neck and his father is carrying him on his back. His father walks slowly and tells Tuum to move his feet. They are in the field across from the house. When he looks back to the house, it isn't his father's but Roong's mistress's house in Khon Kaen. He struggles to move his legs and feet, but he feels nothing below his waist. It is as though only the top half of him exists. The rest is an illusion. He knows his feet are on the ground and that they drag behind his father, but he has no sensations of them. Then the dream shifts, and he and his father are running together. They aren't running very fast. He sweats more than his father and is more out of breath. His father doesn't appear to be straining at all. His father turns to him and smiles and says: "See."

He wakes then and is sweating profusely especially at his wrists. He stays lying on the bed and knows the dream is a warning. He isn't sure yet what it is warning him about but knows in time he will. He remembers then a moment from the accident. He sees a car stop too quickly in front of the motorcycle and feels his arms squeeze his father's waist. Then there is that terrible white light again. He also senses that the memories will trickle back like this whether he wishes them to or not. They have a will that extends beyond his. He doesn't control these workings.

Why did he and his father have that accident? There are still many missing pieces. All of those conversations with his father at the temple were leading up to one about the accident. But now that mystery will remain a mystery unless he finds Roong. He moves to face the hot afternoon sunlight through a large window in the room. He turns away from the light and closes his eyes again.

More memories of the accident flood back. His father turns the motorcycle and shields Tuum with his left arm. Time skips and Tuum is lying on the ground and his father is holding his head and rocking him. His father is sobbing. Deep loud sobs. Tuum tries to lift a hand to his father's cheek but he can't move it. He hears a jumble of voices around him, and the noises of passing vehicles. There are the scents of gasoline and engine oil and rubber. Then it all goes white. He opens his eyes again and the bright sunlight has gone from the window. He hears Roong in the room with him.

"*Maa Ghin Khao,*" (The food's ready. Come and eat.) she says, her voice is as clear as if she were really here. A phrase he's heard her say many times now. She heaps portions of sticky rice onto plates and then tops them with steaming green curry. "*Aroi,*" (Delicious), she says after several mouthfuls.

Why is she always serving him food? Why is she fiddling with the dishes? He knows these are images from another life not this one. This is not his Roong and yet it is.

He can't fight his mind any more than he can stop the rain.

"Eat," she says.

"Okay," he says, and wishes he could reach out and touch her but knows that isn't part of what's being allowed even as the room fills with the scent of green curry and rice.

"I am not here anymore," she says, and the images vanish.

Later he goes outside onto the sidewalk and it is raining. He doesn't attempt to escape the rain and instead he walks directly in it.

"I am beside you," Roong says.

But he's alone. The rain darkens everything and further east in the middle of Chiang Mai there is more rain and more dark.

"I am coming to you," he says.

"Good," she says.

He walks east without an umbrella, without a raincoat, and lets the rain soak through his clothes, and even as he feels that dampness, he continues to walk.

"This is the right direction, my love," she says. "Now you are on your way."

And soon he isn't just crossing streets, he's crossing time.

## CHAPTER 18

### *Hua Hin*
### *Present Day*

A MONTH LATER and before they leave for Canada, they take a beach holiday in Hua Hin. In the taxi to the beach on the last day they are there, Nan leans closer and says: "A man walked a water buffalo across a wooden suspension bridge. Halfway across he met another man walking a water buffalo going the other way. The bridge was too narrow to allow each to pass. The man who was on the bridge first insisted that the other man should back up his buffalo and allow him and his buffalo to pass. The other man disagreed and said that he had been there first and that the other man should back up instead. Both men stood with crossed arms and refused to move.

"In time a monk joined them on the bridge. He listened to both men's arguments and he suggested that they both back up and that he would wait in the middle and, when he meditated and decided who should go first, he'd wave them onto the bridge.

"'How will you determine that?' the first man asked, feeling he was the one entitled to go first.

"'Buddha will determine that,' the monk said.

"Both men thanked the monk but neither volunteered to back up. The monk then said that they were beyond his help and they'd have to let Buddha decide and continued on his way. The two men didn't budge from where they stood. In time a strong wind blew across the bridge and it swayed so much that one span snapped and then the other and both men and their buffalos plunged into the water below. The buffalos were quickly carried away in the strong current but each man was able to swim to his respective bank and so they then stood facing each other across the water. But now that their buffalos had been washed away, each man turned and walked home.

"What do you suppose that means?" she asks him.

"I don't know except that perhaps Buddha decided in the end."

"Not Buddha. No, not Buddha. Those water buffalos were too heavy. It was bound to turn out that way. It's a love story, don't you think?"

"How so?"

"There is a bridge and all that water. Stubbornness. The fall. Those are all the phases of love."

"A bridge?"

"Love means building bridges. I read that somewhere. Not very good, true or honest, but I like the sound of it. Something snarky to it."

He likes it that she says the word "snarky."

"The monk who told me that story smiled and asked me to chant with him afterward. He later said that he had been the monk on the bridge and that on his way back home the next day he discovered that the bridge had collapsed. It was never rebuilt, he said. That was the point. Not all bridges are rebuilt. Some stay ruined and people have to swim across. That's the lesson, he said. Not just to those two stubborn men but for everyone who relied on the bridge to cross the river.

"I asked him if he swam across and he said he did. Many times. Lucky it was a narrow river, he said, even if in some places the current was strong enough to sweep away a water buffalo. Both buffalos drowned and their bloated bodies washed up down river. Each landed on the wrong side so each man had to deal with the corpse of the other man's buffalo. I asked him if he made that part up and he said that he never made anything up. There was no need to. There were plenty of true stories like that he could draw upon."

Ed isn't really certain what she wishes him to take from her story and says as much.

"I love you," she says. "That's the point."

He says he loves her too. Just then the taxi reaches the beach.

Since burning the hut, he's thought about Run's message regarding it. He and Nan have occasionally spoken about their past lives connected to it. *That was us then. It is us who have found them not they who have found us,* Nan has said. There are only the days going forward, the years yet to live. *I have found you and you have found me,* she also said. *That is how it is different.*

They walk slowly toward the beach. There is much sun here and much glare on the water and he is happy. He is rooted at last.

Nan and Ed hold hands as they enter the Gulf of Thailand together. They wade in until the water is up to Nan's neck. Ed bends his knees so they are both at eye level. In this moment, surrounded by warm ocean water, he feels his heartbeat quicken. He grips her hands and she firmly grips back. They could both submerge now and come up together either thousands of kilometres away or exactly where they are. At this moment, both outcomes are equally possible. He finally understands what determines the difference.

The lingering details of their past lives remain locked in *soul memory.* The rest is but one of a million, million possibilities. This life is proof that there have been others.

Neither lets go of the other, and then, as though each has counted to three in their head, they both slip beneath the surface at exactly the same time.

## *Acknowledgements*

THE FIRST TWO chapters of the novel were previously published at *The Write Launch* and I wish to thank to Sandra Fluck for her editing suggestions regarding those chapters. I would also like to thank Gary Clairman for his astute editorial guidance. I also wish to thank Michael Mirolla, Connie McParland and everyone at Guernica Editions for believing in this book.

## *About the Author*

ROBERT HILLES AND his wife Rain divide their time between Nanaimo, BC and Khon Kaen, Thailand. He won the Governor General's Award for Poetry for *Cantos from A Small Room*. His first novel, *Raising of Voices*, won the George Bugnet Award for best novel and his second novel, *A Gradual Ruin*, was published by Doubleday Canada. His books have also been shortlisted for The Milton Acorn People's Poetry Prize, The W.O. Mitchell/City of Calgary Prize, The Stephan Stephansson Award, and The Howard O'Hagan Award. He has published seventeen books of poetry, four works of fiction, and two nonfiction books. His latest poetry collection is *Shimmer.* He is currently working on a new novel, and a book of prose poems tentatively called, *A Piece of Rag Wrapped Gold.*

# *Books by Robert Hilles*

## Poetry

*Look the Lovely Animal Speaks*
*The Surprise Element*
*An Angel in the Works*
*Outlasting the Landscape*
*Finding the Lights On*
*A Breath at a Time*
*Cantos from a Small Room*
*Nothing Vanishes*
*Breathing Distance*
*Somewhere Between Obstacles and Pleasure*
*Higher Ground*
*Wrapped Within Again: New and Selected*
*Slow Ascent*
*Partake*
*Time Lapse*
*Line*
*Shimmer*

## Fiction

*Raising of Voices*
*Near Morning*
*A Gradual Ruin*
*Don't Hang Your Soul on That*

## Non Fiction

*Kissing the Smoke*
*Calling the Wild*

This book is made of paper from well-managed FSC® - certified forests, recycled materials, and other controlled sources.